Linking Girl Education with Women Empowerment and Development

Linking Girl Education with Women Empowerment and Development

Vol-III

Deepa Awasthi

KALPAZ

ISBN: 978-93-5128-178-8

Price: ₹ 880

First Published, 2016

Published by

Kalpaz Publications

C-30, Satyawati Nagar,
Delhi – 110052
E-mail: kalpaz@hotmail.com
Ph.: 9212142040

Printed at: G. Print Process, Delhi

Cataloging in Publication Data—DK
Courtesy: D.K. Agencies (P) Ltd. <docinfo@dkagencies.com>

Awasthi, Deepa, author.
Linking girl education with empowerment and development. Vol-III / Deepa Awasthi.
pages cm
Inludes bibliographical references.
ISBN 9789351281788

1. Girls—Education—India. 2. Women in development—India. 3. Economic development—India. I. Title.

LC2322.A93 2016 DDC 370.82 23

Contents

Acknowledgements

It is my immense pleasure to acknowledge all the learned authors from all over the country who have contributed their valuable articles and research papers written by them with utmost pain, efforts and investment of time. Without their sincere and devoted thinking about the serious issue of "Girl Education" it would have been almost impossible to come up with the desired result. I am also obliged to the distinguished panel of reviewers who invested their precious time and hard work in evaluating the contributions from various authors and further guiding them to make their writings focused, clear and appropriate for this book series. I am also thankful to all my friends, teachers from University of Lucknow and family members who encouraged me from time to time to remain adhered to the mission of publishing a series of book on one of the most discussed and utmost important issue - "Girl Education." Last but not the least, I thank God and all who helped me directly or indirectly at every step and provided me emotional support to compile this edited book series.

—Deepa Awasthi
(Editor)

Authors' Introduction

1. Dr Deepa Awasthi (Editor)

Ph. D.- Education, University of Lucknow, UP.

(Editor of Book volume and series and contributor of article: National Mission for Empowerment of Women-2010: Providing Educational Base for Socio-Economic Development of Women)

Dr Deepa Awasthi, Editor of this edited book series, is a freelance researcher. She is Doctorate in Education and Post Graduate in Education, Sociology and Economics. She has qualified UGC – JRF in Education and Sociology as well and has equal command on both the subjects. She has participated and presented her research papers in more than 45 national and international seminars and conferences. She has also edited a book entitled "Eve Teasing: A Social Epidemic." Her publication work also involves 05 chapters in edited books, 03 research papers in the form of conference and seminar proceedings and 17 research papers and articles in various journals of national and international repute. Her keen interest areas include the sociological issues related to women and various issues related to the field of Education.

2. Mukesh Kumar Malviya

Assistant Professor, Department of Law, Banaras Hindu University, Varanasi, UP.

(Contributed article: Gender Empowerment through Education: Mirage or Reality?)

Author has completed his LL.M and Ph.D. from Department of Law, Barkatullah University, Bhopal and M.Phil. (Law) from School of Law, Devi Ahilya Vishwavidyalaya, Indore. He has been a Gold Medal holder throughout in LL.B, LL.M and M.Phil (Law). He joined

Banaras Hindu University, Varanasi as an Assistant Professor in Law in July, 2010. He also served as a M.P. Govt. Guest faculty in New Govt. Law College Indore (2009). He has more than six years of teaching experience. He has guided and supervised more than 5 LL.M dissertations. He is the Editor in Chief of *Jurist* (An International Research Refereed Law Journal), *Adhikar, 15Days, The Public: Problem and Solution and International Research and Reviews* (International research refereed multidisciplinary journals). His area of interests include Jurisprudence, Legal Research Methodology, Indian Constitutional Law, Human Rights Law, Law and Social Transformation, Judicial Process, Law of Interpretation, Law of Evidence, Hindu Law, Muslim Law, Environmental Law, Professional Ethics and Public Interest Litigation etc.

3. **Nutan Sharma**

Assistant Professor, Sri Sai College of Education, Badhani, Pathankot, Punjab

(Contributed article: Women Empowerment and Role of Education)

Nutan Sharma is Assistant Professor in Sri Sai College of Education, Badhani, Pathankot, Punjab, with more than nine years teaching experience. He is pursuing Ph.D in Education from Himachal Pradesh University, Shimla. He is NET in education and post graduate in Mathematics. His keen interest areas include value education, philosophy, teacher education, teaching of mathematics and women empowerment. He has attended more than 23 national and international seminars and conferences. He has published more than 20 research papers in national and international journals and has guided more than 20 students at postgraduate levels.

4. **Sharabani Mazumdar**

Lecturer, Department of Education, Institute for Education, Kolhan University, Jharkhand

(Contributed article: Role of Education in Women Empowerment)

Sharabani Mazumdar is an aspiring writer and avid reader. She holds a master degree in English from Indira Gandhi National Open

University and Master in Education from Kolhan University. She taught English in Jamshedpur Women's College for one and a half year and is currently working as a Lecturer in B.Ed College where she is teaching Psychology and Education Technology. She has attended and presented papers in various national seminars. During her studies, she made several trips around different parts of Bihar, Jharkhand and West Bengal where she came across different people and their cultures that ignited her passion for acquisition of knowledge of people and their customs. Her keen interest area includes socio cultural development of India and various issues related with women. She is an ardent lover of music, a painter, and loves travelling. In her spare time, she loves to spend time with nature, friends and family.

5. Ruchi Dhyani

Research Scholar, Department of Education & community service, Punjabi university, Patiala, Punjab

(Contributed article: Journey of Women Education towards Empowerment)

Ruchi Dhyani is a Research Scholar in Department of Education and Community Service of Punjabi university. She is post graduate in Education, Commerce and Economics. She has been awarded UGC-JRF in Education. She also worked as lecturer in Education in Punjab College of Education. She has participated and presented the papers in 12 National/International seminars and conferences. 03 research papers written by her have been published in reputed international journals.

6. Ruchi Shivam

Research Scholar, Department of Education, BHU, Varanasi, UP.

(Contributed article: Women Empowerment through Education: Pre and Post Independence Era)

Ruchi Shivam is a research scholar in Department of Education, Banaras Hindu University, Varanasi. She is pursuing her Ph.D. on topic "A Comparative Study of Use of Blended Learning by Senior Secondary Students." Her publication includes 03 research papers in national and international journals. She has attended 10 national and international Seminars and 01workshop.

7. **Arpeeta Anand**

M. Phil scholar, National University of Educational Planning and Administration, New Delhi.

(Contributed article: Education and Women Empowerment in India)

Arpeeta Anand is a M.Phil scholar at National University of Educational Planning and Administration, New Delhi. She is post graduate in Education. Her keen interest is in issues related to women and child. She has attended and presented papers in various national and international seminar and conferences. She has published 04 articles and research papers in various journals.

8. **Prabina Kumar Padhi**

Research Scholar, Department of Economics, Berhampur University, Ganjam, Odisha

(Contributed article: Education and Empowerment of Women in Odisha: A Case Study of Ganjam District)

Prabina Kumar Padhi is a Research Scholar in Department of Economics, Berhampur University, Ganjam, perusing his Ph.D. on topic "Public Expenditure Tracking of Elementary Education Sector in Odisha: A case Study of Ganjam." His keen interest areas include elementary education, industrial economics, banking, etc. His publication includes 04 research papers in national and international journals. He has contributed 02 chapters in edited book. He has attended 15 national and 05 internationals seminars and 02 workshops.

9. **Umesh Chandra Panigrahi**

Professor and Course Coordinator, Dept. of MBA, Kalam Institute of Technology, Berhampur, Ganjam, Odisha.

(Co Contributer of article: Education and Empowerment of Women in Odisha: A Case Study of Ganjam District)

Author is Doctorate in Economics with 24 years of teaching experience. At present he is working as Course Coordinator,

Department of MBA, Kalam Institute of Technology, Berhampur, Ganjam, Odisha. He is post graduate in Economics and Political Science. His keen interest area involves Socio political development of India and issues related to women and child. He has attended and presented papers in various national and international seminars and conferences. He has published more than 17 articles and research papers in various journals.

10. Pooja Singh

Research Scholar, Faculty of Commerce, BHU, Varanasi, UP.

(Contributed article: Role of Education in Women Empowerment in India)

Pooja Singh is a Research Scholar in the Faculty of Commerce, BHU, Varanasi. She is pursuing Ph.D. from Faculty of Commerce, BHU. Her main area of interest is Human Resource Management and Human Resource Development. She has attended and presented her research papers in various national and international seminars and conferences.

11. Palwinder Kaur

Senior Research Fellow, Department of Education, Punjabi University, Patiala, Punjab.

(Contributed article: Women Empowerment through Education)

Author is a Senior Research fellow in Department of Education, Punjabi University, Patiala. She is Post Graduate in Education and Political Science and has been awarded UGC- JRF in Education and UGC-NET in Political Science. She has completed her M.Phil. in Political science. She has participated and presented papers in 12 national /international seminar and conferences. 03 articles written by her on various issues have been published as seminar/conference proceedings and in national /international journals. She has contributed one chapter in distance education departmental notes, Punjabi University, Patiala. She has also worked as field investigator in state of nation survey 2008 – 2009, conducted by Lokniti and sponsored by CNN-IBN and The Indian Express.

12. Priyanka

Junior Research Fellow, Faculty of Management studies, BHU, Varanasi, UP.

(Contributed article: Role of Education in Women Empowerment)

Author is NET-JRF in Human Resource Management and Management, she is at present Junior Research Fellow pursuing her Ph.D. from Faculty of Management Studies, Banaras Hindu University, Varanasi. She has participated in more than fifteen seminars and conferences and four articles and research papers written by her have been published in reputed journals.

13. Amit Kumar Dutta

Assistant Professor in Management at Indian Institute of Legal Studies (IILS), Siliguri, West Bangal.

(Contributed article: The Role of Education in Empowering Muslim Women in South Asia)

Amit Kumar Dutta is Assistant Professor in Management at Indian Institute of Legal Studies (IILS), Siliguri. He has around 04 years of teaching experience. He is Post Graduate in Business Administration with first class from ICFAI University, Dehradun and is also a Post Graduate in Commerce. Author has a diploma in International Business Operations and has qualified UGC NET in Management. Till date, he has participated and presented papers in 05 National Seminars and 01 International Conference. He has also published 02 papers as Seminar Proceedings in National Journals and has contributed a chapter in an edited book. He is a freelance writer and has a special interest in gender and development issues.

14. Meenakshi Dwivedi

Post-doc Research Scholar in Department of Education, University of Lucknow, UP.

(Contributed article: Women Empowerment through Distance Education: An Accelerating Action)

Author is currently a Post-doc Research Scholar in Department of Education, University of Lucknow, working on the Project for the Education of students suffering from Autistic Syndrome Disorder. She has completed her doctoral thesis on Pains and Gains of Visually Impaired Students Studying in Mainstream Higher Education. She is Post Graduate in Education, Mathematics and Physics. She has also worked as Assistant Professor (B.Ed) for around seven years. She has participated and presented the papers in 12 national/International seminars and conferences including 102nd Indian Science Congress. More than 09 research papers and articles written by her on various issues have been published in reputed national/international journals. She has also contributed one chapter for an edited book. The teaching and research work of the author is focused on Special Education, Psychology and Mathematics.

15. Yogendra Pal Bharadwaj

Research Scholar, Department of Commerce, Aligarh Muslim University, Aligarh, UP

(Contributed article: Empowered Women, Empowered Nation - Still a Dream in India)

Yogendra Pal Bharadwaj is a Research Scholar in the Department of Commerce, Aligarh Muslim University, Aligarh (U.P.) India, pursuing his Ph.D. on topic "An Appraisal of Human Resource Management Policies and Practices in Delhi Metro Rail Corporation (DMRC)." He has been awarded ICSSR fellowship for his research work. He holds the credit of publishing around 14 research papers in National and International Journals and has also contributed in edited books and attended various conferences, seminars and workshops. He has twice won All India Essay Writing Competition conducted by Competition Success Review. He has also been an executive and organising member of various academic and non-academic programs in the Aligarh Muslim University, Aligarh.

16. Swati Basak

Assistant Professor - History, Mahishadal Raj College, East Midnapore, West Bengal.

(Contributed article: Women, Education and Empowerment: Anandibai Joshi, The Brave Woman)

Swati Basak is an Assistant Professor of History at Mahishadal Raj College, East Midnapore, West Bengal since one year. Previously she worked as Assistant Professor at City College and Vidyasagar College for Women, Kolkata. She has completed M.A. and M. Phil from Jadavpur University, Kolkata. She has deep interest in gender studies, social, economic and cultural history. She has completed her M. Phil dissertation on women domestic workers and she has also written some articles on this topic in International and National journals

17. Mehnaz Najmi

Program-Chair-cum-HOD of Political Science Department, School of Humanities and Social Sciences, Galgotias University, Greater Noida, UP.

(Contributed article: Role of Girl Education in Socio-Economic and Political Development of India)

Author is a Program Chair-cum-HOD of Political Science Department at School of Humanities and Social Sciences, Galgotias University, Greater Noida, UP. She is Ph.D in Political Science from Jamia Millia Islamia, New Delhi; M.A. in Political Science, Jawaharlal Nehru University, New Delhi; B.A. (Hon) Political Science, Daulat Ram College, Delhi University. She has 07 years of experience in research and teaching. She has participated and presented papers in various National/International seminars and conferences. Her special areas of interests are Indian politics, poverty, slum studies, women in political process, minority affairs and other women issues.

18. Meera Thakur

Research Scholar, Department of Education, Himachal Pradesh University, Shimla, HP.

(Contributed article: Girl Education and Development of India)

Meera Thakur is a Research Scholar, pursuing her Ph.D. from Department of Education, Himachal Pradesh University on topic "Teacher's Effectiveness as related to Cognitive Style and Emotional Competence. Her keen interest areas include issues related to women empowerment. Her publications include 03 research papers in national and international level journals and she has contributed 01 chapter in edited book. She has attended 07 state/national/international level seminar and 01 national level seminar cum workshop.

19. Anupama Katoch

Research Scholar, Department of Education, Himachal Pradesh University, Shimla

(Co Contributor of article: Girl Education and Development of India)

Anupama Katoch is a Research Scholar, pursuing her Ph. D. from Department of Education, Himachal Pradesh University on topic 'Organisational Climate and Occupational stress as Pridictors of Teacher Effectiveness at Secondary School Level.' Her keen interest areas include issues related to women empowerment. She has published 01 research paper in international level journals and contributed 01 chapter in edited book. She has attended 05 state/national/international level seminars and 01 national level seminar-cum-workshop.

20. Madhusmita Sahoo

Lecturer, Department of Anthropology and Tribal Studies in North Odisha University.

(Contributed article: Girls Education and Development: A Case Study on the Juang in Odisha)

Author is M.Phil and Ph.D in Anthropology from Pondicherry University, at present working as a lecturer in the Department of Anthropology and Tribal Studies in North Odisha University, Odisha. Her area of specialisation is socio-cultural anthropology and she has done research work on tribal development. Till now she has guided 07 M.A. students and 04 M.Phil students. Basically her research areas include the tribal socio-cultural practices with respect to their economy, health and educational development. She has presented papers in various National and International seminars and her publication involves 04 articles and research papers in reputed journals.

21 Rashmi Gahlowt

Assistant Professor, Department of Mass Media, Usha Pravin Gandhi College of Management, Mumbai, Maharashtra.

Contributed article: Contribution of Girl Education in Nation Building: Challenges and Solutions

Rashmi Gahlowt is working as Assistant Professor in the Department of Mass Media at the Usha Pravin Gandhi College of Management, Vile Parle (West), Mumbai. She is also a freelance script writer, recently having written dialogues and script for the Zee TV show "Fear Files." She has also developed content and edited it for education portals like e-gurukul. She has also written content for lifestyle portals having written on women's and children's issues. She has authored and presented papers on various subjects and themes like mass media, civic issues and English literature at various national and state level platforms.

Introduction

Girl Education has been one of the most discussed topics among all global issues during the last two centuries because civilised society believes that education is the most powerful instrument to bridge the gender gap existing in our society. Although a lot of efforts have been made in this field but due to several reasons, out of which social negligence and lack of political will power are the most prominent, the desired results could not be achieved. A number of scholars have made this issue as part of their study and recommended a number of suggestions, but unfortunately as we move to the implementation part, we find unsatisfactory efforts at ground level. Indian society and culture has proved as the most devastating museum where centuries old evil traditions are still preserved as part of day to day life especially with respect to gender issues related to education, employment or any other field. The book also suggests all possible strategies which have been followed till now and those which can play a decisive role in improving status of girl education in the near future if incorporated in our system with true spirit and intention. Mission of resolving the challenges in girl education in India has still many miles to cover.

This edited book series titled **"Girl Education in India – Still Miles to Cover"** has been divided in to 03 volumes including 06 sections, containing 52 chapters.

A. Understanding Status of Girl Education in India.

B. Gender Issues in Education

C. Girl Education: Challenges and Strategies.

D. Girl Education Promotion: Initiatives and Schemes.

E. Girl Education: Gateway to Women Empowerment

F. Linking Girl Education with National Development

The present **Vol. III - "Linking Girl Education with Women Empowerment and Development"** presents the sections E and F termed respectively as "**Girl Education: Gateway to Women Empowerment"** and **"Linking Girl Education with National Development"** Total 19 chapters are included in this volume especially covering the various aspects and prospects, Linking Girl Education to Women Empowerment and Development.

Section E includes 14 chapters that deal with the various aspects and issues associated with women education. This section also tries to reveal as to how education can lead to women empowerment.

05 chapters are included in Section F which links the development of country with the status of Girl Education.

Content Glimpses

In the first chapter of this book **"Gender Empowerment through Education: Mirage or Reality?"** author ***Mukesh Kumar Malviya*** has stressed on the limited representation of women from Gram Panchayat level to parliament level. He also points out the initiatives at government level to promote women welfare in different five year plans. Through comparison of literacy rates of males and females since 1901 to 2011, he finds that although female literacy has increased to a great extent but still is not satisfactory as compared to female literacy rates of other countries. According to him educating the women is not going to work alone, what is really needed is increasing their participation in employment which will bring real empowerment. An employed woman will certainly contribute in the development of country equivalent to her male counterpart.

In the next chapter **"Women Empowerment and Role of Education"** author ***Nutan Sharma*** describes what does women empowerment mean and how it is helpful in controlling an individual's thinking, ideology and action which ultimately leads to greater external capacity, growth in intrinsic capacity, greater self confidence and transformation of one's consciousness. Author has explained the women empowerment by quoting UNIFEM. Author also stresses on the role of education in empowering the women which will help in socio economic development of the country. He further links the low education level of women with increasing incidences of crime and violence against women.

In the third chapter of the book "**Role of Education in Women Empowerment**", author ***Sharabani Mazumdar*** has defined the term 'women empowerment' and importance of education to achieve goal of women empowerment. She has very well detailed the prospects and challenges in girl education. Author has tabled the gender disparity in overall literacy rate all over the country and steps taken by Government of India to fill that gap. According to author, early marriages, big families, higher dropout ratio, conservative attitude of parents are the main hurdles in the path of educating and empowering the women in India. She further suggests that empowerment automatically follows once women are educated, aware of their rights and able to develop their skills. This empowerment enables them to respond to challenges and to change their life accordingly as per their expectations and needs.

Next chapter of this book "**Journey of Women Education towards Empowerment**" authored by ***Ruchi Dhyani*** has detailed the historical overview of women empowerment and work done in this field at the universal level. According to her increasing cost of education, poor school environment, low status of women in society, conflicts and social exclusion are the main challenges in the provision of free access to education for girls. She further explains the need of social, economical, political empowerment separately. She has figured the number of schemes and initiatives taken by government to achieve the goal of women empowerment through education. She has also highlighted the universal commitment to reduce gender disparity in recent years that have been expressed through various declarations and conventions.

Ruchi Shivam in her next chapter **"Women Empowerment through Education: Pre and Post Independence Era"** suggests that since women constitute almost half of the population of the country, investment on their education can be advantageous for the development of the nation. She observes a shift in government policy which during the fifties was focused was on women welfare and during seventies the focus was on women development, since nineties the focus has been on women empowerment. Author has also tried to illuminate the historical overview of status of girl education in the country. She has detailed the various commissions appointed by the Government of India from time to time for uplifting the status of women. She further expresses the provisions mentioned in the constitution of India that reflect the intention and commitment of government towards the well being of women.

In the sixth chapter of the book **"Education and Women Empowerment in India"** author ***Arpeeta Anand*** focuses on the historical background of status of women in India right from Vedic era to the current twenty-first century. She points out that in spite of a number of social reforms Indian patriarchal society expects women to perform traditional duties at home. Situation is even worse in rural and remote areas where hardly they get the chance to come out of the four walls of homes. She further stresses that woman empowerment is no more a local issue limited to India only. It is a global issue as when compared with the other developed nations we find that we are lagging far behind with respect to women empowerment.

Prabina Kumar Padhi and ***Umesh Chandra Panigrahi*** in their chapter "**Education and Empowerment of Women in Odisha: A Case Study of Ganjam District**" have collected the primary data through survey method and direct observation method and have come to the conclusion that there is an important relationship between education and women empowerment. They have conducted their study at Ganjam district of Odisha state. They have detailed the various schemes and programmes that are being carried by Odisha state government and Central government for the improvement of girl education and women empowerment. Study includes the comparison of number of enrolments and dropouts in Ganjam district. Based on the study, some useful suggestions have been made regarding educating and empowering the women.

In the eighth chapter of the book **"Role of Education in Women Empowerment in India"** author ***Pooja Singh*** has focused on the importance of education in women empowerment. With the help of secondary data author has tried to link girl education and development of nation. She also mentions that in India vocational education and job oriented training courses can help women to improve their skills so as to benefit themselves, family, society and nation.

Palwinder Kaur in the ninth chapter of the book "**Women Empowerment through Education"** has gone through the present status and historical overview of women education. She has further detailed the various barriers in women education and linked it with women empowerment. Author has divided the women empowerment in to five components – sense of self worth, right to have and determine choices, right to have access to opportunities and resources, right to have the power to control their life within and outside home, ability to influence direction of social changes so as to create a more just, social and economic order at national and international level. She further stresses on the impact of education towards women empowerment and relationship between them.

In the tenth chapter of the book "**Role of Education in Women Empowerment"** author ***Priyanka*** has detailed and explained women empowerment and present status of women in the country. She expresses how education can play a vital role in women empowerment. She emphasises that women empowerment is need of the hour as women plays a central role in society and family as daughter, wife, and mother. She has compared the Global gender index where India is ranked 114 out of 134 countries, much below than other developing countries.

Amit Kumar Dutta in his chapter "**The Role of Education in Empowering Muslim Women in South Asia"** expresses that although Islam supports the equal status of women in society but after comparing the work force participation of women of different communities in rural as well as urban areas he finds that still Muslim women's participation in employment is largely lagging behind. His comparative study further suggests that in India still a very small percentage of girls of Muslim society are able to complete their education up to university level. With the help of secondary data he proves that status of women in the neighbouring countries Pakistan or Bangladesh is not much better as compared to India. Author also suggests that for the low status of women in South Asian region, religion has hardly any role to play because Islam does not support the deprivation of girls from education. It is the regional patriarchal setup and culture based on male domination which acts as the main barrier to girl education.

Next chapter **"Women Empowerment through Distance Education: An Accelerating Action"** authored by ***Meenakshi Dwivedi*** explains the extent of gender disparity Indian women have faced from centuries to modern era. She also discusses the real meaning of women empowerment and its need for women, especially in rural areas. She stresses on the role of distance education to be used as effective tool to empower women in orthodox community like India where due to social restrictions girls are unable to carry on their education. She has also taken into account the role of distance education for women who have been deprived of their right to education in the past.

Thirteenth chapter of the book **"Empowered Women, Empowered Nation - Still a Dream in India"** authored by ***Yogendra Pal Bharadwaj*** compares the female work force percentage of India as mentioned in corporate gender gap report of world economic forum and finds that India has lowest percentage of female employees as compared to other developed and developing countries. He has also studied the barriers in the way of women empowerment. Author has tried to exemplify the factors which led to prominence of women empowerment. He also suggests that for developing country like India women empowerment is a quantitative as well as qualitative challenge. The author observes that though India is the world's largest democracy it is the world's most gender skewed country. He has also pointed out some specific areas that need to be focused for educating and empowering women.

The next chapter authored by ***Swati Basak*** **titled "Women, Education and Empowerment: Anandibai Joshi, the Brave Woman"** has been dedicated to Anandibai Joshi – the first Indian woman Doctor awarded with MD degree from USA. Chapter details the life history of Anandibai who started the journey of her life as an illiterate Brahmin girl, married at the early age of nine years, the death of her child at fourteen was the driving force behind her decision to become a Doctor and thereby be able to provide proper medical facilities to thousands of girls and women. Author also praises Gopalrao, the husband who helped Anandibai positively and encouraged her to fulfil her dreams. Through this story author has tried to establish a link between role of education and women empowerment. She emphasises that although patriarchy is considered as the most formidable inhibitor in the way of women empowerment but patriarchal setup have sometimes also acted as an enabler of women empowerment as in the case of Anandibai Joshi, hence positive patriarchal mentality can act in the favour of women.

In the fifteenth chapter of the book **"National Mission for Empowerment of Women-2010: Providing Educational Base for Socio-Economic Development of Women**" author ***Deepa Awasthi*** has detailed the various features of NMEW- National Mission for empowerment of Women – 2010, launched by Government of India on International Women's Day 2010 to promote overall development of women in the country. According to her promoting education among the girls of all age group is the main objective of NMEW. She has also highlighted the various facilities available to girls and women in the primary, secondary, higher and technical educational levels. According to her this scheme has emerged to a great extent as a chief instrument of social change to eliminate gender disparity and create equal opportunity for women in society. The approach and efforts made under the umbrella of NMEW reflects the commitment of Government of India to empower each and every woman of the country so that she can decide her own destiny as well as the destiny of her motherland.

In the next article "**Role of Girl Education in the Socio Economic and Political Development of India**", author ***Mehnaz Nazmi*** has focused on the constitutional provisions to bring equality in women education and power of state to adopt special measures of positive discrimination in favour of women for neutralising the cumulative socio economic, educational and political disadvantage faced by them since centuries. She also finds RTE - 2009 as helpful in affecting the long awaited reforms in the field of education. Author also feels that still serious efforts are needed to bring the literacy rate of women equivalent to men. According to her, gender discrimination in education hinders the economic, social and political development of an individual, family, society and nation. She advocates for investing more and more on girl education so as to break the vicious cycle of poverty especially in developing countries like India. Author has favoured the Human Capital Theory which suggests that human capital acquired through education improves productivity. She further explains how education can be used as an instrument in bringing political empowerment among women not only as voters but also as representative of democracy.

In the seventeenth chapter "**Girl Education and Development of India**", authors ***Meera Thakur*** and ***Anupama Katoch*** have detailed the role and importance of education in an individual's life. The authors feel that the utility of education for girls is much more beyond employment as they can utilise their education for the welfare of their family and children. The authors further favour the Acts and legislations passed by governments from time to time to promote girl education in the country. Authors have studied the census data since 1901 comparing literacy rate of men and women. They have found that although literacy rate of women have comparatively increased in nineteenth and twentieth century but continuously increasing literacy gap is a matter of concern for policy makers and also that low literacy rate of women is in the root of various socio-economic problems prevailing in the country. The article explains the challenges associated with girl education and details the various schemes and initiatives taken by central government to meet these challenges.

Madhusmita Sahoo in the next chapter **"Girls Education and Development: A case Study on the Juang in Odisha"** focuses on the educational status of girls in tribal areas of Odisha state. She has studied the status of girl students' enrolments and dropouts at educational complex developed by Government of India for promoting education among girls belonging to Juang – a primitive tribe in Gonashika area of Keonjhar district. Through review of literature, she has collected secondary data for the chapter. By studying census data she has successfully established that literacy rate of tribal population of Odisha is much below than the average national literacy rate and also the average literacy rate of Odisha state. She further suggests the introduction of more reforms in tribal education system so that boys as well as girls belonging to scheduled tribe category can improve their skills to become useful human resources and thereby contribute duly in the economic development of the country.

In the last chapter of the book **"Contribution of Girl Education in Nation Building: Challenges and Solutions"** author ***Rashmi Gahlowt*** states that the vast regional differences in educational progress, differences in educational level of rural and urban areas and gender gap in education are the three main hurdles in achieving the ideal objectives of education. Chapter also explains how promoting girl education can play a vital role in bringing down the poverty level of the country. In her chapter author further discusses the challenges in girl education and various steps taken by government and NGOs to address the problem. Author focuses on the socio cultural and economic factors responsible for miserable condition of girl education in the country. She has also suggested how condition of girl education can be improved.

(SECTION – E)

GIRL EDUCATION: GATEWAY TO WOMEN EMPOWERMENT

Chapter-1

Gender Empowerment through Education: Mirage or Reality?

—*Mukesh Kumar Malviya*

Abstract

Since 1947 Government of India has executed tremendous efforts in the field of educating the women so as to empower them. Few of the critics continuously criticise the women empowerment endeavours in India by saying that result achieved are not satisfactory. They are harsh enough to expect the whole process to get completed instantly as if by moving a magic wand. The salient elements of this chapter is to focus on the policies of Indian government and non-government organisations that endeavour to ensure the empowerment of women through education and also to study whether these are beneficial for women, hence author would like to glance over the reasons which makes education a priority matter for the development of the country.

Key Words: *Empowerment, Policies, Priority, Development.*

Women and Empowerment

"The share of women parliamentarians was 10.96 per cent in 2011. In 2008 out of 26, 45,883 representatives of Gram Panchayat, 9,75,057 (36.9 per cent) were women. The share of women representatives at the Intermediate Panchayat was 37.1 per cent (58,191 out of 1,56,794) and it was 37.2 per cent (5810 out of 15,613) at the District Panchayats. The three Panchayats taken together, the share of women in the total Central Government employment has increased from 7.53 per cent in 2001 to 10.04 per cent in 2009. Allocations for women as reflected in the Gender Budget Statement shows gradual increase and the number of Central Government Ministries coming out with statements of increased allocations for women has also shown an increasing trend.

The aforementioned statistics sounds very pleasant as it shows that the number of women representatives has been increasing day by day and this development ensures the changing status of women in the Indian society. In parliament, women's participation has amplified than ever before and their valuable presence in Gram Panchayat, the Government and non-government sectors cannot be ignored. Hence, we witness their snail but continuous pace of development which will empower them someday which is not very far. Hence, women empowerment is the matter of concern and is much talked issue in the seminars and the conferences. Now I would like to caste a light over different Five Year Plans that assure the women of our country their identity, rights and empowerment.

Empowerment of women is an enabling process which helps them to move on their path to social makeover which will imbue them with purpose of The Sixth Five Year Plan (1980 to 1985) which includes welfare plans and programmes for women's health, education and employment. Probably it was high time when our country realised that women should be paid heed to. The span of The Eight Five Year Plan was from 1992 to 1997 and this scheme emphasised the 'empowerment' of women. Then only their issues were considered under 'a distinct strategy'. With the launch of The Ninth Five Year Plan in 1997 to 2002, government invested a large sum of money for the plans and schemes made for women. It also focused on the promotion of Self-Help Groups and proposed the participation of people in plan and projects. This project was helpful for the women living below poverty line. Gender disparity in literacy, wage rates and human development were the main eminent components in The Tenth Five Year Plan (2002 to 2007). This plan consisted of mainly three strategies – 'of social empowerment, economic empowerment and providing gender justice so as to create enabling environment of positive economic and social policies for women and eliminating all forms of discrimination against them and thus advance gender equity goals'. Eliminating gender inequality '...by ensuring access to basic physical infrastructure as well as health and educational services to all, recognise gender as a cross - cutting theme across all sectors' was one of the noteworthy proposal of The Eleventh Five Year Plan which states that 'gender equity requires adequate provisions to be made in policies and schemes across Ministries and Departments. It also entails strict adherence to gender budgeting across the board'.

"Empowerment of women is a socio-political ideal, encompassing notions of dignity and equality, envisioned in relation to the wider framework of women's rights. It is a process of gaining control over self, over resources and over existing societal perceptions and attitudes and would be achieved only when an improvement in the 'condition' of women is accompanied by an advancement in their 'position' by enlarging the economic, social and political freedoms and choices available to them." Innumerable plans and schemes were made to make the women of India empowered and one of them was Swayamsidha which was planned to strengthen them '...through formation of women into Self-Help Groups (SHGs).' This was started with the budget of Rs 116.30 in Feb 2001 across the country but was discontinued because of the lack of interest of UTs. With the help of these self help groups several plans were executed in the society such as social awareness, social empowerment, political empowerment and economic empowerment.

Education and Women

'Education for women is equality'. The number of literate women among the female population of India was between 2-6 per cent from the British Raj onwards till the formation of the Republic of India in 1947. Concerted efforts led to improvement from 15.3 per cent in 1961 to 28.5 per cent in 1981. By 2001 literacy for women had exceeded 50 per cent of the overall female population though these statistics were still very low compared to world standards and even male literacy within India.

Education is an instrument which can transform not only the individual but also the society therefore it's mandatory for a country to educate its citizen without any discrimination of caste, creed, sex or religion. That's why education is considered radical and vital in our constitution. It helps a country to make it a knowledge based society. It's significant to study progress of literacy in women of India during 1951-1981 according to Census:

Literacy Rate in India from Year 1901 to 2011.

No.	*Census Year*	*Total per cent*	*Male (per cent)*	*Female (per cent)*
1.	1901	5.35	9.83	0.60
2.	1911	5.92	10.56	1.05
3.	1921	7.16	12.21	1.81
4.	1931	9.50	15.59	2.93
5.	1941	16.10	24.90	7.30
6.	1951	16.67	24.95	9.45
7.	1961	24.02	34.44	12.95
8.	1971	29.45	39.45	18.69
9.	1981	36.23	46.89	24.82
10.	1991	42.84	52.74	32.17
11.	2001	64.83	75.26	53.67
12.	2011	74.04	82.14	65.46

Source: Census of India 2011.

The data mentioned above reveals gender disparity in the education of males and females that has lessened but is still inadequate and it's compulsory to be eliminated otherwise women who are working shoulder to shoulder with men won't be able to benefit the nation which will be the loss of all of us.

Mahila Samakhya (1986) is imbibed in the National Policy of India and has been introduced to ensure women education and empowerment. It started in 10 districts of UP, Gujarat and Karnataka in 1988-89 "Mahila Samkhya endeavours to create a learning environment where women can collectively affirm their potential, gain the strength to demand information and knowledge, and move forward to change and take charge of their lives."

Mahila Samakhya considers education as life long process of acquiring knowledge and empowerment and also helps them to be active beneficiaries. It comprehends that mere literacy won't solve the purpose but looking after all the requirements of rural women may result into tremendous positive result because of its positivity, it has benefitted almost 2 lakh women and a huge number have been impacted indirectly. But its implementation was a challenge so it had to be modified according to the needs of the States.

"The Right to Education' (RTE) Act came into effect in 2009 which was a wonderful effort to fulfil our need of education. Because of RTE, people especially in rural areas also comprehended the value of education. 'The ASER 2010 report shows that for the age group 6-14 years in all of rural India, the percentage of children who are not enrolled in school has dropped from 6.6 per cent in 2005 to 3.5 per cent in 2010.The proportion of girls in the age group 11-14 years who were out of school has also declined from 11.2 per cent in 2005 to 5.9 per cent in 2010." Recently the Indian Government has launched Sakshar Bharat Mission (September 8th, 2009) for Female Literacy. This mission aims to bring down female literacy by half of its present level.

The following data from Census 2011 proves that the gender disparity still exists and eradicating this and to educate women should be our main priority and then only we can claim to empower women of this country.

Since 1947 the Indian Government has tried to provide incentives for increasing attendance of girls in schools through facilities like midday meals, free books, and uniforms. The welfare thrust raised primary enrolment between 1951 and 1986. In 1986 the national policy on Education decided to restructure education in tune with the social framework of each state and with larger national goals. It emphasised that education was necessary for democracy and central to improvement of women's condition. The new policy aimed at social change through revised texts, curricula, increased funding for schools, expansion in the number of schools and policy improvements. Emphasis was placed on expanding girls' occupational centres and primary education; secondary and higher education; and rural and urban institutions. The report tried to connect problems like poverty, and the dependence on girls for household work and sibling day care. The National Literacy Mission also worked through female tutors in villages. Although the minimum marriage age is eighteen for girls, many continue to be married much earlier. Therefore at secondary level, female dropout rates are high.

Balika Samridhi Yojna was a new scheme which Government of India launched in 1997. The scheme was introduced for the development of girls belonging to Below Poverty Line (BPL). To promote education, such girls were facilitated with a scholarship of Rs 300 to 1000 up to class 10th. This was a fantastic initiative taken by the government but according to Planning Commission '...the scheme was known to very few villagers, in fact the scheme exits more on janapad files than having any impact in villages'. Therefore we can figure out how this idea becomes ineffective in absence of insufficient awareness programme in the rural areas.

Rajeev Gandhi Scheme for Empowerment of Adolescent Girls-Sabla:

This comprehensive proposal was planned for the holistic development of adolescent girls (AGs) in the age group of 11-18 years. The scheme was launched in 205 districts across the country in 2010. The pivotal elements in Rajeev Gandhi Yojna are: Nutrition provision @' 5 per day for 300 days in a year, Iron and Folic Acid supplementation, Health check-up and education referral services, guidance on family welfare, life skills education and vocational training. This central scheme is paramount in terms of making women empowered. It's implemented through the state government with 100 per cent financial assistance granted from the central government for all inputs but only 50 per cent of the financial norms are shared by the government of India for nutrition which is not adequate.

Our government launched Sarva Siksha Abhiyan (2001-02) to educate each and every one in the society without any discrimination. This campaign left a profound impact on the society as Gender Parity Index (GPI) in primary (0.94) as well as upper primary (0.92) education. There came an incredible increment in the enrolment of girls at primary by 8.67 level per cent (86.91 per cent in 2001-02 to 104.7 per cent in 2009-10) and upper primary level by 13 per cent (52.1 per cent to 65.1 per cent in 2004-05). But the assumption could never turn into reality and we are still confronting the challenges as attendance rates were not very high and according to India Human Development Report 2011 the attendance rates were not very high, during 2007-08 attendance rates were 82 per cent and 60 per cent respectively while the enrolment was 96 per cent (Data from planning commission). The quality of mid-day meal has worsened about which we keep getting news almost daily. The schools don't have facilities; here I would like to give a reference of a news reported in The Tribune in the on-line edition published on September 28th, 2001 which revealed the pathetic condition of the government schools. The government launched a radio education programme and provided only one radio for each school to make students hear and the result was futile as it didn't help the students. The other mission was Sakshar Bharat Mission to reach out to the adult especially women for whom education is not accessible. The impact of this project was tremendous as "it led to an increase in literacy, amongst women, from 53.67 per cent (Census 2001) to 65.46 per cent (Census 2011). It was also for the first time that of the total of 217.70 million literates added during the decade, women (110.07 million) over numbered men (107.63 million)."

Another such example is the news which was published on January 10th, 2011 in The Hindustan Times, New Delhi. The news read that since 2011 more women have been opting for engineering courses for their higher studies.

The budget of National Department of Education for 2005-2012 was Rs 99,057 crores which in US currency is $ 16 billion. This sounds impressive as it seems to give the lion's share to the women for which they have been claiming since long. But sometimes they feel a bit hesitant and depressed to express the heinous deeds of society against them such as foeticide, violence, patriarchal mindset, lack of freedom and gender disparity etc. Moreover they know that they themselves will have to step ahead to remove the impediments on their way and then only they will be able to access the opportunities being made available to them.

According to a news article published in The Times of India, January on 30, 2014, 42 per cent women are employable against 30 per cent men. 'Only 30 per cent grads job worthy' was stated in a report of a survey conducted across 28 states by online assessment firm Wheebox. Various skills of 1 lakh graduate and postgraduate students were evaluated. The result was very astonishing as it showed that mere '34 per cent people were employable in which women fared better than men in the tests'. So this news usher us to the bright future of women in India even when they have limited resources.

So if women will have education, surely they will participate in the country's progress and will gain economic independence and then only they will have the ability of decision making. Education is the best medium which can give them 'Midas Touch'. 'Investing in girls is smart', so said Word Bank President, Robert Zoellick–and that 'this investment in education is an unsurpassed and excellent and fundamental exercise'. If effective policies of a nation are blended with sustainable investment in education, not only women but the whole nation will get the positive results of the endeavours as thereby the individual and group entitlements will become accessible.

References

- SAARC Development Goals, www.mospi.nic.in
- Programmes for Women, Chapter 2, 12th Five Year Plan Report of the Working Group on Women's Agency and Empowerment, www.planning-commission.nic.in
- Agarwal S. P., Women's Education in India, Present Status, Perspective Plan, 1995-98 With Global View, Chapter 1, Volume 3.
- "Crude literacy rate" in India from 1901 to 2011, census of India 2011.
- Faster, Sustainable and More Inclusive Growth, An Approach to the Twelfth Five Year Plan 2012-17, www.planningcommission.nic.in
- Education in India, www.en.wikipedia.org
- Victims of Social Injustice, Chapter 3, Pg 29 www.planningcommission.nic.in
- Ministry of Women and Child Development, Government of India, Annual Report 2012-13, www.wcd.nic.in
- 12th Five Year Plan Report of the Working Group on Women's Agency and Empowerment, www.planningcommission.nic.in
- Getting to Equal: How Educating Every Girl Can Help Break the Cycle of Poverty.

Chapter-2

Women Empowerment and Role of Education

—Nutan Sharma

Abstract

Globalisation has presented new challenges in the realisation of the goal of empowering women. Women empowerment has become the slogan and motto of many social reformers, governmental agencies and voluntary organisations. There is a long cherished wish among all the women to have better avenues in order to lead the life in a more fruitful way. There are number of elements which deprive women of their basic rights in every society, state and nation, but these elements lack the awareness. If we enlist such elements from the society, then women would be on the top of this list. As a consequence of this growing tendency of underestimating women such as to make them occupy a secondary position in society and to deprive them of their basic rights, the need for empowering women was felt. Women education in India has also been a major pre-occupation of both the government and civil society as educated women can play a very important role in the development of the country. The growth of women's education in rural areas is very slow. This obviously means that still large segment of womenfolk of our country are illiterate, weak, backward and exploited. Education of women is the most powerful tool to change the society. Education also reduces the inequalities and improves their status within the family. Education is milestone of women empowerment because it enables them to respond to the challenges, to confront their traditional roles and change their life. Hence, importance of education can't be neglected in the context of women empowerment.

Key Words: *Globalisation, Development, Exploited.*

Introduction

In recent years globalisation has presented new challenges in the realisation of the goal of empowering women. Women empowerment has become the slogan and motto of many social reformers, governmental agencies and voluntary organisations. There is a long cherished wish among all the women to have better avenues in life in order to lead the life in a more fruitful way. Today we enjoy the benefits of being citizens of a free nation, but we really need to think whether each of the citizens of our country is really free or enjoying freedom, in the true sense of the term. If we consider our country, each Indian citizen is given certain basic rights. The Constitution of our nation doesn't discriminate between men and women, but our society has deprived women of certain basic rights, which were bestowed upon them by our Constitution. Due to such current situation, it was needed to make women free from all the shackles and to empower them as well. This is nothing but empowerment of women.

Empowerment

Empowerment means creating of social environment in which one can make decisions and make choices either individually or collectively for social transformation. It strengthens the innate ability of the individuals by way of acquiring knowledge, power and experience. Empowerment is the process of enabling the individual to think, take action and control his or her work in an autonomous way. It includes control over resources (physical, human, intellectual and financial) and over ideologies (beliefs, values and attitudes). It is not merely a feeling of greater extrinsic control, but also the realisation of an intrinsic capacity, greater self-confidence and an internal transformation of one's consciousness that enables one to overcome external barriers to accessing resources or changing traditional ideology.

Women's empowerment is very essential for the development of society. As per the United Nation Development Fund for women (UNIFEM), the term women's empowerment means:

(i) To acquire knowledge and understanding of gender relations and the ways in which these relations may be changed.

(ii) To develop a sense of self-worth, a belief in one's ability so as to secure desired changes and the right to control one's life.

(iii) Gaining the ability to generate choices and exercise bargaining power.

(iv) Developing the ability to organise and influence the direction of social change, to create a more just social and economic order, nationally and internationally.

In other words empowerment can be summarised as:-

- Self decision-making power.
- Access to information and resources for taking proper decision.
- Ability to exercise assertiveness in collective decision making.
- Positive thinking on the ability to make change.
- Ability to learn skills for improving one's personal or group power.
- Ability to change others' perceptions by democratic means.
- Increasing one's positive self-image and overcoming stigma.

Hence, empowerment is a psychological sense of personal control or influence and a concern with actual social influence, political power and legal rights. It is a multi level construct referring to individuals, organisations and community. It is an international, ongoing process centred in the local community, involving mutual respect, critical reflection, caring and group participation, through which people lacking an equal share of valued resources gain greater access to the control over these resources.

Women Empowerment and Education

It is through education that one realises what is good and what is bad, what is proper and what is not, what is just and what is unjust, etc.. It is education which gives a voice to injustice. Women's empowerment is not limited only to the Indian society; women's empowerment has now become a topic of global discussion. Therefore, literacy should spread amongst women. The literacy rate amongst the women in the post-Independent Era is not as per the expectations. We, as a nation, dream of becoming a Super Power by 2020. For becoming a Super Power, each element of our society/nation should contribute in the nation building process. But if women, who constitute almost half of the population of this society, aren't literate then we can't expect to become a Super Power. Therefore, it is urgent for us to know the importance of women's education, which would, in turn, give an impetus to the process of women's empowerment.

"***There is no chance of the welfare of the world unless the condition of women is improved. It is not possible for a bird to fly on one wing.***"

—Swami Vivekananda

Education as means of empowerment of women can bring about a positive attitudinal change. It is therefore, crucial for the socio-economic and political progress of India. The Constitution of India empowers the State to adopt affirmative measures for prompting ways and means to empower women. Education significantly makes difference in the lives of women. Education is important for everyone, but it is a critical means of empowerment for girls and women. This is not only because education is an entry point to opportunity but also because a woman's educational achievements have positive ripple effects within the family and across generations.

Education increases the number of economic, social and political opportunities available to women. It leads to direct economic benefits in the form of higher lifetime earnings for women. The society and community also benefit from the higher productivity of its labour force. Besides improving human capital and increasing economic growth, female education also reduces the fertility rate. Keeping women illiterate clearly retards economic growth. Societies that do not invest in girls' education pay a price for it in terms of slower growth and reduced incomes. Investments in female education start a virtuous cycle that leads to improved levels of income, growth and gender equality. Inequality in education is like an asset distorted that misallocates resources, thereby reducing economic growth.

Education increases women's knowledge about controlling fertility and access to family planning services and often encourages them to delay the age at which they marry. The political commitment behind many education campaigns has remained unfulfilled. Disparities in education between various social groups defined by region, area, caste, sex, class, disabilities etc. still exist. They are indicative of government's failure to deal with the problem of enabling the right to education. There is an urgent need to convert the government's commitments regarding education into action. Only then it will be possible to use education as a key instrument for bringing changes in social and cultural attitudes in relation to human rights.

Challenges

Indian societies have received notoriety for being unsafe for women. Whereby the fair sex is not only being hassled, stalked and raped but incidents of immoral trafficking also are very high. Add to this the heinous practice of female foeticide and infanticide wherein nearly 10 million baby girls have been killed in the last twenty years alone (Greater Kashmir, 2013). In fact, the level of atrocities against women is an indicator of the coercion of our society and underscores that we are a suppressed society. Clearly, safety is an obsolete word in today's India. In India, women are devalued traditionally and the men's image is reified.

Sen, in his work "Securing the Future We Want: Gender Equality, Economic Development, and Environmental Sustainability" alongside the 67th UN General Assembly stressed that empowering women and girls with more choices and more freedoms is crucial to achieving a better future for all. He also added that women agency and freedom are among the crucial means for enhancing development (Sen, 2012). But unfortunately women are victimised through dowry, kidnapping, rape, sexual harassment, female infanticides and sex selective abortions, domestic violence, trafficking, etc. Instead of getting proper justice and favour, women are deprived of justice because of the non-availability of witness, discontinuance of suits, difficulty of proving the incidents etc. So, empowering or strengthening the woman is the need of the hour and her status should be uplifted. To enable her to utilise her potential power she should be strengthened mentally, physically, culturally, politically so as to contribute in the all round development of our country.

Social norms and family structures in developing countries like India, manifests and perpetuate the subordinate status of women. There are several constraints, mentioned as follows:–

- One of such inhibiting norm is the continual preference for the birth of a male child. This preference is present in almost all societies and communities and its hold has strengthened rather than weakened and its most glaring evidence is in the falling sex ratio (Seth, 2004). The society is more biased in favour of male child with respect to provision of education, nutrition and other opportunities. The root cause of this type of attitude lies in the belief that male child inherits the clan in India.
- Women often internalise the traditional concept of their role as natural, thus inflicting an injustice upon their own selves.
- Poverty is the reality of life for the vast majority of women in India. It is another factor that poses challenge in the way of realising women's empowerment. In a poor family, girls are the main victims; they are malnourished and are denied the opportunity of better education and other facilities. But if women become financially independent or acquire greater control over the resources then they exhibit greater autonomy both in the household and in public sphere and are no longer victims of poverty.
- Lack of awareness about legal and constitutional provisions and failure in realising it, is another factor that hinders the process of empowerment. Most of the women are not aware of their legal rights. Even women who are aware, lack the courage to take the legal step. The legislation has almost failed in case of immoral trafficking and indecent exposure of women. There are numerous incidences of indecent exposure of women in all forms of media with hardly any prosecution. Although the legal rights are in place to create an enabling atmosphere these have not been successfully implemented in realising women's empowerment.
- Other problems against women education includes the familiar problems like lack of funds, inadequate facilities, inadequate

manpower, sexual harassment, conflicting societal role expectations, and lack of political will power to implement the entire educational programme.

- There are some other major constraints, like lack of confidence, lack of business acumen and know how, lack of financial support, inhibiting socio - cultural customs etc., that hinder women from becoming self employed and instead become dependent on wage employment outlets. Highly educated, technically sound and professionally qualified women should be encouraged for managing their own enterprise, the unexplored talents of young women should be identified, trained and used for various types of industries so as to increase the productivity in the industrial sector.
- Structural barriers in the economic, social, political and environmental spheres produce and reinforce these inequalities. Obstacles to women's economic and political empowerment, and violence against women and girls, are barriers to sustainable development and the achievement of human rights, gender equality, justice and peace.

Conclusion

Women empowerment is an essential element in national development. Since women constitute half of the population there can be no development unless the needs and interests of women are fully taken into account. In fact, empowered women are a nation's strength. Since development means improvement in the living conditions of the society, as a whole, it is logical to expect that this also means improved status for women. The effective management and development of women's resources, their capabilities, interests, skills and potentialities are of paramount importance for the mobilisation of human resources. In order to create a sustainable world, it is the need of the hour to educate and empower women and girls. Empowering women empowers her family and in turn her community which translates to a powerful force that can change the world in significantly positive ways. Also, bringing more equality to mankind balances the strengths and weaknesses of men and women so as to complement each other. Now it is cleared that only literacy is not the ultimate solution but women should be highly educated to know their rights and duties. But it is also mandatory that there should be proper implementations of policies and different programmes regarding women empowerment. The need of the hour is to identify those loopholes or limitations which are obstructing the realisation of empowerment of women and this initiative must be started from the women folk itself so as to set into motion the objectives imbibed in the policy initiatives of the State and society. Governments should undertake all appropriate steps towards the elimination of any stereotyped concepts in all forms of education. Let us take the oath that we want an egalitarian society where everybody whether a man or a woman get the equal opportunity to express and uplift one's well-being and well-being of the society as a whole.

References

- Baruah, B. (2013). Role of Electronic Media in Empowering Rural Women Education of N.E. India. *ABHIBYAKTI: Annual Journal,* 1, 23-26.
- Deshpande, S., and Sethi, S., (2010). Role and Position of Women Empowerment in Indian Society, *International Referred Research Journal,* 1(17), 10-12.
- Goswami, L. (2013). Education for Women Empowerment, *ABHIBYAKTI: Annual Journal*, 1, 17-18.
- Greater Kashmir (2013). Let women script their own destiny.www.greaterkashmir.com
- Gupta, N. L. (2003). *Women's Education through Ages.* New Delhi : Concept Publications Co.
- Hall, C. (1990). *Women and Identity: Values Choices in a changing World.* New York: Hemisphere Publishing Corporation.
- Kadam, R. N. (2012). Empowerment of Women in India- An Attempt to Fill the Gender Gap, *International Journal of Scientific and Research Publications,* 2(6), 11-13.
- Maslak, M. A. & Singhal, G. (2008). The identity of educated women in India: Confluence or divergence. *Gender and Education,* 20(5), 481-493.
- Nagaraja, B. (2013). Empowerment of Women in India: A Critical Analysis. *Journal of Humanities and Social Science* 9(2), 45-52.
- Sen, A. K. (2012). Speech on Securing the Future We Want: Gender Equality, Economic Development, and Environmental Sustainability, www.undp.org
- Seth, M. (2004). *Women and Development- The Indian Experience,* New Delhi: Sage Publication.

- Suguna, M., (2011). Education and Women Empowerment in India, *International Journal of Multidisciplinary Research,* 1(8), 19-21.
- Verma, J. (2006). *Gender, Girls and Women Education.* New Delhi: Murari Lal & Sons.
- http://www.slideshare.net/puneetsharma5688/women-empowermentpuneet-sharma
- http://womeninislam.ws/en/status-of-women_indian-society.aspx
- http://womenroleinsociety.blogspot.in/2010/06/status-of-women-in-indian-society.html
- http://www.bu.edu/wcp/Papers/Huma/HumaSing.htm

Chapter-3

Role of Education in Women Empowerment

—*Sharabani Mazumdar*

Abstract

Education is the means to voice injustice. It is the indispensible tool through which women empowerment can be achieved. In India empowerment of women became a serious concern of both the government and civil society as women are the better half of the human race. If women are educated then they can contribute in the social, economic and political development of the country. The term empowerment in relation to women defines her raised status with respect to spiritual, political, social and economic development. It is only education which enables them to responds to the challenges, to confront their traditional roles and change their life as well as the life of their families. In rural areas the growth of women education is very slow and needs to be improved. It means that most of the women in the country are illiterate, weak, exploited and backward. Only education can bring a tremendous change. Through education only, women can get equal status in society. The most needed qualities with in women like self dependence, self-confidence, ability to take decisions, positive way of thinking, and take active participation in the transformation process should be the main goal of empowerment of education. Therefore, it is necessary to spread literacy amongst women. To become a super power India should provide education to women who constitute almost half of the population in the world. An educated woman has the skills, information and self-confidence needed to be a better parent, worker and citizen. Access to education of women can change the present scenario of the society and nation.

Key Words: *Education, Women Empowerment, Female Literacy Rate.*

Introduction

There are members within the society who are deprived of their basic rights in every society, state and nation. This is due to their lack of awareness as a consequence of which there is a growing tendency of underestimating women, assigning them a secondary position in society and depriving them of their basic rights; due to such injustices being met out to women the need for empowering them was strongly felt.

Definition

"Women's empowerment is defined as the process in which their spiritual, political, and socio-economic status is raised." This also includes the right to raise their level of confidence regarding their own capabilities. Empowerment includes the following aspects:

1. The ability to take their own decisions,
2. Right to seek information and have other facilities at their disposal which would enable them to take proper decisions.
3. Access to wide choices (Not only 'Yes/No' and 'If/Else' choices.
4. Firmness while taking collective decisions.
5. Possessing positive way of thinking regarding the ability to bring about transformation.
6. The ability to bring about improvement in one's own capabilities.
7. The competence to modify other's attitudes in a democratic manner.
8. The right to participate in continuous and self-propagated development process and to take active participation in the transformation process.
9. The ability to control negative factors and build up a positive image of oneself.

The word 'Education' has a very wide connotation. According to Nunn, "Education is the complete development of individuality so that an individual can make an original contribution to the human life to his/her best capacities." Education may be visualised as a process of self-realisation which has been well emphasised by Gandhi Ji. It is the light which clearly shows the difference between the good and the bad. It is education which gives a voice to injustice.

Importance of Education for Women Empowerment

Women Empowerment is a global issue and discussion on political right of women are at the fore front of many formal and informal campaigns worldwide. Women constitute almost half of the population in the world. But the hegemonic masculine ideology in different parts of the world has made them suffer a lot as they were denied equal opportunities. Access to education has been one of the most pressing demands of women's rights movements. Concept of empowerment began to arise within the women's movement in the mid 1970s. The similarities among oppressed groups in different parts of the world are considerable because the oppressed face the common problem of limited willingness of those in control to see the seriousness of their condition and to work to solve it. Under the circumstances, the oppressed must themselves develop power for change to occur. It is believed that empowerment would follow if women understood their conditions, knew their rights and learn skills that have been traditionally denied to them. This is possible through education which is mile stone of women empowerment because it enables them to respond to the challenges, to confront their traditional roles and change their life. Education is the tool for self realisation which is the most important need of women.

Women Education Prospects and Challenges

Women education in India has also been a major concern of both the government and civil society as educated women can play a very important role in the development of the country.

India is poised to emerge as one of the most develop nation by 2020, more literate, knowledgeable and economically at the forefront. No doubt, women will play a vital role in contributing to the country's development. Women power is crucial to the economic growth of any country. Though India could well become one of the largest economies in the world, it is being hindered due to a lack of women's participation.

India presently accounts for the largest number of illiterates in the world. Literacy rate in India has risen sharply from 18.3 per cent in 1951 to 64.8 per cent in 2001 in which enrolment of women in education have also risen sharply from 7 per cent to 54.16 per cent. Despite the importance of women education, unfortunately only 39 per cent of women are literate as compared to 64 per cent of the men. Within the framework of a democratic polity our laws, development policies, plans and programmes have aimed at women's advancement in different spheres. In recent years, the empowerment of women has been recognised as the central issue in determining the status of women. The National Commission of Women was set up by an Act of Parliament in 1990 to safeguard the right and legal entitlements of women. The 73rd and 74th Amendments (1993) to the constitution of India have provided for reservation of seats in the local bodies of Panchayats and Municipalities for women, laying a strong foundation for their participation in decision making at the local level.

In spite of several forceful intervention by - a bastion of female privileges, feminist critics, constitutional guarantees, protection laws and sincere efforts of the state governments and central government through various schemes and programmes over the last 62 years and above all the United Nation's enormous pressure for mitigating the plight of women - women education is still in the state of an enigma in India for several reasons. The growth of women's education in rural areas is very slow. This obviously means that still large womenfolk of our country are illiterate, weak, backward and exploited. Moreover education is also not available to all equally. Gender inequality is reinforced in education which is proved by the fact that the literacy rate for the women is only 54 per cent against 76 per cent of men as per 2001 Census.

Despite improvements in girls' education, immunisation, and access to credit significant gaps remain in gender equality and economic empowerment in developing countries like India. There are strong correlation among girls' education, marriage age, maternal health, and fertility. Girls who marry early are likely to have less education, poorer health, higher fertility, and more unequal relations within the household. Understanding the impact of these constraints is important for designing effective interventions to address these gender gaps. Equally important is to understand the links among them. Due to mainly a lack of comparative and long-term data, there is also limited knowledge about how these factors — alone or in combination — can keep women from getting jobs or succeeding as entrepreneurs. This project addresses these knowledge gaps by assessing the causal impact of reducing various barriers — such as limited access to education and information, early marriage, poor financial skills, a lack of savings, lack of attention, foetus killing — that shape women's prospects for empowerment from an early age.

Literacy Rate in India

To know development in a society, Literacy is another proper indicator of economic development. For purpose of census, a person in age limit of seven and above, who can both write and read with understanding in any of the language is considered as a literate in India.

As per Population Census of India 2011, the literacy rate has shown as improvement of almost 9 per cent. It has gone up to 74.04 per cent in 2011 from 65.38 per cent in 2001, thus showing an increase of 9 per cent in the last 10 years. Total literacy rate consists of male literacy rate at 82.14 per cent and female literacy rate at 65.46 per cent. Kerala with 93.9 per cent literacy rate is the top state in India with respect to literacy attainment. Lakshadweep and Mizoram are at second and third position with 92.3 per cent and 91.06 per cent literacy rates respectively. Bihar with 63.08 per cent literacy rate is the last in terms of literacy rate in India.

Ranking of States in India by Literacy Rate

S. No	*State*	*Literacy Rate (2011 Census)*	*Male Literacy Rate (2011 Census)*	*Female Literacy Rate (2011 Census)*
1.	Andaman & Nicobar Islands	86.3 per cent	90.1 per cent	81.8 per cent
2.	Andhra Pradesh	67.7 per cent	75.6 per cent	59.7 per cent
3.	Arunachal Pradesh	67.0 per cent	73.7 per cent	59.6 per cent
4.	Assam	73.2 per cent	78.8 per cent	67.3 per cent
5.	Bihar	63.8 per cent	73.5 per cent	53.3 per cent
6.	Chandigarh	86.4 per cent	90.5 per cent	81.4 per cent
7.	Chattisgarh	71.0 per cent	81.5 per cent	60.6 per cent
8.	Dadra & Nagar Haveli	77.7 per cent	86.5 per cent	65.9 per cent
9.	Daman & Diu	87.1 per cent	91.5 per cent	79.6 per cent
10.	Delhi	86.3 per cent	91.0 per cent	80.9 per cent
11.	Goa	87.4 per cent	92.8 per cent	81.8 per cent
12.	Gujarat	79.3 per cent	87.2 per cent	70.7 per cent
13.	Haryana	76.6 per cent	85.4 per cent	66.8 per cent
14.	Himachal Pradesh	83.8 per cent	90.8 per cent	76.6 per cent
15.	Jammu and Kashmir	68.7 per cent	78.3 per cent	58.0 per cent
16.	Jharkhand	67.6 per cent	78.5 per cent	56.2 per cent
17.	Karnataka	75.6 per cent	82.8 per cent	68.1 per cent
18.	Kerala	93.9 per cent	96.0 per cent	92.0 per cent
19.	Lakshadweep	92.3 per cent	96.1 per cent	88.2 per cent
20.	Madhya Pradesh	70.6 per cent	80.5 per cent	60.0 per cent
21.	Maharashtra	82.9 per cent	89.8 per cent	75.5 per cent
22.	Manipur	79.8 per cent	86.5 per cent	73.2 per cent
23.	Meghalaya	75.5 per cent	77.2 per cent	73.8 per cent
24.	Mizoram	91.6 per cent	93.7 per cent	89.4 per cent
25.	Nagaland	80.1 per cent	83.3 per cent	76.7 per cent
26.	Orissa	73.5 per cent	82.4 per cent	64.4 per cent
27.	Puducherry	86.5 per cent	92.1 per cent	81.2 per cent
28.	Punjab	76.7 per cent	81.5 per cent	71.3 per cent
29.	Rajasthan	67.1 per cent	80.5 per cent	52.7 per cent
30.	Sikkim	82.2 per cent	87.3 per cent	76.4 per cent
31.	Tamil Nadu	80.3 per cent	86.8 per cent	73.9 per cent
32.	Tripura	87.8 per cent	92.2 per cent	83.1 per cent
33.	Uttar Pradesh	69.7 per cent	79.2 per cent	59.3 per cent
34.	Uttarakhand	79.6 per cent	88.3 per cent	70.7 per cent
35.	West Bengal	77.1 per cent	82.7 per cent	71.2 per cent
-	**INDIA**	74.04 per cent	82.14 per cent	65.46 per cent

Steps Taken by Government of India to Improve Literacy Rate in India

- Free education programs to poor people living in villages and towns.
- Setting up of new schools and colleges at district and state levels.
- Several committees have been formed to ensure proper utilisation of funds allotted to improve literacy rate.

In India, it was found that there is a large disparity between female literacy rates in different states. For example, while Kerala actually has a female literacy rate of about 86 per cent, Bihar and Uttar Pradesh have female literacy rates around 55-60 per cent. These values are further correlated with health levels of the Indians, where it was found that Kerala was the state with the lowest infant mortality rate while Bihar and Uttar Pradesh are the states with the lowest life expectancies in India. Furthermore, the disparity of female literacy rates across rural and urban areas is also significant in India. Out of the 24 states in India, 6 of them have female literacy rates of below 60 per cent. The rural state Rajasthan has a female literacy rate of less than 12 per cent.

In India, higher education is defined as the education of an age group between 18 and 24, and is largely funded by the government. Despite women making up 24-50 per cent of higher education enrolment, there is still a gender imbalance within higher education. Only one third of science students and 7 per cent of engineering students are women. In comparison however, over half the students studying education are women.

Why Women in India are not Educated?

India has a biased outlook towards the education of women. The Indian society feels that a woman is a liability who will get married and will not contribute to the economic and social development of the family. The society perceives that a woman cannot do other duties apart from her duties of cooking and housekeeping. As a result the society has considered home training more important as compared to formal education.

Another factor is the rapid growth of the population. Most Indian household have a number of children which leads to the neglect of the girl education and put more emphasis on the education of the boy child.

Women have a much lower literacy rate than men. Far fewer girls are enrolled in the schools, and many of them drop-out. In the patriarchal setting of the Indian family, girls have lower status and fewer privileges than boy children. Conservative cultural attitudes prevent some girls from attending schools.

The number of literate women among the female population of India was between 2–6 per cent from the British Raj onwards to the formation of the Republic of India in 1947. Concerted efforts led to improvement from 15.3 per cent in 1961 to 28.5 per cent in 1981. By 2001 literacy of women had exceeded 50 per cent of the overall female population, though these statistics were still very low compared to world standards and even male literacy within India. Recently the Indian government has launched "Sakshar Bharat Mission" for Female Literacy. This mission aims to bring down female illiteracy by half of its present level.

Importance of Education in India

Women education in India plays a key role in the social and economic development of the country. Educating a woman uplifts her life as well as the quality of life of her entire family. It is a fact that any educated woman will definitely support the education of children especially a girl child to provide a better guidance to her children. An educated woman will easily foster an independent and progressive outlook in her children. An educated woman in a society like India will assist in reducing the infant mortality rate and control the booming of the population.

As it was said by Emmaline Pankhurst that freeing a woman is freeing a half of the human race because they represent a half of the population. On the other side Nellie Mcclung advices the society never to underestimate the power of a woman.

Education is one of the most critical areas of empowerment of woman. Among children not attending school there are twice as many girls as boys, and among illiterate adults there are twice as many women as men. An educated woman is, for example, likely to marry at a later age and have fewer children. Cross-country studies show that an extra year of schooling for girls reduces fertility rates by 5 to 10 per cent and the children of an educated mother are more likely to survive. In India, for example, the infant mortality rate of babies whose mothers have received primary education is half that of children whose mothers are illiterate.

An educated woman will also be more productive at work — and better paid. Indeed, the dividend for educational investment is often higher for women than men. Studies from a number of countries suggest that an extra year of schooling will increase a woman's future earnings by about 15 per cent, compared with 11 per cent for a man.

Over recent decades there has certainly been significant progress in girls' education. Between 1970 and 1992, combined primary and secondary enrolment for girls in developing countries rose from 38 per cent to 68 per cent — with particularly high rates in East Asia (83 per cent) and Latin America (87 per cent). But there is still some way to go. In the least developed countries enrolment rates are only 47 per cent at the primary level and 12 per cent at the secondary level.

When girls are allowed to go to school, they have a significant impact on their family and community. According to Camfed, when you educate a girl she will earn up to 25 per cent more and reinvest 90 per cent of her income in her family. This reinvestment in her family means her children will more likely go to school and be immunised, leading to healthier and more productive individuals and communities.

Measures Taken to Improve Education Level of Women

- The government has made it mandatory for an Indian child between the ages of 6 to 14 years to attend school. In addition, the government has made available free food specially lunch across the country for the underprivileged school going children.

- Welfare and Support Services are being extended through programmes like Hostels for Working Women, Short Stay Homes and Family Counselling Centres etc. So far, 840 hostels have been constructed all over the country to provide accommodation for more than 75,000 working women and their dependent children. At present around 360 Short Stay Homes all over the country are taking care of 12,000 women and girls in distress. The mid-term appraisal recognises the increasing demand for these services and suggests expansion.
- The Ninth Plan attaches great importance to the awareness generation and gender sensitisation programmes to change the mind-set of the people besides projecting positive image of women and the girl child. Efforts are also being made to gender sensitise the policy makers, planners, administrators, implementers, enforcement machinery etc.
- The other enabling measures that are being strengthened and expanded to reach the un-reached include - (i) safeguarding the rights and interests of women through the efforts of the National Commission for Women; (ii) extending micro-credit to poor and assetless women through the efforts of Rashtriya Mahila Kosh (RMK); and (iii) extending grant-in-aid to NGOs to promote voluntary action through Central Social Welfare Board (CSWB).
- Towards empowering women, efforts are being made–(i) to finalise the draft 'National Policy for Empowerment of Women'; (ii) to legislate reservation of not less than 1/3 seats for women in the Lok Sabha and in the State Legislative Assemblies and thus ensure adequate representation of women in decision making; (iii) to adopt an integrated approach towards empowering women through effective convergence of existing services, financial and human resources, and infrastructure in both women-specific and women-related sectors; (iv) to adopt a special strategy of 'Women's Component Plan' to ensure funds/benefits flow to women

from other relevant sectors; and (v) to organise women into Self-Help Groups and thus mark the beginning of a major process of empowering women.

- A Committee on Empowerment of Women was constituted in March 1997 by Lok Sabha to review the progress of empowering women from time to time. The Committee has, so far, reviewed the progress of the development schemes for rural women.
- A Group of Ministers was set up in July, 2000 to examine/finalise the proposal of the formulation of a National Policy on Empowerment of women.
- A Task Force on Women and Children was constituted in August, 2000 to review all the related aspects of empowering women, besides drafting a programme for celebrating 2001 as 'Year of Women's Empowerment.'
- A review of the implementation of Women's Component Plan in August, 2000 has brought forth that – (i) a few Central Ministries/Departments like Health and Family Welfare, Education, Labour, Agriculture, Rural Development, Urban Affairs and Employment, Small Scale and Agro Industries, Non-conventional Energy Sources, Science and Technology are already channelizing the flow of funds/benefits to women; and (ii) States like Karnataka, Kerala, Gujarat and Himachal Pradesh have also taken initiatives for earmarking funds under Women's Component Plan.
- To organise women into Self-Help Groups (SHGs) and equip them with the services of awareness generation and income generation through training, employment, credit and marketing linkages to small women entrepreneurs etc., programmes like Indira Mahila Yojana (IMY) and Rural Women's Empowerment and Development (RWDEP) have been launched. Of the total Ninth Plan target of 50,000, more than 37,000 Groups were set up benefiting about 8 lakh women.
- Towards promoting employment and income generation - programmes like Support for Training and Employment (STEP) , Training-Cum-Production Centers (popularly known

as NORAD), Socio-economic Programme (SEP) and Condensed Courses of Education and Vocational Training (CCEVT) have been benefiting more than 5 lacs women both in traditional and non-traditional sectors.

- On the suggestion of the Planning Commission, action has already been initiated to merge all the training-cum-employment-cum-income generation programmes under one single umbrella programme viz., Integrated programme for Training and Employment for Women.

Conclusion

Taking an overview of all the above aspects, we come to know that the transformation is needed, accepting at the same time that its pace may be less than the desired pace. For giving this process a right momentum, education is indispensable. If women need to be empowered then we need to charge the weapon of education through which we can uplift the life and quality of women in all aspects.

References

- J. C. Aggarwal, (2010), Theory And Principles of Education, 13th edition Vikas Publication House Pvt. Ltd., New Delhi.
- Girl's education: A lifeline to development Women, Education and Empowerment: Pathways towards Autonomy edited by Carolyn Medel - Anonuevo (1993).
- UNESCO Institute for Education, Hamburg.
- Women's Empowerment Through Education, Jitendra Shinde, National Refereed Journal of Research in Arts & Education, www.abhinavjournal.com

Chapter - 4

Journey of Women Education towards Empowerment

—*Ruchi Dhyani*

Abstract

Education is a weapon that gives self confidence and power to take decisions in life without getting influenced by others. The society has always given priority to men and has accorded a secondary position to women. Women even don't enjoy their basic human rights. They often cannot actively take decisions concerning their own lives. Women empowerment means equal representation of women in all activities of societies. Empowerment means enforcing transition from enforcing condition of powerlessness to a position of power. Education helps a woman to write her own destiny with her own will. Education defines and gives the true worth and respect to women in society and enable them to stand as equal to men. Brigham Young has said, "If you educate a man; you educate a man. If you educate a woman; you educate a generation." Societies which discriminate by gender have to face poverty, less economic development, injustice and other social ailments. Women are equally important as men and they have equal rights to live their lives as they seek to.

Key Words: *Women, Education, Empowerment, Equality, Society.*

Introduction

"***Societies that discriminate on the basis of gender pay a significant price...... in terms of higher poverty, lower quality of life,***

Slower economic growth and weaker governance......Educating girl is strategic for achieving development."

—Elizabeth King

Article 26 of the Universal Declaration of human rights adopted by the United Nation General Assembly in 1948, proclaims that everyone has the right to education and enshrines this right alongside other basic rights such as freedom of expression and equality before the law. The Beijing Declaration and Platform for Action (1995) made specific reference for the first time towards ensuring the right of women and girls to education by setting a universal target and ensuring commitments of governments towards: provision of universal access to basic education by the year 2000 and completion of primary education by at least 80 per cent of primary school age children; closure of the gender gap in primary and secondary school education by the year 2005; provision of universal primary education in all countries before the year 2015. In April 2000 at Dakar, the Dakar Education for All (EFA) Framework for Action, Goal 5 (2000) further articulated that the efforts of the international community should be directed at, "Eliminating gender disparities in primary and secondary education by 2005 and achieving gender equality in education by 2015 with a focus on ensuring for the girls full and equal access to achievement in basic education of good quality."

Education is an essential means of empowering women with the knowledge, skills and self-confidence necessary to fully participate in the development process. Sustainable development is only possible when women and men enjoy equal opportunities to reach their potential. Okeke (1995) observed that education is a sure pathway to the liberation of the mind and the improvement of the socio-economic status of people. History, the world over, is replete with the achievements of men folk and their contributions to the development processes and from time immemorial the position of women in the structure of society has never been considered on the same plane as that of men, they have been regarded as a second-fiddle. "Women perform 66 per cent of the world work and produce 50 per cent of food yet earn only 10 per cent of income and own 1 per cent of the property. Whether the issue is improving education in the developing world or fighting global climate change or addressing nearly any other challenge we face empowering women is a critical part of the equation."(Bill Clinton, 2009).

Challenges to Girl Education

There are five main challenges that make it difficult for girls to access education. These include:

(1) **The cost of education:** there is need to ensure that communities, parents and children can afford schooling.

(2) **Poor school environments**: girls should have access to a safe school environment.

(3) **The weak position of women in society:** society and parents should be prompted to value the education of girls.

(4) **Conflict:** children who are excluded due to various conflicts should have access to schooling.

(5) **Social exclusion:** education inclusion programmes should ensure that girls are not disadvantaged on the basis of caste, ethnicity, religion or disabilities.

Meaning of Women Empowerment

Empowerment means enforcing transition from a condition of powerlessness to a position of power. Empowerment also refers to the equitable representation of women in decision-making structures - both formal and informal, and in the formulation of policies affecting their societies (Lopez-Claros et. al., 2005). The World Bank (2002) defines empowerment as the "expansion of the assets and capabilities [of individuals]... to participate in, negotiate with, influence, control and hold accountable institutions that affect their lives." According to Wallenstein (2001) empowerment is a social action process that promotes participation of people, organisation and communities towards the goal of increased individual and community control, political efficacy improved quality of community life and social justice. Women empowerment is one of the most important issues in the present day world. Though women have made a great contribution in the development process, they have low status as compared to men specifically in the developing world (Khan et al., 2010). According to the UN Population Information Network (1995) women's empowerment involves "their right to have the power to control their own lives, both within and outside the home; and their ability to influence the direction of social change to create a more just social and economic order, nationally and internationally." The parameters of empowerment have been identified as:

(a) Developing the ability for critical thinking.
(b) Fostering decision-making and action through collective processes.
(c) Ensuring equal participation in developmental processes.
(d) Enhancing self-esteem and self-confidence in women.

Thus, on the basis of above mentioned parameters of empowerment, women empowerment can also be conceived as shown in the below diagram.

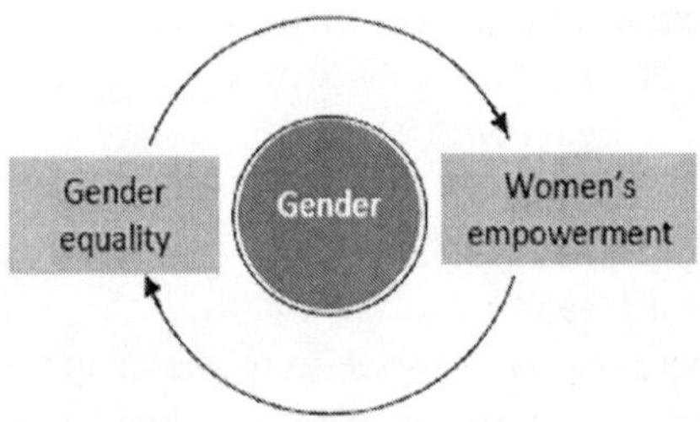

Education of girls and women helps them to access their human rights. Education empowers women to fight for their rights and realise their own worth. Education can also improve the bargaining power of women in the household by increasing their potential as earners from the labour market. The improved bargaining position may help women to take positions which do not conflict with their well-being. Individuals with more education command higher earnings in the labour market, and the return to education is higher in developing countries (Psacharopoulos 1994, Schultz 2002). Education can bring new opportunities and new dimensions in the life of every woman. It helps women in taking decisions concerning their own lives. Increased knowledge, self-confidence and awareness of gender equity are indicators of empowerment process (Murphy-Graham, 2008). There is evidence that these components are usually developed during and as a result of higher education (Maslak and Singhal, 2008). Education is a weapon that guarantees equity in society. Pandey and Singh (2008) investigated the role of employment and personal values in reproductive health status of women. Questionnaires to assess women empowerment, personal values, health and reproductive health behaviour were administered to 30 employed and 30 unemployed women. Results revealed that employed women felt more empowered and were superior on social, democratic, hedonistic and power values than their unemployed counterparts. They adopted family planning and reported better reproductive health status. Empowerment and personal values emerged as strong predictors of reproductive health.

Telescoping the Pathway from Education to Adolescent Transitions to Development

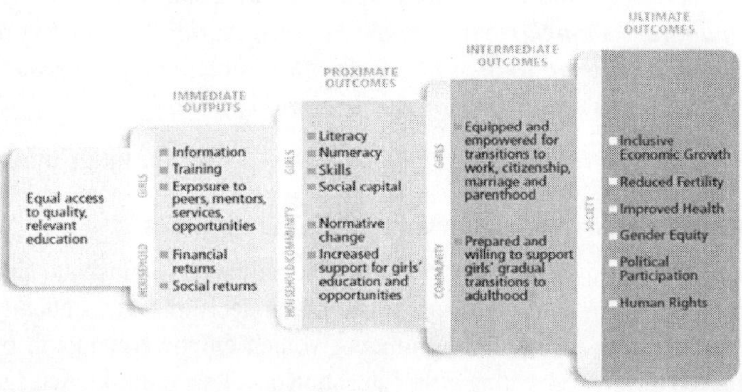

As shown in the diagram education propels girls towards the attainment of their basic human rights, equips them with basic skills, increases their participation in all the important sectors of society, empowers them for taking up rewarding work, enhances the worth of their citizenship, and enables them to take their own decisions concerning marriage, parenthood and other matters. All these transitions effect the attainment of the ultimate outcomes which is social, economic and political empowerment at the macro level.

Social Empowerment: The Social Empowerment is about changing society outlook so that women's place within it is respected and recognised on the terms by which they want to live, not on terms dictated by others. A sense of autonomy and self value is fundamental to be able to make choice independently - over sexual relations, marriage and having children.

Economic Empowerment: The Economic Empowerment is about women's capacity to contribute and benefit from economic activities on terms which recognise the value of their contribution, respect their dignity and also provide them equal opportunity for working conditions.

Political Empowerment: The Political Empowerment is concerned with the equity of representation in political institutions and the freedom of women to exercise the right to raise voice for their own welfare as till today they are being exploited by others.

"Women have been suppressed under customs and law for which man was responsible and in the shaping of which she had no hand... woman has as much right to shape her own destiny as man has to shape his...It is up to men to see that they enable them to realise their full status and play their part as equal of men."

—Mahatma Gandhi

Government Schemes for Women Empowerment

Women empowerment can be possible only when women are able to access their right to education and take their decisions independently without getting influenced by others. Women empowerment can be achieved through educating girls. Education develops skills, knowledge and confidence in women that can help them in achieving opportunities in the economy. Fee concession and needy scholarship for girls at schools has helped a lot in increasing the number of educated women. Vocational training programs can help in providing better skills and good jobs to women (Tornqvist, A., & C, Schmitz, 2009). Government also realises the importance of education in empowering the women that's why it has started many schemes for providing them educational opportunities like:

Kasturba Gandhi BalikaVidyalayaYojna: This program is especially for promoting girls education. There are 3500 Kasturba Gandhi Balika Vidyalaya in which 3.6 lakh girls are studying. These schools also have hostel facility for girls of 5th to 8th class. Launched in July 2004, the KGBV sets up residential schools at the upper primary region- primarily for girls from SC, ST and OBC families as well as minority communities. The scheme is being implemented in Educationally Backward Blocks where the female literacy is below the national average. 75 per cent of the seats in KGBVs are reserved for SCs, STs, OBCs and minorities. The remaining 25 per cent of the vacancies are filled with girls of BPL families.

Kanya Saaksharta Protsahan Yojna: Objective of this scheme is to reduce the drop-out rate and to increase the interest of Tribal Girl Students to continue their studies. Rs 500 is given to those girls who continue to study in class VI, Rs 1000 to girls who get admission in class IX and Rs 2000 to girls who gets admission in class XI.

Rajiv Gandhi Scheme for Empowerment of Adolescent Girls (RGSEAG) – 'Sabla': A Centrally-sponsored scheme was approved by the Government on August 16, 2010. The scheme is being implemented in 200 districts across the country on a pilot basis. In the remaining districts, Kishori Shakti Yojana (KSY) continues to be operational as before. However, SABLA has completely replaced Nutrition Programme for Adolescent Girls (NPAG) as all districts of NPAG are now part of the 'Sabla'. The scheme, interalia, aims at vocational training for girls above 16 years of age for their economic empowerment.

Rashtriya Mahila Kosh – (National Credit Fund for Women): The Rashtriya Mahila Kosh (National Credit Fund for Women) was set up in 1993 with a corpus of Rs 31 crores, against the backdrop of socio-economic constraints faced by poor women to access micro – credit from the formal financial system in the country, especially those in the rural and in unorganised sectors. The principal corpus was increased to Rs 100.00 crore by 2009-10. The main objective of setting up of Rashtriya Mahila Kosh (RMK) under the Department of Women and Child Development (now Ministry) was to provide micro-credit to poor women for various livelihood support and income generating activities at concessional terms in a client-friendly procedure to bring about their socio-economic development.

Gender Budgeting and Economic Empowerment of Women: Refers to Budgets which influence the overall level of national income and employment and reflect the priorities of the government regarding public investment, also promote gender equality within the national development framework. The Government of India is committed to promoting gender equality and has adopted Gender Budgeting (GB) as a tool to address the inequalities faced by women. The purpose is to ensure the translation of Government's policy commitments on gender equity into budgetary allocations.

Rajiv Gandhi National Crèche Scheme: With a view to encourage women to join/continue with gainful employment, Rajiv Gandhi National Crèche Scheme for children of working mothers (RGNCS) was introduced in 2006. The scheme seeks to provide day care facilities to children in the age group 0-6 years from families with a monthly income of less than Rs 12,000. In addition to being a safe space for the children, the crèche provide services like supplementary nutrition, preschool education, emergency health care etc.

Support to Training and Employment Programme for Women (STEP): A Central Sector Scheme launched in 1986-87, seeks to upgrade skill of poor and asset less women and provide employment on sustainable basis by mobilising them into viable cooperative groups, strengthening marketing linkages, providing support services and access to credit.

Central Social Welfare Board (CSWB): In order to address the socio-economic needs of the women and children of selected eight most backward districts in the North Eastern region in the economic arena, Central Social Welfare Board has formulated the Integrated Scheme for Women Empowerment (ISWE).

National Programme for Education of Girls at an Elementary Level (NPEGEL): The National Programme for Education of Girls at an Elementary Level was started in September 2003 as an integral component of the Sarva Shiksha Abhiyan. It sought to distribute free textbooks to girls till Class VIII, construct separate toilets for girls and to conduct bridge camps for older out-of-school girls. The NPEGEL aimed at ensuring that 50 per cent of the newly recruited teachers were females and that learning materials be gender sensitive. NPEGEL also intends to mobilise intensive community efforts and constitute an innovation fund (for better enrolment and retention) per district. As such, the NPEGEL provides additional provisions for enhancing the education of underprivileged/disadvantaged girls at an elementary level through more intense community mobilisation, development of model schools in clusters and the provision of need based incentives like textbooks and uniforms.

Swadhar: Aims to support the cause of women in becoming independent - in spirit, in thought, in action - and to have full control over their lives than be the victims of other's actions. The Swadhar Scheme purports to address the specific vulnerability of women in difficult circumstances through a Home-based holistic and integrated approach.

Swayamsiddha: This is one such scheme for empowering the Indian women both socially and economically so as to enable them to live with dignity and self-reliance. It is a Self Help Groups based programme with emphasis on convergence activities. The objective is to ensure that members of the Self Help Groups are able to avail the benefit of all schemes and services in an integrated and holistic manner.

Status of Women in India

In India women are the image of the worshiped Goddesses. Women are the house makers and they also contribute towards national progress and growth but still are facing discrimination in every facet of life. As per Census 2011, the workforce participation rate for females at the national level stands at 25.51 per cent compared with 53.26 per cent for males. In the rural sector, females have a workforce participation rate of 30.02 per cent compared with 53.03 per cent for males. In the urban sector, it is 15.44 per cent for females and 53.76 per cent for males. In 2011-12, the average wage/salary received by regular wage/salaried employees of age 15-59 years was Rs 201.56 per day for females compared with Rs 322.28 per day for males in rural areas. For urban areas, it was Rs 366.15 and Rs 469.87 per day for females and males respectively. Even in educational sector women are still lagging behind in getting educational opportunities.

As per Census 2011, 73.0 per cent of the population is literate comprising 64.6 per cent females and 80.9 per cent males. The incremental increase over Census 2001 of 10.5 per cent for females is higher than 5.0 per cent for males. The gross enrolment ration (GER) for females at the primary level stood at 116.7 compared with 115.4 for males in 2010-11. At the middle classes level, the GER for female was 83.1 while that for males was 87.7.

Indian women are not free to take the important decisions of their life relating to their health, marriage, family matters and financial matters. According to National Family Health Survey–III (2005-06), currently in the rural sector married women take 26 per cent decisions regarding obtaining health care for herself and 7.6 per cent in case of purchasing major household items. 10 per cent decisions in respect of visiting their family or relatives are taken by females. For urban areas, these figures are 29.7 per cent, 10.4 per cent and 12.2 per cent respectively. In the age group of 15-19 years, 46 per cent of women are not involved in any kind of decision making. In the rural sector, 23.4 per cent females are not involved in any decision-making while, in the urban sector 13.9 per cent of urban resident women are not involved in any decision making. It is found that 32.7 per cent illiterate women, 21.6 per cent unemployed women are not involved in any decision making. For the country as a whole, 59.6 per cent have no access to money.

Conclusion

It has been rightly said "*maa ke pairo me jannat hoti hai*", but we don't really give worth and respect to the creator of man who is a woman and hence will always be superior and greater to men. Women have always been mistreated and exploited by society and have often become victims of discrimination. Their voice has greatly been suppressed so that they cannot stand equal to men. But now the time has come to usher in the much needed change and for women to become empowered and know how to struggle for their basic human rights and break free from the discriminating world around them. Education is the only weapon which can help them to get powerful positions and take decisions concerning their own life without any fear and make it worthwhile.

References

- Khan, T., Mann, A., Zafar, M., Hashmi, N. & Akhtar, S. (2010). Determinants of Women Empowerment: A Case Study from District Rawalpindi, Punjab, Pakistan. *Pakistan Journal of Science,* Vol. No. 62 (1).
- Lopez-Claros, A., Zahidi, S. & Forum, W. E. (2005), Women's empowerment: Measuring the global gender gap. *In*, 2005. World Economic Forum Cologny Geneva.
- Maslak, M. A. & Singhal, G. (2008). The identity of educated women in India: Confluence or divergence. *Gender and Education*, 20, (5), 481-493.
- Okeke E.A.C. (1995) "Women Empowerment and Rural Development" in E .C. Eboh, C. U. Okoye & D Ayichi (Eds) Rural Development in Nigeria: Concepts, Processes and Prospects. Enugu. Auto-Century pp. 152-163.
- Pandey, S., Singh, M. (2008). Women empowerment & personal values as predictors of reproductive health. *Journal of the Indian Academy of Applied Psychology*, 34(2), 309-316.
- Psacharopoulos, George. (1994). "Returns to investment in education: A global update." *World Development*, 22 (9), 1325-1343.
- Schultz, T. Paul. (2002). "Why Governments Should Invest More to Educate Girls," *World Development,* 30 (2), 207-225.
- Sharma, R., & Afroz, Z. (2014). Women empowerment through higher education, *International Journal of Interdisciplinary and Multidisciplinary Studies*, 1(5), 18-22.
- Tornqvist, A., & C, Schmitz. (2009). Women's economic empowerment: scope for Sida's engagement Sida (Swedish international corporation agency) working paper, Sida, Stockholm.
- United Nations Population Information Network (1995)."Guidelines to Women's Empowerment" in Guidelines for the United Nations Resident Coordinator System, September1995. www.un.org
- Wallersterin, N. (2001). Powerless, Empowerment & Health: Implication for health promotion programs: *American Journal of Health Promotion*, 6 (3), 197-205.
- World Bank (2002). *Empowerment and Poverty Reduction: A Sourcebook.* PREM: May1, 2002.
- www.e-learningup.org.in
- www.mhrd.gov.in
- www.mospi.nic.in
- www.siteresources.worldbank.org
- www.indianresearchjournals.com
- www.nfhsindia.org
- www.ohchr.org
- www.equalityindia.wordpress.com

Chapter-5

Women Empowerment through Education: Pre & Post Independence Era

—Ruchi Shivam

Abstract

A woman is dynamic in every role she plays. The status of women in India has been subject to great changes over the past eras. From equal status with men in ancient times to low status in the medieval period and then to the promotion of equal rights by many reformers, the history of women in India has been eventful. Even the Vedas, Upanishads and other religious texts have appreciated women for their beauty and intelligence. From pre-independence to post-independence era women have been considered eligible for education. Even the constitution of India provides equal status and right to education for women. Special provision and amendment has been made in our constitution to increase the participation of females. Various commissions from time to time have been emphasising on the importance of women education at all the three levels (primary, secondary, university). Through this chapter author has tried to show the stages towards women empowerment through education in Pre and Post independence era. The chapter also deals with the recommendations of the various commissions on women education.

Keywords: *Women empowerment, Education, Pre Independence, Post independence.*

Introduction

"O learned lady! All life is dependent on you, because you impart education to all"

—Rig Veda

Scholars believe that in ancient India, women enjoyed equal status with men in all fields of life. Some others hold contrasting views regarding equal status. Scholarly works by ancient Indian grammarians such as *Patanjali* and *Katyayana* suggest that women were educated in the early Vedic Period. Rig Veda suggests that they were highly educated and independent enough to take their own decisions. As per the Vedic texts in the Vedic period many learned ladies conducted religious rituals and sacrifices. The Indian women's position in the society deteriorated during the medieval period yet in spite of the severe conditions of the medieval era, some women excelled in the field of politics, literature, education and religion. In South India many women administered villages, towns, divisions and heralded social and religious institutions. The early beginnings of renaissance of the Indian womanhood can be seen in the life history of Pandit Ramabai or Anandibai who ventured to go abroad for education, and the humble but heroic efforts of social reformers like Karve (S.P. Agrawal and J.C. Agrawal). After independence we notice drastic change in society with special reference to women education. Many separate arts colleges for women and institutions imparting knowledge in home science, applied sciences and poly techniques too were established. Educationally equipped women have lots of opportunities and fruitful carrier potential in various fields like administration, advertising, aeronautics, business and commerce etc. In the post independent era women in education were no fewer in number and not limited to certain fields only. The picture became broader and clearer with respect to women education.

The need to bring women into the main stream of the development has been the prime concern in India. Its history can be traced back from ancient India till after gaining independence of India. It is so because they are the principle providers of care and support to infants and children. As we know that women constitute almost half of the population in the world, thus the investment towards women capacity building and empowering them to exercise their choice is not only valuable in itself but also a surest way to contribute to economic growth and overall development of the society through development of human resource.

In order to improve the well being of humanity in society, the government has made a significant shift in the approach from "welfare during fifties" to "development during seventies" and "empowering during nineties." During the nineties major thrust in respect of women was to make them economically independent and self-reliant while with respect to children, efforts were made to ensure their survival, protection and development with special focus on the girl child and adolescent girl.

The principle of gender equality is enshrined in the Indian constitution in its preamble, fundamental rights, fundamental duties and directive principles. The constitution, not only grants equality to women but also empowers the State to adopt measure of positive discrimination in favour of women. Within the framework of a democratic politics, our laws, development policies, plans and programmes have aimed at women advancement in different spheres. From 5th five year plan (1974 - 78) onwards there has been a marked shift in the government's approach regarding the issue of women. In recent years the empowerment of women has been recognised as the central issue in determining the status of women. In ancient India, Gargi and other ladies were considering as jewels among women for their intellect. They were highly educated and perfect scholars of the Veda. If the husbands were well educated and the wives were ignorant or vice-versa, there would be a state of constant struggle between them. Thus, the importance of women education was equally emphasised in ancient era.

Women Education before Independence

In this section of the article women education in different time periods has been briefly discussed to show the actual picture that existed and also to show the change in the educational condition.

Before 200 B.C.: During this period women were eligible for the study of the Vedas and the performance of sacrifices. Upanayana sanskaar of girls was as common as of boys. There were several women scholars in the vedic age like Vishvavara, Atreyi, Apala, Indrani, Savitri, who remained unmarried for a long time and devoted themselves to higher studies. Many woman opted teaching as their profession. There were boarding houses for girl students probably under the superintendence of women teachers.

200 B.C. - 1200 A.D.: This was the time of a great setback for female education due to the deterioration of the religious status of women and lowering of the marriage age. The girls gradually lost the privilege of Upanayana, the Vedic initiation and were not considered fit to recite Vedic mantras or perform Vedic sacrifices. This was the period of downfall in women education.

1200-1800 A.D.: Female literacy rate went down very rapidly during the Muslim rule. Society on the whole became against women education. The pardah system stood in the way of girls beyond a certain age being sent to schools, though some schooling was possible for the very young girls. One of the most educated princesses of this time was Razia Sultan who was provided liberal education by the Mughal emperors. During this period some prejudices against education of women prevailed among the people. The mentality of people became narrow. Women were now no more considered fit for education.

1800-1854 A.D.: During this period several great Indians supported the opening of girls' schools and protested against various traditions against women education. Among them, Raja Ram Mohan Roy and Pandit Iswarchandra Vidyasagar played an important role. Now women education was promoted and female were motivated towards studies. By 1850 the stage was set for change in the state policy. Various orders were later confirmed by the educational despatch of 1854.

1854-1882 A.D.: With the educational despatch of 1854, the state promised financial assistance and even direct action. The establishment of municipalities and levy of the local fund aiding the primary education helped the establishment of special primary school for girls between 1870 and 1882. Now no more rules against women education were there and girls' schools were opened to promote female education.

1882-1902 A.D.: The recommendation of the Indian education commission (1882-83) on women education included the cause of supporting of girls' schools from public funds, the offer of free scholarships etc. Due to lack of funds, the progress of women education mostly depended upon private enterprises. The lady Dufferin fund was created during this period for developing medical education for women.

1902-1921 A.D.: This was the period of transference of education to Indian control in 1921. The transition showed better progress in the education of women mainly due to the greater public awakening and the First World War. Large number of women took up commercial and technical careers during this period. This naturally increased the educational opportunities for girls and their continuance in schools and colleges.

1921-47 A.D.: During this period the age of marriage was raised. Nonetheless it was also a period of financial stringency and political struggle. In spite of difficulties women education made considerable progress. By 1947 good increment was seen in girls studying in mixed schools.

Women Education after Independence (1947)

The university education commission (1948-49) made certain recommendations regarding women education. But the most important development regarding this cause was the setting up of a National Committee on Women's Education in 1958, entrusted with the responsibility of examining the problem of women education very comprehensively. As a result of recommendations of the committee a National Council for Education was setup in 1959. The Education Commission 1964-66 also made valuable recommendations regarding women education in India. Thus various recommendations by education committees were made regarding women education during this period. This was the period of women enlistment. Participation of women was seen in different fields. Many customs and traditions were changed and reformed. The table below shows the literacy rates of male and female population. A great hike is noticed in the literacy rate of female population. From 1901 to 2011 regular rise in the literacy percentage can be seen, thus showing the empowerment of female population.

Table: Male and Female Literacy Rates

Year	*Persons*	*Males*	*Females*
1901	5.3	9.8	0.7
1911	5.9	10.6	1.1
1921	7.2	12.2	1.8
1931	9.5	15.6	2.9
1941	16.1	24.9	7.3
1951	16.7	24.9	7.3
1961	24.0	34.4	13.0
1971	29.5	39.5	18.7
1981	36.2	46.9	24.8
1991	52.1	63.9	39.2
2001	65.38	76.0	54.0
2011	74.04	84.14	65.46

In the above table we can see that the literacy percentage of female population rose to 65.46 from 0.7. Though it took a long time still the positive sign of women empowerment can be seen. From the above table it can be concluded that if the literacy percentage of women continues to rise at the same pace then in the coming years it will overtake the rise in male literacy percentage.

Commissions on Women Education (After Independence)

Various commissions on women education have been framed from time to time to support women education and bring changes in the society. As the position of females in any society is a true index of prosperity level, thus necessary changes are required to empower the women. Some of the important commissions and their recommendations are given below:

University Education Commission (1948-49): This commission noted the importance of women's education and stated that "There cannot be educated people without educated women. If general education had to be limited to men or to women that opportunity should be given to women for then it would surely be passed on to the next generation."

Recommendations

1. There should be no curtailment in educational opportunities for women, but rather a great increase.
2. Women teachers should be paid the same salaries as men teachers for equal work.
3. Standards of courtesy and social responsibility should be emphasised on the part of men in mixed colleges.

Secondary Education Commission (1952-53): This commission felt that there was no special justification required to deal with women education. During the course of visit to different institutes and universities it found that women had found admission to nearly all the faculties which a generation ago would have been considered as unsuitable for them or beyond their reach.

Education Commission (1964-66): It included the recommendation of the three committees which had examined the problem of women education in the recent past years. These committees were:

1. The National Committee on the education of women under the chairmanship of Smt. Durgabai Deshmukh.
2. The committee on differentiation of curricula between boys and girls under the chairmanship of Smt. Hansa Mehta.
3. The committee under the chairmanship of Shri. M. Bhaktavatsalam.

Recommendations

1. The education of women should be regarded as a major educational programme for some years to come. Determined effort should be made to face the difficulties involved and to close the existing gap between the education of men and women in very short time.
2. Special schemes and fund requirement should be made on the priority basis.
3. There should be special machinery to look after the education of girls and women.

National Policy on Education (1986): This policy stated that education will be used as an agent of basic change in the status of women. In order to neutralise the accumulated distortions of the past, there will be a well conceived edge in favour of women. The policy of non-discrimination will be pursued vigorously to eliminate sex stereo-typing in vocational and professional courses and to promote women's participation in non-traditional occupations as well as in existing and emergent technologies.

National Commission on Self-employed Women and Women in the Informal Sector (1987-88): According to this commission education is an important instrument for increasing and bettering the chances of women's employability and for empowering women.

Recommendations

1. Greater emphasis has to be given on the vocational aspect of education.
2. It would be preferable to have a regular crèche attached to the primary school where the younger children could be taken care of so that the older child can attend the school.
3. It is necessary to convince the parents of poor girls regarding the relevance of education to the lives of their daughters.
4. For vocational training of girls there should be a revolving fund.

Various such recommendations were given by the commission for the betterment of women. All the above mentioned commissions focused on women education and enlistment. The main aim of these commissions was to bring women to the main stream. The representation of women was seen in all the sectors. The efforts showed a remarkable growth in mainstream women participation. However few lacunas existed due to improper implementation of the recommendations made by the commissions.

Women in the Constitution of India

Women in the constitution of India have also been given equal status. In the entire article there is provision of equal representation for both the sexes. The article also states that no discrimination should be done on the basis of religion, race, caste or sex and provides for the Reservation of seats for women. The constitution of India not only grants equality to women but also empowers the state to adopt positive discrimination in favour of women. Articles, 14, 15, 15(3), 16, 39(a), 39(b), 39(c), 42 are few articles of significant importance. Some articles are listed below to show the equal representation of women in the constitution:

Article 14: Establishes the 'Equality before law' principle. Every individual is equal in the eyes of law and no discrimination or injustice is supported by the law.

Article 15 (1): Maintains that the State should not discriminate against any citizen on grounds of religion, race, caste, **sex**, place of birth or any of them. In the preamble, fundamental rights and fundamental duties there is provision of equality. Thus any kind of discrimination is against the law.

Article 15 (3): Maintains that the State is eligible to make special provisions in favour of women and children. Though there is provision for equality but the constitution also provides special rights to the State for formulating special rules or laws for women.

Article 16: Upholds the equality of opportunity for all citizens in matters relating to employment or appointment to any office under the State. The constitution also provides for equal opportunities to all in employment or appointment in any government post.

Article 23: Provides for the prohibition of trafficking of human beings and forced labour. Human trafficking and forced labour is considered as crime in Indian constitution.

Article 39A: Provides for equal justice and free legal aid. There is provision of equal justice and free legal aid. No individual can be denied for this facility.

Article 42: Provides rights to the State for making provisions for securing just and humane conditions of work and for maternity relief.

Article 44: Maintains the applicability of Uniform civil code for all citizens. Civil code is uniform for all citizens and every person has to follow the same rules and regulations.

Article 46: Provides rights to the State to promote with special care the educational and economic interests of the weaker sections of the people and to protect them from social injustice and all forms of exploitation.

Article 47: Provides rights to the State to take measures for raising the level of nutrition and the standard of living of its people. The article holds that the State is totally responsible for the level of nutrition and standard of living of its people and can from time to time frame special provisions for the betterment of its people.

Article 325: Upholds that no person is ineligible for inclusion in, or claim to be included in a special electoral roll on grounds of religion, race, caste or sex.

Article 326: Upholds that election to the house of the people and to the legislative assemblies of states to be on the basis of adult suffrage.

The above articles in the constitution of India show the special position of women granted by the highest authority of the country. All these efforts have been made to empower women and create a better world. A woman not only owns a special place in a family but also deserves great respect in society for her devotion and sacrifices.

Conclusion

Education is milestone of women empowerment because it enables them to respond to challenges, to confront their traditional roles and change their life. We can't neglect the importance of education with reference to women empowerment. From child rearing to family management the need of women is felt in every step of life. Education of women is the most powerful tool of change of position in society. Education also brings a reduction in inequalities and functions as a means of improving the status of women within the family

India is set to emerge as one of the most developed nations by 2020 - more literate, knowledgeable and economically at the forefront. No doubt, women will play a vital role in contributing to the country's development. Women power is crucial to the economic growth of any country. In India this is yet to meet the requirements despite reforms. Little has been achieved in the area of women empowerment, but chain of reforms is still required. Though India could become one of the largest economies in the world, its course is being hindered due to a lack of women's participation. Thus the call of the hour is to increase the women participation in all the spheres of life. The more empowered a women is the more prosperous a country will be.

"The union of man and woman will represent a perfect co-operation in the building up of human history on equal terms in every department of life."

Rabindranath Tagore (1861-1941)

References

- Adult education of women in the changing pattern of society: Seminar working paper, 1968, *Indian journal of adult education,* 29(10) October, p. 6-9.
- Suguna, M. (2011), Education and Women Empowerment In India, *International Journal of Multidisciplinary Research*, December 2011, p. 198-204.
- Government of India, Census of India 2001.
- R. K. Rao, 2001, Women and Education, Kalpaz Publications, Delhi.
- Khan, N. (2013), women Security and Safeguards in India, *Journal of Business Management & Social Sciences Research,* April 2013, p 1-7.
- Anonuevo, C. M. and Bochynek, B. (1993). The international seminar on Women Education and Empowerment in Anonuevo, C. M. Women, Education and Empowerment: Pathways towards Autonomy. Hamburg. UNESCO.
- Patel, C. L. (1996). 'Empowerment of Women and Law', *Central India Law Quarterly,* Vol. IX: IV, New Delhi.
- Prajanya Trust, (2010). Gender Violence in India : *A Prajnya Report* 2010, Prajanya Trust, Chennai.
- Agrawal, S. P. and Aggarwal, J. C. (1992). Women's Education in India. New Delhi. Concept Publishing Company.

Chapter – 6

Education and Women Empowerment in India

—*Arpeeta Anand*

Abstract

Women education in India has been a major preoccupation of both the government and civil society as educated women can play a very important role in the development of the country. Education is milestone of women empowerment because it enables them to respond to the challenges, to confront their traditional roles and change their life. So that we can't neglect the importance of education in reference to women empowerment, India is poised to become a superpower, a developed country by 2020. The growth of women's education in rural areas is very slow. This obviously means that still large womenfolk of our country are illiterate, weak, backward and exploited. Education of women is the most powerful tool to change women's position in society. Education also brings a reduction in inequalities and functions as a means of improving their status within the family. This chapter is an effort to assess the current size of the gender gap by measuring the extent to which women have fared with respect to men in critical areas such as economic participation, economic opportunity, political empowerment and educational attainment. The National Policy for Empowerment of Women 2001, as well as the Twelfth Five Year Plan, illustrates the Indian Government's commitment to women's empowerment and welfare. Social empowerment aims to provide women easy and equal access to all the basic minimum services so as to enable them to realise their full potential. Economic empowerment aims to make all women economically independent through training, employment and income generation activities.

Keywords: *Education, Female Literacy Rate, Women Empowerment, Society, India.*

Introduction

"If you educate a man you educate an individual, however, if you educate a woman you educate a whole family. Women empowered means mother India empowered."

Pt. Jawaharlal Nehru

Women, who constitute a sizeable proportion of a country's population, are subjected to gender bias and indignities arising out of the age-old patriarchal tradition. Despite worldwide evidence of the low levels of female participation in social, educational, economic and political spheres, there is still a tendency not to see it as a real problem. Women constitute almost half of the population in the world. Access to education has been one of the most pressing demands of these women's rights movements. Women education in India has also been a major preoccupation of both the government and civil society as educated women can play a very important role in the development of the country.

The 12th Five Year Plan Working Group (WG) on 'Women's Agency and Empowerment' builds on the view that development is a process of expanding freedoms equally for all individuals, and considers gender equality as a core development goal in itself. It expands the definition of women's empowerment by looking at it as a process, which enables women to have a notion of dignity and self worth, bodily integrity, freedom from coercion and control over resources. It affirms that empowerment is achieved when, along with the condition of women, their position improves and their freedoms and choices are enlarged economically, socially and politically.

Empowerment must enable *all* women to negotiate these freedoms and increase their capabilities. The overall framework takes steps to advance substantive equality by addressing the causes and consequences of social, economic and political exclusion of all women especially the dalits, tribal, minorities, women with disabilities, migrants, displaced and trafficked women, women in the unorganised workforce, women infected and affected by HIV/AIDS, single and excluded women especially widows and women in conflict zones. Many projects taken on the task of women's empowerment through micro-enterprises in recognition of the impact it can have on women, their families and poverty alleviation.

The 12th Plan document defines different aspects of women's empowerment. Social empowerment aims to provide women easy and equal access to all the basic minimum services to enable them to realise their full potential. Economic empowerment aims to make all women economically independent through training, employment and income generation activities. Employment opportunities for women support for self-employment and women's enterprises came to be recognised as essential for releasing women's economic potential, allowing women to enjoy not only the de-jure but also the de-facto rights and fundamental freedom on par with men in all spheres. Cultural parameters are not mentioned in the Tenth Plan but refer to the concept of empowerment in relation to respect of rights of indigenous people and inclusion of their knowledge and practices. The dimensions of power are not specifically considered but are important in the context of women's empowerment in India. These include women's collectivisation and greater participation in the political processes.

In India women education is yet to meet the requirements despite reforms. Little has been achieved in the area of women empowerment, but for this to happen, this sector must experience a chain of reforms. Though India could well become one of the largest economies in the world, it is being hindered due to a lack of women's participation.

Status of Women in India

Through gender bias exists in every country, it is more evident in some South Asian countries, with India being one of them. The history of Indian women is not linear, nor does it have a well organised structure. Women's duties as good daughters, good wives and good mothers are well defined in the Indian patriarchal society. The good woman is sweet, loving, caring and ever sacrificing. Wifehood and motherhood are accepted as pivotal roles for women by implication, these roles complete in themselves and women need not pursue any specialised discipline of knowledge or profession. It is believed that in the Vedic era women enjoyed the same position as men. In the intellectual field they were given equal recognition. Some of the Vedic poets were women and there were women philosophers and women mathematicians as well. The girls received education and went through the brahmacharya discipline like boys. Vedic sacrifices were performed jointly by husband and wife and singing hymns was considered as one of the most appropriate functions of the wife. In brief, women enjoyed freedom of socio-economic rights as much as men. The permission of love marriage indicated freedom of movement and choice of life partner. Women were highly respected within and outside homes. In later eras unethical customs put women in an abysmal state, especially during the middle age the glorious status of women declined. However, historical process through the ages brought considerable changes in the status of women. The Indian society became more patriarchal and male supremacy dominated. Women receded indoors. Health, education, employment and empowerment became almost exceptions. This long period of subjugation of women by the stereotyped patriarchal mindset caused gender inequality in society.

The principle of gender equality is enshrined in the Indian Constitution and finds a place in the preamble, fundamental rights, fundamental duties and directive principles. The Constitution not only grants equality to women but also empowers the States to adopt measures of positive discrimination in favour of women. Since independence, the government of India has been making various efforts to empower women. In its various plans issues regarding women empowerment have been given priority. From the fifth Five Year Plan onwards there has been a remarkable shift from a welfare oriented approach of women empowerment to a development approach. The year 2001 was declared as the Year of Women's Empowerment for enhancing their status. The National Commission for Women was set up in India by an act of parliament in 1990 to safeguard the rights of women. The 73rd and 74th Amendments to the Constitution of India provided an opportunity to women to take part in active politics. To achieve these goals the Indian government introduced different programmes, identified strategies, established different institutions and made various legal provisions but they remained invisible. Ironically women's work is generally undervalued and the additional development they promote is usually unrecognised. Here, gender related human development index lags behind the general human development index. Gender discrimination and gender gaps are ubiquitous. Yet it is a fact that they are often the victims of social and domestic violence. Women's work is of tremendous value to family, society and state, but it has always remained invisible.

An Indian woman has a multifaceted personality. She is the pivot around whom a whole household revolves. Hard working and dedicated, she shares many of the duties and responsibilities of a family. Though she makes substantial contribution to the family income through home-based activities, this is treated as supplemental and hence it goes unnoticed. The mainstream concept of the role of a woman seems to be best described in an anonymous Sanskrit couplet. "She is like a mother while cooking and serving food, a secretary while she is working, a servant at his feet, a courtesan in his bed and earth-like in forbearance." The Indian women are a marginalised race and they continue their fight for survival, recognition, respect and dignity. The woman is expected mainly to give birth and look after the children and the family, through her gender defined domestic role. Reality spells that both the family and community expect largely from married women to perform their duties at home. A woman has to carry out a set of expected duties. The diverse roles that a woman is expected to play makes her a multi-mother-provider, counsellor and social worker, causing a strain that leads to disgruntlement.

The situation is much worse in the rural and remote areas of the country. In spite of pursuing higher education, women continue to face subjugation from their male counterparts. The incidences like early marriage, dowry, rape, bride burning, molestation, female feticides and infanticide, kidnapping, etc... are very frequent and the record of crime against women indicates an increasing trend.

The Indian society is torn between traditional expectations from women and their recently achieved assertiveness and capabilities in various roles. Although the benefits of women's work are there for all to see, there persists some reluctance towards completely freeing them to pursue their careers and accepting that their success involves some curtailments on the part of both the society and family. There seems to be an unwritten but vigorous accord about what women can and should do, and influenced challenges experienced by women in their socio-cultural life get replicated in the domain of the office, albeit in slightly different formats. Besides having to balance employment and family life, women often find that they have to struggle to be taken seriously. Long standing traditions in both the domains place women at the very bottom of the hierarchy and provide them minimal access to positions of authority. Women are suffering from womb to tomb in this country. At the time of Lord Krishna, Kansa killed only one baby girl, but today there is female infanticide by Kansas in every third house; even if the girl survives, she is subjected to humiliation, discrimination, abuse from every corner every day. Even our rituals are against daughters. No celebration is organised on the birth of a girl.

Importance of Education

If it is said that education is the key to all problems, then it won't be improper. Thinkers have given a number of definitions of education but out of these definitions, the most important definition is that which was put forth by M. Phule. According to M. Phule, "Education is that which demonstrates the difference between what is good and what is evil." If we consider the above definition, we come to know that whatever revolutions that have taken place in our history, education is at the base of them. It is through education that one realises what is good and what is bad, what is proper and what is not (just and unjust etc.). It is education which gives a vent/ voice to injustice. The 3-fold formula which Dr B. R. Ambedkar gave to Indian society includes that the most important thing is to be educated. In other words, he has emphasized upon the importance of education.

History of Women Education in India

Although in the Vedic period women had access to education in India, they gradually lost this right. However, in the British period there was revival of interest in women's education in India. During this period, various socio religious movements led by eminent persons like Raja Ram Mohan Roy, Iswar Chandra Vidyasagar emphasised on women's education in India. Mahatma Jyotiba Phule, Periyar and Baba Saheb Ambedkar were leaders of the lower castes in India who took various initiatives to make education available to the women of India. However, women's education got a fillip after the country got independence in 1947 and the government has taken various measures to provide education to all Indian women. As a result women's literacy rate has grown over the decades and the growth of female literacy rate has in fact been higher than that of male literacy rate. While in 1971 only 22 per cent of Indian women were literate, by the end of 2001 54.16 per cent females were literate. The growth of female literacy rate is 14.87 per cent as compared to 11.72 per cent male literacy rate.

Importance of Education in Women Empowerment

The cause of women's empowerment is not limited only to the Indian society. If we consider the global scenario in this regard, we see that women are now being given equal treatment in developed nations due to several women activist movements in the past. In fact, if we take a retrospect of history, we come to know that women have always been given secondary position in society in most countries. The difference between men and women created by the Nature is misinterpreted and distorted by the stereotyped mentalities. It is only through education that women realise this fact and that they are also entitled to the same rights as men. When American women realised the injustice being meted out to them by the society for just being born as women, they opposed by way of a huge movement through which they asked for equal rights. For eradicating this injustice, the UNO (United Nations' Organisation) framed a Convention/Charter which is called 'The Convention on the Elimination of all Forms of Discrimination against Women' (CEDAW), which further led to the formation of Women's Commission.

Taking an account of this background, we come to know that women's empowerment has now become a topic of global discussion. Seeing all the aspects of this discussion, we will realise that education is the only means for empowerment of women. Therefore, literacy should spread amongst women. The literacy rate amongst the women in the post-Independent Era is not as per the expectations. We, as a nation, dream of becoming a Super Power by 2020. For becoming a Super Power, each element of our society/nation should contribute in the nation building process. But if women who are a major faction of this society aren't literate then we can't expect to become a Super Power. Therefore, it is imperative for us to know the importance of women's education which would in turn give an impetus to the process of women's empowerment.

Importance of Women Education in India

Women education in India plays a very important role in the overall development of the country. It not only helps in the development of half of the human resources, but in improving the quality of life at home and outside. Educated women not only tend to promote education of their girl children, but also can provide better guidance to all their children. Moreover educated women can also help in the reduction of infant mortality rate and growth of the population.

Obstacles

Gender discrimination still persists in India and lot more needs to be done in the field of women's education in India. The gap in the male-female literacy rate is just a simple indicator. While the male literary rate is more than 75 per cent according to the 2001 Census, the female literacy rate is just 54.16 per cent.

Women's Education Prospects and Challenges

Women education is still in the state of an enigma in India for several reasons in spite of forceful interventions that include provision of a bastion of female privileges, voicing by feminists, constitutional guarantees, protection laws and sincere efforts by the state governments and central government through various schemes and programmes over the last 62 years and above all the United Nation's enormous pressure for uplifting the condition of women. The 2011 Census report indicates that literacy among Indian women is only 65.46 per cent; it is virtually disheartening to observe that the literacy rate of women in India is much lower to the total national average literacy rate of. 74.04. The growth of women's education in rural areas is very slow. This obviously means that still large womenfolk of our country are illiterate, weak, backward and exploited. Moreover education is also not available to all equally. Gender inequality is reinforced in education which is proved by the fact that the literacy rate for women is only 65.46 per cent against 82.14 per cent of men as per 2011 Census.

Table -1 Literacy Rate in India

Year	*Persons*	*Males*	*Females*
1901	5.3	9.8	0.7
1911	5.9	10.6	1.1
1921	7.2	12.2	1.8
1931	9.5	15.6	2.9
1941	16.1	24.9	7.3
1951	16.7	24.9	7.3
1961	24.0	34.4	13.0
1971	29.5	39.5	18.7
1981	36.2	46.9	24.8
1991	52.1	63.9	39.2
2001	65.38	76.0	54.0
2011	74.04	82.14	65.46

Source: Census of India (2011).

According to the Table-1 the pre-Independence time literacy rate for women had a very poor spot in comparison to literacy rate of men. This is witnessed from the fact that literacy rate of women rose from 0.7 per cent to 7.3 per cent where as the literacy rate of men rose from 9.8 per cent to 24.9 per cent during 1901 to 1941. During the post-independence period literacy rates have shown a substantial increase in general. However, the literacy rate of males has almost tripled over the period, from 25 per cent in 1951 to 76 per cent in 2001. Surprisingly the female literacy rate has increased at a faster pace than the male literacy during the decade 1981 - 2001. The growth is almost 6 times e.g. 7.9 per cent in 1951 and 54 per cent in 2001. From this analysis one can infer that still the female literacy rate (only half of the female population are literates) is waddling behind male literacy rate (three fourth of the male population are literates).The rate of school drop outs is also found to be comparatively higher in case of women. This higher rate of illiteracy of women can undoubtedly be attributed to dependence of women on men and them playing a subordinate role. The lack of education is the root cause for women's exploitation and negligence. Only literacy can help women to understand India's constitutional and legislative provisions that have been made to strengthen them. Thus promoting education among women is of great importance for empowering them to accomplish their goals and be at par with men in the different spheres of life.

Educational Equality

Another area in which women's equality has shown a major improvement as a result of adult literacy programs is the area of enrolment of in schools. As a result of higher participation of women in literacy campaigns, the gender gap in literacy levels is gradually getting reduced. Even more significant is the fact that disparity in enrolment of boys and girls in neo-literate households is much lower as compared to the non-literate households.

Table -2 State-Wise Percentage of Female Literacy in the Country as per Census - 2011

Sl. No.	*Name of the State*	*Female Literacy*
1.	Andhra Pradesh	59.7 per cent
2.	Arunachal Pradesh	59.6 per cent
3.	Assam	67.3 per cent
4.	Bihar	53.3 per cent
5.	Chhattisgarh	60.6 per cent
6.	Delhi	80.9 per cent
7.	Goa	81.8 per cent
8.	Gujarat	70.7 per cent
9.	Haryana	66.8 per cent
10.	Himachal Pradesh	76.6 per cent
11.	Jammu and Kashmir	58.0 per cent
12.	Jharkhand	56.2 per cent
13.	Karnataka	68.1 per cent

(Contd...)

14.	Kerala	92.0 per cent
15.	Madhya Pradesh	60.0 per cent
16.	Maharashtra	75.5 per cent
17.	Manipur	73.2 per cent
18.	Meghalaya	73.8 per cent
19.	Mizoram	89.4 per cent
20.	Nagaland	76.7 per cent
21.	Orissa	64.4 per cent
22.	Punjab	71.3 per cent
23.	Rajasthan	52.7 per cent
24.	Sikkim	76.4 per cent
25.	Tamil Nadu	73.9 per cent
26.	Tripura	83.1 per cent
27.	Uttar Pradesh	59.3 per cent
28.	Uttarakhand	70.7 per cent
29.	West Bengal	71.2 per cent
Union Territories		
1.	Andaman & Nicobar Islands	81.8 per cent
2.	Chandigarh	81.4 per cent
3.	Dadra & Nagar Haveli	65.9 per cent
4.	Daman & Diu	79.6 per cent
5.	Lakshadweep	88.2 per cent
6.	Pondicherry	81.2 per cent
	All India	**65.46 per cent**

Source: Census of India (2011).

According to the Table -2 the state-wise female literacy rate had an average of 65.46 per cent in 2011 census, an 11 per cent increase from 54.16 per cent over the previous census year. The highest women literacy rate is 92.0 per cent in Kerala and least women literacy rate is 52.7 per cent in Rajasthan as per 2011 census Women have grown well in the last 10 years with respect to education. Government of India has been taking various steps, especially for women, in its every endeavour.

Conclusion

According to the Country Report of the Government of India, "Empowerment means moving from a weak position to a position of being able to execute power." Education of women is the most powerful tool to change their position in society. Education also brings a reductioh in inequalities and functions as a means of improving the status of women within the family. To encourage the education of women at all levels and for dilution of gender bias in education there is a need for establishment of more schools, colleges and universities even exclusively for women. To bring more girls, especially from marginalised families of BPL, into mainstream education, the government is providing a package of concessions in the form of free books, uniforms, boarding and lodging, clothing, midday meals, scholarships, free cycles and so on.

References

- Government of India, Census of India 2011.
- Gupta, N. L. (2003). Women's Education Through Ages, Concept Publications Co., New Delhi.
- Rao, R. K. (2001) Women and Education, Kalpaz Publications, Delhi.
- Agarwal, S. P. (2001) Women's Education in India (1995-98) Present Status, Perspective, Plan, Statistical Indicators with Global View, Vol III Concept Publications Co, New Delhi.
- Twelfth Five Year Plan, 2012-2017, Report of the Working Group on Women's Agency and Empowerment.
- Women in India, (2001). Department of Economics and Statistics, Thiruvananthapuram.

Chapter - 7

Education and Empowerment of Women in Odisha: A Case Study of Ganjam District

—Prabina Kumar Padhi and
Umesh Chandra Panigrahi

Abstract

Education leads human beings from ignorance to enlightenment, from social backwardness to brightness of social amelioration and a nation from underdevelopment to faster social and economic development. The great appearance of education in the lives of humans explores the way for a sustained improvement in wellbeing of the entire human race. Women Empowerment implies equality of prospect and equity between not only the genders, but also among the cultural groups, social classes and age groups. It gives emphasises on a society wherein women can live without the fear of intimidation, exploitation, discrimination and the general feeling of harassment. Education is one of the most important means of empowering women with the knowledge, skills and self-confidence necessary to participate fully in the development process. Educating a woman uplifts her life and her entire family; an educated woman will easily foster an independent and progressive outlook in her children. In these regards the chapter aims to probe the role of education in empowering women in Odisha. Chapter also explains the various schemes on education which will be supportive for augmenting the women empowerment in our economy. Here analysis is made regarding the women empowerment in Ganjam district with special reference to enrolment and drop-out ratio of girls during the study period of 2009-14.

Keywords: *Women Empowerment, Education, Ganjam, Economic Development.*

Introduction

"Education, in the present day context, is perhaps the single most important means for individuals to improve personal endowments, build capability levels, overcome constraints and in the process, enlarge their available set of opportunities and choices for a sustained improvement in well-being."

Human Development Report, India. 2002

Education, by its very nature, influences and gets influenced by the whole development process. There is hardly any field of activity or sector of development which is not influenced by education in some form or other. Empowerment facilitates the individuals or a group of individuals to recognise their complete uniqueness and influence in all spheres of existence. It creates awareness for improved decision making. Empowerment of women generally means equal status to women through increased awareness of their rights and duties as well as admittance to resources as a significant step en route to greater security for them. It includes advanced literacy levels and education for women, better health care for women and children, equal ownership of industrial resources, enlarged involvement in economic and commercial sectors, consciousness of their rights and responsibilities, improved standards of living and acquiring self-reliance, self-esteem and self-confidence. Education is an effective instrument through which transformation of processes and social change come to existence. Indian States are under Constitutional obligation to provide free and compulsory education to all children up to the age of 14. The Government of Odisha has formulated a number of goals for the education sector like Universalisation of Elementary Education (UEE) in the State by 2010, universal literacy, development of secondary and higher secondary education, skill development through vocational education in higher secondary schools and modernisation of technical education. There has been a steady improvement in the literacy rates of the State over successive decades, which is a result of expansion of educational infrastructure, both quantitative and qualitative. All these provisions have been made to facilitate the empowerment of the masses especially women in all respects. This present study is an attempt to show the impact of education on women empowerment especially in Ganjam District during the study period 2009-14.

Objectives of the Study

Education is an essential means of empowering women with the knowledge, skills and self-assurance which accelerates the development process. Sustainable development is only possible through women empowerment. By taking these aspects into account this present study focuses on the following objectives –

- To study the impact of education on women empowerment.
- To study different associated schemes of women empowerment.
- To analyse level of empowerment by means of enrolment and drop-out in girls education in the Ganjam District.

Significance of the Study

Empowerment of women is an essential condition for socio-economic improvement of any society. Education is one of the foremost objectives of women empowerment because it enables to deal with their long-established roles and change their life. For this reason the present study is an endeavour with regard to women education in the Ganjam district of Odisha and as to how it contributes to the women empowerment.

Literature Review

Different literatures have discussed women empowerment and the development process achieved by it. Some of these are mentioned below:

M. Haimanti (2008) in his study tries to investigate responsibility of education in the empowerment of women in particular references to the district of Malda, West Bengal, India. In the article he tries to express the attitude of the society towards girls' education and problems hindering the education of women.

M. Suguna, (2011), in her article has given stress on the role of education that makes women competent enough to face the various difficulties their lives. So her article stresses that the importance of education with reference to women empower-ment cannot be neglected and more so as India is poised to becoming a superpower, a developed country by 2020.

Patil, P.D. (2008), in her deliberation has stressed on the need for education for a self sustained Women empowerment process. She has highlighted the participation of the State Governments through the various schemes which gives encouragement for the education of the girl child.

Sehrawat, J. (2014), in her paper made an attempt to analyse the concept of women empowerment and the various problems faced by them and the forefront possibilities that can be actualised for achieving women empowerment through education.

Research Methodology

The secondary data for the current study has been collected from various published and unpublished sources, reports, economic surveys, journals, magazines and old official records. For the impact assessment of education and women empowerment Ganjam district of the state of Odisha has been taken into conside-ration. Survey method has been used to collect primary data. Sampling has been completed in two phases. In first phase 9 different blocks have been selected through random sampling and in second phase 10 primary and upper primary schools have been selected from each block. Thus total 90 schools have been selected. Average enrolment and dropout has been taken in consideration for analysis. The time period for the study was from 2009-14.

Women Empowerment through Education:

The role of education in facilitating social and economic progress is well accepted. Education leads to empowerment by securing the means of creating a social environment in which one can make decisions for social and individual transformation. It strengthens innate ability through knowledge, power and experience enabling an individual to think, act and control human, intellectual and financial resources. It develops intrinsic capacity, inner transformation of one's consciousness to overcome barriers, access resources and change traditional ideologies. Women's empowerment in India is greatly reliant on many diverse variables that comprise of geographical location, educational status, social status, and age. Policies on women's empowerment exist at the national, state, and local levels in many sectors, including health, education, economic opportunities, gender-based violence, and political participation. The persistent low educational participation of girls till recently has had an adverse impact on women's quality of life and empowerment. This educational backwardness has cost both the individual and national advancement, producing a skewed national progress. The major consequences of education for attaining women empowerment are as follows –

- Education stimulates more social exposure and understanding which help women to improve decision making capabilities.
- Education promotes awareness on health, hygiene, nutrition and family care which leads to a better standard of living in the society.
- Education enhances wisdom as well as equips the adolescent girls to improve/upgrade home based and vocational skills.
- Education enables accomplishment of a better understanding of social environment for becoming a better competitor in the society.

Education in Odisha

Odisha has been at the forefront of education and research. Before the creation of modern Odisha, the foundation of the education system were the Sanskrit Pathsalas, and the Maktabs, which existed in Cuttack, Balasore, Puri, Angul and Sambalpur and local Chatasalis to cater to grass root level education, as well as being advanced centres of Oriental learning. The ruins of a major ancient university, like Takshashila and Nalanda universities, Puspagiri are great examples of the great educational culture of Odisha. Gender equality is a prerequisite for advancing growth and reducing poverty which can be achieved only when women and men enjoy the same opportunities, rights and obligations in all spheres of life. Empowered women contribute to the health and productivity of whole families and communities, which boost the prospects for the next generation. Empowerment through proper education provides the monetary sovereignty towards realising personal ambitions. The state has accorded high priority in ensuring gender equity in education, political participation as well as in economic and employment opportunities. Several definitive measures have been taken by the State Government in order to improve the status of women in society. Initiatives like 50 per cent reservation of women in Panchayati Raj institutions and urban local bodies, 33 per cent reservation in Government jobs, and special incentives to girls for taking up education are some of the progressive steps for furthering the status of women. The female literacy has increased by 26 per cent between 2001 and 2011 which in itself is remarkable.

Schemes Associated with Women Education and Empowerment of Odisha

Policies relating to women's education have had a positive trajectory in the past few decades with the central government articulating many progressive measures to advance gender equality in social, economic, and political arenas.

Kishori Shakti Yojana: Kishori Shakti Yojana aims at the empowerment and holistic development of adolescent girls by improving their self perception and creating opportunities for realising their full potential through Balika Mandals. The scheme primarily aims at breaking the intergenerational life cycle of nutritional and gender disadvantage and providing a supportive environment for self development. In its target group are included the adolescent girls (11-18 yrs.) - both school going and out of school girls.

Mission Shakti: Empowerment of women is one of the key development initiatives identified by the Government of Odisha It is also well known that women are better-placed to overcome the pessimistic social pressures and gender biases operating against them and to unleash themselves through group identity and activity. Promotion of Women's Self-Help Groups (WSHGs) has therefore been adopted as a key strategy for achieving women's empowerment. A Mission approach has been adopted for this purpose through launching of 'Mission Shakti' aimed at promotion of Women's Self-Help Groups and providing them the necessary technical support.

Rajiv Gandhi Scheme for Empowerment of Adolescent Girls (RGSEAG): The scheme aims at covering all out-of-school adolescent girls in the age group of 11 to 18 years who are brought together at the Anganwadi Centres on a fixed day at regular intervals. The others, i.e., school-going girls, meet at the AWC at least twice a month, and more frequently (once a week) during vacations/holidays. Here they receive life skills education, nutrition and health education, awareness about socio-legal issues, etc. This scheme provides an opportunity for diverse group interface between school-going and out-of-school girls, motivating the latter to also join school and help the school going girls to receive life skills. This scheme mainly aims at lowering the dropout rate of adolescent girls by escalating their literacy rate and work participation.

Mahila-Samakhya: Mahila Samakhya Programme (Education for Women's Empowerment) aims at creating an environment for women to seek knowledge and information with a view to bringing about a change in their perception about themselves and that of the society. Mahila Samakhya launched in 1989 covers about 6,877 villages in 51 districts of 8 States namely, Uttar Pradesh, Gujarat, Karnataka, Andhra Pradesh, Bihar, Assam, Madhya Pradesh and Kerala.

Kasturba Gandhi Balika Vidyalaya (KGBV) Scheme: KGBV is a scheme launched in July 2004 for setting up residential schools at upper primary level for girls belonging predominantly to the SC, ST, OBC and minority communities. It is being implemented in educationally backward blocks of the country where female rural literacy is below the national average and gender gap in literacy is above the national average. The scheme provides for a minimum reservation of 75 per cent for girls from SC, ST, OBC or minority communities. For the remaining 25 per cent, priority is accorded to girls from families below poverty line.

National Programme for Education of Girls at Elementary Education (NPEGEL): Government of India is committed to achieving Universalisation of Elementary Education by 2010. The NPEGEL is a focused intervention of Government of India, to reach the "Hardest to Reach" girls, especially those not in schools. Launched in July 2003, it is an important component of SSA, which provides additional support for enhancing girls' education above the investments for girls' education through normal SSA interventions.

Education and Women Empowerment: A Study of Ganjam District

Ganjam district is a district in the Indian state of Odisha situated on the boundary of Andhra Pradesh. Its total area is 8,070 km^2 (3,116 mi^2). Its population is approximately 2,704,056. Ganjam is known for its beaches bordering the Bay of Bengal. The most populous city in Ganjam is Behrampur famous for silver filigree and silk sarees woven with gold and silver threads. The district headquarters is in Chhatrarpur. Ganjam is divided into three sub-divisions - Chhatrapur, Behrampur, and Bhanjanagar. As of 2011 it is the most populous district of Odisha (out of 30). Ganjam district is named after the Old Township and European fort of Ganjam. The name Ganjam comes from the word Gan-i-aam which means Granary of the Common People. It spreads over the geographical area of 8070.60 square km. in Odisha. There are 22 blocks, 475 Grampanchayats, 18 Urban Local bodies, 3229 villages, 29 Police Stations and 13 Assembly Constituencies.

Table 1: Average Enrollment of Boys and Girls

Block	*2009-10*		*2010-11*		*2011-12*		*2012-13*		*2013-14*	
	B	*G*	*B*	*G*	*B*	*G*	*B*	*G*	*B*	*G*
1. Bellaguntha block	45	44	44	41	43	40	42	37	40	35
2. Bellaguntha N.A.C	61	42	58	38	54	38	49	38	47	38
3. Berhampur Municipal Corporation	58	49	57	45	54	44	50	45	50	40
4. Buguda Block	95	85	97	76	90	82	84	82	82	78
5. Buguda N.A.C	50	63	48	50	40	43	38	45	50	38
6. Patrapur	45	54	45	50	45	44	45	41	44	40
7. Polasara Block	49	58	50	61	48	50	50	56	54	50
8. Rangeilunda Block	50	47	43	50	49	40	40	44	38	42
9. Sanakhemundi block	88	81	83	82	83	79	81	77	80	76

The above Table 1 gives a brief idea regarding the average enrolment of boys and girls from 2009-14 in the different blocks of Ganjam District. In each block the enrolment of both boys and girls are decreasing with the time interval. But the rates of enrolments, in case of girls, are minimum as compared to boys. In 2009-10 the average no of girls are 44 as compared to 35 in 2013-14 and boys are 45 and it has decreased up to 40 in numbers which shows that girls percentage of enrolment is low in relation to boys in Bellaguntha block in Ganjam. However in other blocks the results are moderate but not satisfactory. By educating the girls the path of women empowerment is encouraged. If the government will take more necessary steps the decreased rate of enrolment of girls can be controlled to a great extent. In this way education can also be helpful towards women empowerment.

Table 2: Drop-out of Boys and Girls

Block	*2009-10*		*2010-11*		*2011-12*		*2012-13*		*2013-14*	
	B	*G*	*B*	*G*	*B*	*G*	*B*	*G*	*B*	*G*
1. Bellaguntha block	32	38	26	30	13	15	27	29	28	28
2. Bellaguntha N.A.C	35	45	32	38	15	25	23	27	08	12
3. Berhampur Municipal Corporation	28	32	23	27	18	22	12	18	24	26
4. Buguda Block	40	51	40	51	30	35	34	42	33	43
5. Buguda N.A.C	26	28	20	25	16	20	17	19	17	19
6. Patrapur	24	26	19	21	29	31	13	17	09	11
7. Polasara Block	47	52	45	54	15	18	10	12	11	11
8. Rangeilunda Block	21	29	16	24	18	22	20	30	19	21
9. Sanakhemundi block	21	39	20	28	17	19	12	27	01	14

Drop-out rate is defined as the proportion of children that cease to remain enrolled in the schooling system. There are a number of methods for estimating drop-out rate. The drop-out ratios of primary and elementary education of India is highlighted in Table-2. The time period varies from 2009-14, in this table we find that in all the blocks and N.A.C. of Ganjam district the drop-out rates are continuous in nature. For instance in Buguda Block in the year 2009-10 the average drop-out student in case of boys are 40 in numbers in comparison to girls which is 51. But the drop-out numbers gradually decreases to boys at 33 and girls at 43 in 2013-14 and in Patrapur block during the year 2009-10 the average drop-out student in case of boys are 24 and girls are 26 and 9 for boys and 11 for girls respectively in the year 2013-14.

In the case of Berhampur Municipal Corporation the situation is little bit encouraging as it reveals that in the year 2009-10 average drop-out student in case of boys are 28 in relation to 32 for girls and in 2013-14 the drop-out rate is just below the 2009-10 numbers i.e 24 for boys and 26 for girls.

Findings

The present study has following findings:

- In the year 2009-10 in Buguda Block the average drop-out student in case of boys are 40 in numbers in comparison to 51girls.
- In case of Berhampur Municipal Corporation in 2009-10 average drop-out student numbers in case of boys are 28 in relation to 32 for girls, in 2013-14 the drop-out rate is just below the 2009-10 numbers i.e. 24 for boys and 26 for girls.
- In 2009-10 the average No. of girls are 44 in comparison to 35 in 2013-14 and boys are 45 and it has decreased up to 40 in numbers which shows that girls' percentage of enrolment is low in relation to boys in Bellaguntha block in Ganjam.
- These results undoubtedly indicate that we should accept the null hypothesis that there is no consistency in the linkage between education and women empowerment during the study period. However, due to improvement in various infrastructure facilities there happens to be a positive output in relation to girls education which shows the endeavours to improve the status women empowerment in the context of Ganjam in the state of Odisha.

Suggestions and the Way Forward

The findings undoubtedly indicate inconsistent enrolment and drop out numbers, the question here is to define a significant change and how to effect a significant positive change and reverse a negative change. The data can be used as a tool for monitoring, control and planning significant impacts. The blocks which show a positive significant change over a time period can be assessed with respect to their endeavours and interventions etc. and learning so attained from their cases can be applied to other blocks as well. Stagnant and negatively performing blocks (with more or less insignificant or significant negative changes in data) should be a matter of concern especially in such areas where education levels are so low; these blocks call for immediate deliberation. Empowerment enables education and education enables empowerment. The task of the various education imparting stake holders should be to provide empowerment so as to enable education and enable education to further empower so as not only to start the process of empowerment but also give it momentum. Here it should also be noted that due to improvement in various infrastructure facilities there are positive signs with respect to girls' education which indicates towards the effectiveness of State endeavours to improve the status of women empowerment in the context of Ganjam in the State of Odisha. The challenge is to maintain consistent and significant growth.

There is a need of purposeful consideration by the Government for achieving sustainability and consistency in progress of women education in Odisha so as to empower them. Following are the major suggestions:

- Publicise the educational system and uphold the objectives of equality for women and their empowerment.
- Identify hurdles in implementing the various State government schemes and ensure their proper implementation.
- Identify and administer means of empowerment so as to increase enrolment and decrease drop out numbers. These may include scholarships, free provisions, neighbourhood educational and training facilities, separate facilities for girls, flexible and suitable timings, women teachers, vocational training etc. Some of these may already be existent in the form of schemes.
- Identify and suitably address security issues that hinder women empowerment and education.
- Identify specific issues, invest wise as per proper plan taking into consideration priority and pressing issues.

- Encourage public participation on the issue of quality of girls' education.
- Women reservation policy should thoroughly be maintained in all aspects like appointment in govt. and semi government offices and admissions in the educational institutions, participating in politics etc.
- General awareness programmes should be conducted among the women of the village areas so as to sensitise them about the modern development of science and technology so that they give up their superstitious beliefs and attitudes.

Conclusion

Education must be used as a driving force to effect fundamental changes in the status of women. It must be a looked upon as a privilege as well as a right that is guaranteed by the State. However, the Government of Odisha has given high priority towards ensuring gender equity in education, political participation as well as in economic and employment opportunities. To promote the education of women at all levels and for dilution of gender bias in the provision of knowledge and education schools, colleges and universities even exclusively for women need to be established in the State. The need of the hour is to necessitate a strong value based education that upholds ideology such as equity, ethics and empowerment.

References

- Kandpal, Eeshani and *et.al,* (2012), "Empowering Women through Education and Influence: An Evaluation of the Indian Mahila Samakhya Program" IZA Discussion Paper No. 6347 pp. 1-53.
- Kumar Ashok, (2006), "Educational Status of Girl Child: A Situational Analysis in Rural India", Kurukshetra, Vol. 55 (1), November, pp. 13-17.
- M. Suguna, (2011), "Education and Women Empowerment in India", Zenith International Journal Of Multi disciplinary Research Vol.1 Issue 8, pp. 198-203.
- M., Haimanti, (2008), "The Role of Education in the Empowerment of Women in a District of West Bengal, India: Reflections on a Survey of Women" Journal of International Women's Studies. Volume 10 Issue 2 pp. 217-225.

- Patil. P.D, (2008) "Empowered Women- Empowered Nation Vol. 52, YOJANA pp. 5-6.
- Peerzade S. A. and Prema Parande, (2005), "Empowerment of Women: A Study" Kurukshetra, Vol. 54, No.1, pp. 7-11.
- Rupali Sharma and Zia Afroz (2014) Women "Empowerment Through Higher Education" International Journal of Inter disciplinary and Multi-disciplinary Studies (IJIMS), Vol 1, No. 5, 18-22. pp. 18-22.
- Yogesh. H.S. and Mahesha. M (2013), "An Analysis Of Growth and Trend Pattern of Enrollments In Elementary Schools Of India" Arth Prabhand: A Journal of Economics and Management Vol. 2 Issue 1, pp. 38-45.
- Schuler, S., and S. Hashemi. (1994), "Credit Programs, Women's Empowerment, and Contraceptive use in Rural Bangladesh." Studies in Family Planning, 25(2): pp. 65-76..
- Sehrawat, J. (2014), "Education and Women Empowerment in India" Indian Streams research Journal Volume-4, Issue-3, pp. 1-7.
- Yamuna. A. and *et. al*, (2013), " Panchayat Raj Institutions as an Instrument For Women Empowerment-A Case Study" IOSR Journal of Humanities and Social Science,Volume 8, Issue 4, pp. 06-09.

Chapter-8

Role of Education in Women Empowerment in India

—Pooja Singh

Abstract

"The aim of education is not the acquisition of information, although important, or acquisition of technical skills, though essential in modern society, but the development of that bent of mind, that attitude of reason, that spirit of democracy which will make us responsible citizens."

Dr Sarvepalli Radhakrishnan

We all know that the role of education in human life is very important. A comprehensive education system would help in shaping the younger generation into one that has a sound ethical base and a strong sense of social responsibility. Culture and education are inseparable and yet complementary with multiple points of interaction. Culture paves the way for education while education is responsible for flavouring the cultural values in life. Therefore, both have to be interwoven in various ways and both play an important role in complete development of a nation and women education in India has been a major preoccupation of both the government and civil society as educated women can play a very important role in the development of the country. In this Chapter the main focus is given on the importance of education (professional education) in women empowerment which is a very important factor for the development of any nation.

Keywords: *Professional education, Cultural development, Social responsibility, Empowerment.*

Introduction

Indian economy is expected to emerge as one of the most developed economy by 2020, in terms of more literacy, greater knowledge base and better economical condition. No doubt, women will play a vital role in contributing to the country's development. Women power is not only crucial for the economic growth of any country but is also essential for cultural development of any society. In India this is yet to meet the requirements despite reforms. Little has been achieved in the area of women empowerment, but for this to happen, this sector must experience a chain of reforms. Though India could well become one of the largest economies in the world, it is being hindered due to a lack of women's participation. Although in the ancient times women had access to education in India, but gradually they lost this right. However, in the British period there was revival of interest in women's education in India. During this period, various socio religious movements led by renowned persons like Raja Ram Mohan Roy, Iswar Chandra Vidyasagar emphasised on women's education in India. Mahatma Jyotiba Phule, Periyar and Baba Saheb Ambedkar were leaders of the lower castes' development in India who took various initiatives to make education available to the women of India.

However, women's education got a fillip after the country got independence in 1947 and since then the government has taken various measures to provide education to all Indian women. As a result women's literacy rate has grown over the decades and the growth of female literacy rate has in fact been higher than that of male literacy rate. While in 2001 only 54.16 per cent of Indian women were literate, by the end of 2011, 65.46 per cent females were literate. The growth of female literacy rate is 11.30 per cent as compared to 6.29 per cent male literacy rate.

A study by the International centre for research on women confirms, "Women are more likely to control their own destinies and effect change in their own communities when they have higher level of education." According to Conference on Population and Development, its programme of action states that: "education is one of the most important means of empowering women with the knowledge, skills and self-confidence necessary to participate fully in the development process."

Government of India has launched The National Mission for Empowerment of Women (NMEW) on International Women's Day in 2010 with the aim to strengthen overall processes that promote all-round Development of women. The mission has the consent to strengthen the inter-sector convergence; facilitate the process of coordinating all the women's welfare and socio-economic development programmes across ministries and departments. The Mission aims to provide a single window service for all programmes run by the Government for Women under aegis of various Central Ministries. In the light of its mandate, the Mission has been named Mission Poorna Shakti, implying a vision for holistic empowerment of Women. The National Resource Centre for Women has been set up to function as a national convergence centre for all schemes and programmes for women. It acts as a central repository of knowledge, information, research and data on all gender related issues and is the main body servicing the National and State Mission Authority.

However, experience has shown that the relationship between education and empowerment is not as simple as it may first appear; while education is undoubtedly a key element contributing to empowerment, the two do not necessarily go hand in hand.

Objectives of the Study

An attempt has been made to highlight the role of education (whether formal academic or vocational education) in women empowerment in India and also role of women in nation building as well as cultural development in society. Women who are educated have greater awareness of their rights, and greater confidence and freedom to make decisions and improve their own and their children's health and increase their chances of survival and boost their work prospects.

Research Methodology

The present study is based on secondary data. The data was collected from various research papers, journals, websites and articles to ensure detailed understanding of the subject and preserve authenticity of information.

Education and Empowerment

Many educational programmes focus on students' acquisition of formal knowledge and training, and often equip them with the technical skills necessary to take up paid employment in a specific sector. In case of girls, this can mean being formally trained in an activity traditionally seen as "women's work", such as sewing, the small-scale production and commercialisation of food products, artisanal production or secretarial skills for the more literate. While it is often important that girls receive vocational training as part of their education, a more holistic approach that places a strong emphasis on enabling girls to develop a wider awareness of them and the external context in which they live is also vital. Having the opportunity to develop an awareness of their own social situation, as well as to gain confidence and self-esteem, means not only that girls are in a better position to deal with the multiple challenges that entry into the labour market can pose, but also an increased empowerment to define and act upon their ambitions.

Education has a unique power to act as a catalyst for wider development goals which can only be fully realised, however, if it is equitable. Women must fully benefit from educational opportunities if they have to enjoy the empowerment benefits that come with it. Education for women and girls has varied benefits towards their empowerment ranging from health, self-defence, political participation, leadership, entrepreneurship, to democracy and governance and employment opportunities. "Empowerment is the process by which individuals and groups gain power, access to resources and control over their own lives. In doing so, they gain the ability to achieve their highest personal and collective aspiration and goals" (Robbins, Chatterjee and Canda, 1998, p. 91).

Education empowers women in several dimensions. Some of these have been discussed as below:

(a) **Equal education creates path to financial independence for women and girls:** Education not only helps women and girls to fight with poverty by developing the skills required to improve their livelihoods, but also generates productivity gains that boost economic growth substantially. For financial independence, however, the education sector needs to overcome inequality by improving the lives of the poorest and marginalised women and girls. Education is a vital tool to achieve this goal because it can help ensure that the benefits of growth are fairly shared with women and girls as well.

(b) **Health and hygiene issues:** Women's education is critical in helping them with an empowered approach to health issues. Uneducated women in rural areas at times die due to health related diseases which can be prevented by providing proper health and hygiene education. Educated women are more likely to avoid these dangers by adopting simple and low cost practices to maintain hygiene, by reacting to symptoms, and by making sure a skilled attendant is present at birth.

(c) **Elimination of malnutrition**: Malnutrition is the underlying cause of more than a third of global child deaths. Educated mothers are more likely to ensure that their children receive the best nutrients to help them prevent or fight off ill health, know more about appropriate health and hygiene practices, and have more power in the home to ensure fulfilment of their children's nutritional needs.

(d) **Enhancing job opportunities:** Education can help in reducing the gender gaps in work opportunities and pay. Educated women are more likely not just to be employed, but to hold jobs that are secure and provide good working conditions and decent pay.

(e) **Education empowers women to overcome gender discrimination:** Women who are educated have greater awareness of their rights, and greater confidence and freedom to make decisions that affect their lives, improve their own and their children's health and chances of survival, and boost their work prospects. Education is also a key factor in hastening the demographic transition to lower birth and mortality rates.

(f) **Education is indispensable tool for strengthening the bonds that hold women in communities and societies together:** Education helps women in understanding democracy, promotes the tolerance and trust that underpin it, and motivates women to participate in politics and claim for leadership positions.

Empowerment is not something which could be made available in the form of a capsule to people whom we think may be in need of it. It is not just a concept that could be defined with the help of some universally accepted parameters. Empowerment is a process and includes components such as equal distribution of resources, prohibition in gender discrimination, freedom from violence, financial independence, freedom in decision making and freedom of choice etc.

The Importance of Women in Nation Building

"Woman is the builder and moulder of a nation's destiny, though delicate and soft as lily, she has a heart, stronger and bolder than that of man, she is the supreme inspiration for man's onward march."

Nation building means the legitimate political process to establish a system of governance and ability to maintain order, guarantee the fulfilment of international obligations and human rights and deliverance of essential social services. It is the establishment of equitable, democratic, and egalitarian society in which the rights of men and women are respected. Empowering somebody for nation building therefore is about giving her, the knowledge, skills and attitudes needed to live more fully and effectively. Life itself is a never ending process of learning, and when this is fully appreciated one is no longer a survivor but an adventurer (Emodi, 2009).

Education is the single most important window that defines the life, values and economic power of a nation. It inculcates the norms of responsible citizenship. Education also plays the most important role in human resource development and empowering the citizen for nation building. In short without education, we will have no society, no democracy, no future and no nation (Emodi, 2009).

The woman is a citizen, a worker, a professional, a director, a nation builder, a mother and a home maker. A nation is a conglomeration of homes and the woman is fully involved from its cleaning to its full management. The well known old adage which posits that "If you educate a man you educate an individual, but if you educate a woman you educate a family (nation)" is still relevant in present time. The message here is that once we know the value of education for men in society, we should allow women to have equal access to it. Education is used here to mean knowing, through formal or informal means, what is right for the spirit, mind and body and acting upon this knowledge.

Women constitute approximately half of the population of India. If she is given the task for the development of the country she can make a wonder. She is more dedicated, hard working, sincere, more devoted to the cause in comparison to men. Many social evils like-dowry, illiteracy among the females, killing of girl child in the womb, negligence of hygienic values etc. can well be tackled by the serious and active involvement of women. Today the educated women have come out of their inferiority complex and are shouldering all kinds of responsibilities, as managers, officers, TV and radio news readers, pilots, ministers, anchors, musicians, clerks, stenographers, and what not? There are veteran woman MPs and Ministers in the centre and the State - Ms. Mayavati, Ms. Jayalalitha, Mrs. Sushma Swaraj, Ms. Mamta Banerjee, Uma Bharti, Mrs. Vijaya Raje Scindhiya have proved to be astute Politicians.

In our society today more women are holding forth in their areas of chosen profession and proving their worth in their various endeavours. It is only justifiable that they be given equal opportunity to empowerment in order to contribute effectively to nation building and development. That is why in this article I want to discuss about women's contribution in Nation Building and the remarkable things they have done.

Literacy in India

Literacy represents a measure of educational status of any community. Literacy rate is estimated as the percentage of people educated to the respective total population. Though literacy is very important for both males and females, these exists a wide gap between both the sexes in India. The 15th official census in India was calculated in the year 2011. In a developing economy like India, literacy is the main foundation for social and economic growth. At the time when British rule ended in India in the year 1947 the literacy rate was just 12 per cent. Over the years, India has changed socially, economically, and globally. After the 2011 census, literacy rate in India was found to be 74.04 per cent. The Male literacy rate is 82.14 per cent and Female literacy rate is 65.46 per cent according to Census 2011. Among the Indian states, Kerala has the highest literacy rate of 93.91 per cent followed by Mizoram at 91.58 per cent. Among the Union Territories, Lakshadweep has the highest literacy rate of 92.28 per cent. Bihar has the lowest literacy rate in India with 63.82 per cent. The Male literacy is highest in Lakshadweep at 96.11 per cent and Kerala at 96.02 per cent. The Female literacy is highest in Kerala at 91.98 per cent and then in Mizoram at 89.40 per cent. Lowest male literacy is in Bihar at 73.39 per cent. Lowest female literacy is in Rajasthan at 52.66 per cent.

Provision of educational opportunities for women has been an important part of the national attempt in the field of education since independence. The National Policy on Education (NPE, 1986) as revised in 1992 was a landmark in the field of policy on women's education which recognised the need to redress traditional gender imbalances in educational access and achievement.

The Programme of Action (POA, 1992) which translates the above guidelines into an action strategy, in the section "Education for Women's Equality" (Chapter-XII, pages 105-107), focuses on empowerment of women as the critical precondition for their participation in the education process. The table given below presents the total literacy rate as well as Male and Female literacy rates in each state and union territory of India.

Indian States	*Total Literacy Rate*	*Male Literacy Rate*	*Female Literacy Rate*	*Indian States*	*Total Literacy Rate*	*Male Literacy Rate*	*Female Literacy Rate*
Jammu & Kashmir	68.74	78.26	58.01	Bihar	63.82	73.39	53.33
Himachal Pradesh	83.78	90.83	76.60	Sikkim	82.20	87.29	76.43
Punjab	76.68	81.48	71.34	Arunachal Pradesh	66.95	76.69	59.97
Chandigarh	86.43	90.54	81.38	Nagaland	80.11	83.29	76.69
Uttarakhand	79.83	88.33	70.70	Manipur	79.85	86.49	73.17
Haryana	76.64	85.38	66.77	Mizoram	91.58	93.72	89.40
Delhi	86.34	91.03	80.93	Tripura	87.75	92.18	83.15
Rajasthan	67.06	80.51	52.66	Meghalaya	75.48	77.17	73.78
Uttar Pradesh	69.72	79.24	59.26	Assam	73.18	78.81	67.27
West Bengal	77.08	82.67	71.16	Andhra Pradesh	67.66	75.56	59.74
Jharkhand	67.63	78.45	56.21	Karnataka	75.60	82.85	68.83
Orissa	73.45	82.40	64.36	Goa	87.40	92.81	81.84
Chhattishgarh	71.04	81.45	60.59	Lakshadweep	92.28	96.11	88.25
Madhya Pradesh	70.63	80.53	60.02	Kerala	93.91	96.02	91.98
Gujarat	79.31	87.23	70.73	Tamil Nadu	80.33	86.81	73.86
Daman & diu	87.57	91.48	79.59	Puducherry	86.55	92.12	81.22
Dadar & nagar haveli	77.65	86.46	65.93	Andman & Nikobar Islands	86.27	90.11	81.84
Maharashtra	82.91	88.82	75.48				

Source: India 2011 Census Report.

Today, the female literacy levels according to the Literacy Rate 2011 Census are 65.46 per cent where as the male literacy rate is over 80 per cent. The literacy rate in India has always been a matter of concern due to which many NGOs are getting involved and several government sponsored ads, campaigns and programs are being used to spread awareness amongst people about the importance of literacy. Also the government has made strict rules for female equality rights. Indian literacy rate has shown significant rise in the past 10 years.

Conclusion

Lastly to conclude with the famous quote that "There is no chance for the welfare of the world unless the condition of women is improved. It is not possible for a bird to fly on only one wing." Education is the only means to pave the path for transformation. Women education in India plays a key role in the social and economic development of the country. Educating a woman uplifts her life as well as the quality of her life (personal and professional) and her entire family. Thus, the need of the hour is a strong system of value based education that upholds principles such as equity, ethics and empowerment in India. As of now, there is neither adequate 'quantitative' nor 'qualitative' representation of women in education. Women not only need to occupy more spaces in education sector but also more meaningful spaces. If we are really committed to creating an environment that is conducive to women's empowerment we have to build into the system of education those values which build respect for women's roles and responsibilities and recognise their contribution to society.

References

- Sugana, M. (2011). "Education and Women Empowerment in India", International Journal of Multi-disciplinary Research, Vol. 1, Issue 8.
- Shinde, J. "Women's Empowerment through Education", National Monthly Referred Journal of Research in Arts & Education, Vol. 1, Issue 11.
- Waris and Viraktamath (2013). "Gender gaps and Women's Empowerment in India- Issues and Strategies", International Journal of Scientific Research Publications, Vol. 3, Issue 9.
- Arogyamma, T. (2014). "Education for Women's Empowerment", Global Journal for Research Analysis, Vol. 3, Issue 8.
- Medel, C. (1995), "Women, Education and Empowerment: Pathways towards Autonomy", UNESCO Institute for Education, Germany.
- Emodi, J. (2009), "Women Empowerment and Nation Building: The Role of Unity Colleges", Anniversary of Federal Government Girls College, Bwari, Abuja.
- Barman, A. and Saurikhia, A. (2011), "Education: A Potent Tool in Emancipation and Empowerment of Indian Women", the First International Conference on Interdisciplinary Research and Development, Thailand.
- www.empowerwomen.org
- www.theguardian.com
- www.nmew.gov.in
- www.census2011.co.in
- www.ncte-india.org
- www.hindustantimes.com

Chapter-9

Women Empowerment through Education

—Palwinder Kaur

Abstract

Always there have been people in the society who have been deprived of their basic rights in every society, state and nation, mainly because these people have lacked awareness of their rights. If we enlist such people from the society, then women would top this list. Woman in society have been considered as secondary citizens and deprived of all basic rights, hence since the ages the need to empower them has been strongly felt by the reformers. Education enables a woman to become strong by giving her knowledge about good health, which ultimately benefits her physical as well as mental health. Women education in India has also been a major preoccupation of both the government and civil society as educated women can play a very important role in the development of the country. We can't neglect the importance of education with reference to women empowerment. India is poised to becoming a superpower, a developed country by 2020. The growth of women's education in rural areas is very slow. This obviously means that still large womenfolk of our country are illiterate, weak, backward and exploited. Education of women is the most powerful tool to change the society. Education also brings a reduction in inequalities and functions as a means of improving their status within the family.

***Key Words**: Education, Female Literacy Rate, Women Empowerment, Society, Development.*

Introduction

Education is a milestone for women empowerment because it enables them to respond to opportunities to challenge their traditional roles and to change their lives. Educating women benefits the whole society. It has a more significant impact on poverty and development than men's education. Education plays an important role in removing economic poverty by opening various job avenues for her so that she can work hand in hand with man and give support to the family, which in the long run strengthens the economy. Education develops the personality and rationality of individuals, qualifies them to fulfil certain economic, political and cultural functions and thereby improves their socio-economic status. The Universal Declaration of Human Rights affirms that all human beings are equal in dignity and rights without distinction of any kind including distinction based on sex. Girl's education is an investment and not expense which gives its returns in a positive way in the long run. Acknowledging the status of women in family is the first step of progress and development. In Indian mythology, women are considered as divine, holy and pure and Goddesses are highly revered and worshiped all over the country. Durga is the symbol of strength, Saraswati denotes knowledge, Parvati is regarded as the goddess of power, and Laxmi the endower of wealth. Despite the fact that India has a strong written constitution that proclaims penalty for those who harrass women - in the form of female foeticide, female infanticide, child labour, child marriage, dowry, sexual harassment, rape, eve-teasing etc. - the crime graph against women is increasing at an alarming rate, according to a report by the National Commission for Woman (NWC) and the Women's Rights Commission.

Status of Women Education

The constitutional directive to provide free and compulsory education to all children up to the age of 14 years has remained unfulfilled till now. Educational experts admit that this failure is mainly due to the slow progress of education among girls. After many years of Independence, there still exists a great disparity between male and female educational status. India is the world's largest democracy where billions of people live and almost half of these are women. If girls are not educated, families suffer too. Educated mothers use their knowledge to improve the health of their children and other family members. Their knowledge about health risks protects their families against illness. Child mortality rate is much higher where mothers lack education than in families where mothers are educated. Girls' education has emerged as one of the top priorities of Indian society "Educating girls is not an option, it is a necessity." We all want to elimilnate gender disparities in education. Adi Shankaracharya, Raja Ram Mohan Roy, Ishwar-Chandra Vidyasagar, Swami Vivekanand, Mahatma Gandhi, Jawaharlal Nehru spoke against the inhuman oppression and crimes perpetrated on women in the name of tradition and religion. Margaret Cousins, worked hard to create social awareness on women's issues and to increase legal and constitutional rights of women. Annie Besant, Mutthulakshmi Reddy, Kamla Devi Chattopadhaya, Durga Bai Deskmukh, Sarojini Naidu are the names of the prominent crusaders who fought for equality of women's rights.

Barriers to Women Education

In Indian families especially in rural areas, girl children play the role of second mother by shouldering the responsibilities of household work such as looking after the sibling, fetching water, collecting wood, cleaning and cooking etc., and are discouraged to go to school. Another prominent social evil - bonded labour system - is also acting as a barrier against girls' education, mainly in the case of the underprivileged families like those of the washer people and landless agricultural labourers. The lower enrolment of girls in school is one of the stumbling blocks in the path of women education. In India, more than 50 per cent of the girls are non-starters. One out of ten of the girls in the age group of 6-11 are still not enrolled in schools. The incidence and prevalence of drop-outs among girls especially in rural, tribal and slum areas seems to be quite high. The reasons mainly cited for the cause of this high rate of drop-out are: the poor academic records of the students which make it difficult for them to cope up with the subjects and comprehend the practical sessions, some of the students/trainees being able to get jobs before the completion of the course, teachers did not teach well and the poor economic background of students. According to available sources, occurrence of drop-out and stagnation amongst girls are nearly twice as that of boys all over India. In India, the school environment for girls is not really interesting and encouraging. The methods of teaching are mostly outdated, rigid and uninteresting. Most schools lack basic facilities such as drinking water and toilet facilities; these schools do not have adequate infrastructure and experienced teachers– especially female teachers who are preferred by parents for the safety of their girl children.

According to the UN sources, India is the most child labour populous nation in the globe with more than 50 million child labourers working in carpet making, domestic works, beedi works, glass bangles, construction etc. In most of these industries girl children are preferred for high productivity and low costs. In many poverty stricken families, especially girls are considered as economic assets as they bring income for livelihood as well for economic crises due to death or incapacity of parents.

Definition of Women Empowerment

"Women's empowerment is defined as the process in which their spiritual, political, social or economic status is raised." This also includes the right to raise their level of confidence regarding their own capabilities. Empowerment includes the following aspects:

1. The ability to take their own decisions.
2. The ability to seek information and have other facilities at their disposal which would enable them to take proper decisions.
3. Having wide choices (besides 'Yes/No' and 'If/ Else' choices).
4. Firmness while taking collective decisions.
5. Possessing positive way of thinking regarding the ability to bring about transformation.
6. The ability to bring about improvement in one's own capabilities.
7. The competence to modify other's attitudes in a democratic manner.
8. The ability to participate in continuous and self-propagated development process and to take active participation in the transformation process.

9. The ability to exercise control on negative factors and build up a positive image of oneself.

Meaning of Women Empowerment

The absence of a democratic context has contributed to slow progress in empowering women, particularly in South Asia. Women's empowerment movements have not survived in authoritarian regimes based on gender subordination and ideologies of male dominance. Approaches in South Asia have necessarily focused on opportunities and services rather than on political power. Conceptualisations of gender discrimination and male domination have been oversimplified and focused on elimination of obvious oppressive practices such as wife beating or dowry demands. Empowerment of women that will have lasting impacts must involve consciousness raising before the social construction of gender - which subordinates women in the family, class, caste, religion, or society–can be changed.

Three experimental approaches to empowerment in South Asia have been tried: integrated development, economic empowerment, and consciousness raising. Consciousness raising has been implemented in awareness groups' and educational programmes that have led to a new consciousness and self worth of targetted population, societal and gender analysis, and access to more skills and information for the targetted groups. The economic empowerment approach has relied on improving women's control over economic resources and strengthening women's economic security. Gramin Bank is one example of an endeavour to organise women for savings and credit, income generation, and skill training activities. Integrated development approaches have encouraged women's collectives that have engaged in development and social problem resolution and formed specialised activity groups as means of mobilisation of women. No one design has assured success. Identification of the poorest and most oppressed in a geopolitical area has provided an entry point for action. Women were encouraged to find a separate time and space for themselves. The three aforementioned approaches have different assumptions about the reason for women's powerlessness and these are: greater poverty and lower access to resources, economic vulnerability, subordination within patriarchal societies and socio-economic inequalities.

Need of Women Empowerment

Empowerment is probably the totality of the following or similar capabilities:

- Having self decision-making power.
- Having access to information and resources for taking proper decision.
- Having a range of options from which one can make choices. (not just yes/no, either/or.)
- Ability to exercise assertiveness in collective decision making.
- Having positive thinking on the ability to make changes.
- Ability to learn skills for improving one's personal or group power.
- Involving in the self-initiated and continuous growth and change process.
- Increasing one's positive self-image and overcoming stigma.

So from the above points we can divide the issue of Women's empowerment into five components, which are self explanatory and indicate the need of women empowerment:—

- Women's sense of self-worth;
- Their right to have and to determine choices.
- Their right to have access to opportunities and resources.
- Their right to have the power to control their own lives, both within and outside the home.
- Their ability to influence the direction of social change so as to create more just social and economic orders, nationally and internationally.

Importance of Education

If it is said that education is the key to all problems, then it won't be improper. Thinkers have given a number of definitions of education but out of these definitions, the most important definition is that which was put forth by M. Phule. According to M. Phule, "Education is that which demonstrates the difference between what is good and what is evil." If we consider the above definition, we come to know that whatever revolutions that have taken place in our history, education is at the base of them. It is through education that one realises what is good and what is bad, what is proper and what is not (just and unjust etc.). It is education which gives a vent/voice to injustice. The three fold formula given by Dr B. R. Ambedkar to Indian society includes that the most important thing is to be educated.

Importance of Education in Women's Empowerment

Women education in India plays a very important role in the overall development of the country. It not only helps in the development of half of the human resources, but in improving the quality of life at home and outside. The first year of New Millennium 2001 was declared as "Women Empowerment Year." Jawaharlal Nehru had said "Education of a boy is the education of one person, but the education of girl is the education of entire family." Education of a woman leads to a better family and ultimately an ideal society and a progressive nation. Educated women not only tend to promote education of their girl children, but also can provide better guidance to all their children. Moreover educated women can also help in the reduction of infant mortality rate and growth of the population. Women Empowerment is a global issue and discussion on women's political rights are at the fore front of many formal and informal campaigns worldwide. A progressive nation is one where all the people of the country irrespective of sex, religion, caste, creed and colour are economically, socially, culturally, politically and through all thoughts are independent.

Within the framework of a democratic polity, our laws, development policies, plan and programmes have aimed at women's advancement in difference spheres .Women's empowerment is not limited only to the Indian society. If we consider the global aspect in this regard, we see that now women are being given equal treatment in developed nations, yet, in fact, if we take a retrospect of history, we come to know that women have always been given secondary position in most societies. Although the difference between men and women created by the Nature is but natural but it is education through which we can protect women from the exploiters. When women in America realised this, they opposed this injustice which was meted out to them by way of a huge movement and asked for equal rights. For eradicating this injustice, the UNO (United Nations' Organisation) framed a Convention/Charter which is called 'The Convention on the Elimination of all Forms of Discrimination against Women (CEDAW)', which further led to the formation of Women's Commission. The concept of women empowerment was given much impetus at the international women conference at NAIROBI in 1985.

Taking an account of this background, we come to know that women's empowerment has now become a topic of global discussion. Seeing all the aspects of this discussion, we will realise that education is the only means for empowerment of women. The literacy rate amongst the women in the post-Independent Era has increased to a great extent. We, as a nation, dream of becoming a Super Power by 2020. For becoming a Super Power, each element of our society/ nation should contribute in the national building process. Therefore, it is urgent for us to know the importance of women's education, which would in turn give an impetus to the process of women's empowerment. The National Commission of Women was set up by an Act of Parliament in 1990 to safeguard the right and legal entitlements of women. The 73rd and 74th Amendments (1993) to the constitution of India have provided for reservation of seats in the local bodies of Panchayat and Municipalities for women, laying a strong foundation for their participation in decision making at the local level.

Relationship between Education and Women Empowerment

Education definitely raises 'Women nation', Women Empowerment Act of Parliament in 1990 was enacted to safeguard the rights of women. Majority of the women in our country are uneducated that is why they are suppressed. It is the duty of school teachers to tell the girls from very beginning that becoming a wife is not their ultimate goal. Their standing up on their feet and being something is more important. Education can bring phenomenal change in women's life resulting in social transformation in the long run by inculcating following attributes among them:

1. Enhancing their confidence

2. Raising their status in the family and society
3. Bring awareness about their rights
4. Boosting their self esteem
5. Increasing their self efficacy
6. Reducing their dependency
7. Better bringing up of their children
8. Enhancing their mobility
9. Opening career opportunities

Increased knowledge, self-confidence and awareness of gender equity are indicators of empowerment process. Women who are educated and employed are in much better position in our society as compared to uneducated women worker. This is a commonly understood view about the role of education in transforming women.

On observing the table given below, we come to know that at no point could the literacy rate of women match with that of men. As a result, even after 67 years of independence, women are occupying a secondary position in our social hierarchy. Inspite of being aware of her position, a woman can't transform the situation due to lack of education. Therefore, women's empowerment can't be effected unless we persuade the importance of women's education.

Table 1. Literacy rate in India

Year	*Persons*	*Males*	*Females*
1901	5.3	9.8	0.7
1911	5.9	10.6	1.1
1921	7.2	12.2	1.8
1931	9.5	15.6	2.9
1941	16.1	24.9	7.3
1951	16.7	24.9	7.3
1961	16.7	24.9	7.3
1971	29.5	39.5	18.7
1981	36.5	46.9	24.8
1991	52.1	63.9	39.2
2001	62.38	76.0	54.0
2011	74.4	82.14	65.46

Conclusion

On the basis of above detailed analysis it could be concluded that there is no doubt about the essential need of empowering women through education. Now it is also clear that only literacy is not the ultimate solution but women should be highly educated so as to at least know their rights and duties.

References

- Batliwala, S. (1994). The Meaning of Women's Empowerment: New Concepts from Action. In Sen, G., Germain, A and Chen, L. (eds.) Population Policies Reconsidered. Health Empowerment and Rights. Cambridge: Harvard University Press, pp. 127-38.
- Government of India, Census of India, 2011.
- Hashemi, S., Schuler, M. & Riley, A. (1996). Rural Credit Programs and Women's Empowerment in Bangladesh. World Development, 24(4), pp. 635-53.
- Heyzer, N. (2005). Making the links: women's rights and empowerment are key to achieving the millennium development goals 01. Gender & Development, 13:1, 9 -12.
- Maslak, M. A. & Singhal, G. (2008). The identity of educated women in India: Confluence or divergence. Gender and Education, Vol. 20, No.5, pp. 481-493.
- N. L. Gupta (2003)Women's Education Through Ages, Concept Publications Co, New Delhi.
- R. K. Rao (2001). Women and Education, Kalpaz Publications, Delhi.
- S. P. Agarval (2001), Women's Education in India (1995-98)Present Status, Perspective, Plan, Statistical Indicators with Global View, Vol. III Concept Publications Co, New Delhi.
- http://www.slideshare.net/puneetsharma5688/women-empowermentpuneet-sharma
- http://womeninislam.ws/en/status-of-women_indian-society.aspx
- http://womenroleinsociety.blogspot.in/2010/06/status-of-women-in-indian-society.html
- http://www.bu.edu/wcp/Papers/Huma/HumaSing.htm
- http://www.civilserviceindia.com/subject/Essay/women-empowerment-challenges-and- prospects.html faculty.wcas.northwestern.edu/.../research/Doepke_Tertilt_0411.pdf
- http://bahai-library.com/kingdon_education_women_development
- http://zenithresearch.org.in

Chapter-10

Role of Education in Women Empowerment

—*Priyanka*

Abstract

The empowerment of a person or group of people is the process of giving them power and status in a particular situation. Empowering women implies enabling them to develop themselves in economic, social and political fronts. Women empowerment involves the building up of a society, a political environment, wherein women can breathe without the fear of coercion, mistreatment, apprehension, discrimination and the general feeling of persecution which goes with being a woman in a traditionally patriarchal society. Empowerment of women in the context of knowledge societies necessitates building up the abilities and skills of women so that they can gain insight into the issues affecting them and also building up their capacity to voice their concerns. In this context education is a powerful tool for gender empowerment in many developing countries. Education can dramatically change the situation. Education can enable direct interactive communication even with those who lack skills, who are illiterate, lack mobility and have little self-confidence. Proper education can only empower women in the true sense.

Key words- *Empowerment, Women Empowerment, Education, Patriarchal, Society.*

Introduction

"If you educate a man you educate an individual, however, if you educate a woman you educate a whole family. Women empowered means mother India empowered."

Pt. Jawaharlal Nehru

The empowerment of women has been extensively acknowledged as an important goalmouth in a nation's development, but the meanings and context associated with this concept vary. The UNICEF Women's Equality and Empowerment Framework underlines women's access, awareness of causes of inequality, capacity to direct one's own interests, and taking control as well as action to overcome obstacles to reducing structural inequality (UNICEF 2001).

Empowering women means enabling them to develop themselves in socio economic and political dimensions. Women empowerment involves the building up of a society, a political environment, wherein women can breathe without the fear of oppression, exploitation, apprehension, discrimination and the general feeling of persecution which goes with being a woman in a traditionally patriarchal structure. Women can be empowered by welcoming them in the mainstream of development and declaring their access to productive assets, regulations warranting them equal social and political position, educating them about their rights, assuring their participation in decision making and providing them a platform for expressing their complaints, integrating their issues into the mainstream of the decision making process and fighting for the cause of poor and oppressed women in the society in particular. However, in all the policies provision of education is the central link which holds the key to women empowerment.

India will develop itself as one of the most developed nations by 2020, more literate, knowledgeable and economical at the forefront and undoubtedly women will play a vibrant role in contributing to the country's growth and development. Women power is crucial to the economic growth of any country. In India this is yet to meet the requirements despite the introduction of a number of programmes, policies and reforms for women. Slight achievements can be seen in the area of women empowerment, but for this to happen significantly, this sector must experience a chain of reforms. Though India could well become one of the largest economies in the world, it is being hindered due to a lack of women's participation.

Empowerment- Concept and Definitions

The concept of empowerment came into knowledge in the middle of 17th century and the meaning was 'to invest with authority'. Afterwards people started to use it in a more general way meaning "to enable or permit." This idea of empowerment is an outgrowth of the discourse on human development and it came into fame after 1980s. The dictionary meaning of empowerment is "the empowerment of a person or group of people is the process of giving them power and status in a particular situation. (Collin's Dictionary). Different authors and scholars have described the concept of empowerment differently as per their need and their work. Some of them are:

According to Narayan, 2002 and World Development Report, 2002, Empowerment has been defined as to infuse people with power.

As per Sen, 1999, Empowerment is an expansion in individual's agency i.e. expansion in one's ability to act and bring about change, whose achievement can be judged in terms of her own values and objectives.

As per Kabeer, 2005, Empowerment refers to the processes by which those who have been denied the ability to make choices acquire such an ability, that means people who exercise a great deal of choice in their lives may be very powerful, but they are not empowered in the sense they have never been empowered in first place.

As per Malhotra, Schuler & Boender 2002, Empowerment is a dynamic process. The process can be separated into components (such as enabling factors, agency and outcomes).

Women Empowerment–Status in India

"There is no chance of the welfare of the world unless the condition of women is improved. It is not possible for a bird to fly on one wing."

Swami Vivekananda

India is a country of majestic inconsistencies. On the one hand it is a global leader in the knowledge economy, and on the other side more than half of its population is poor and illiterate, most of whom are women. In India, the status of Women Empowerment cannot be envisioned with a single dimension. It requires a multidimensional assessment in terms of various components of a woman's life. Empowerment of women in the context of knowledge societies entails building up the abilities and skills of women to gain insight into the issues affecting them and also building up their capacity to voice their concerns. In this context education is a powerful tool for gender empowerment in many developing countries. Education can dramatically change the situation.

"If women are unhappy, individual homes, society and the nation will not prosper," so said former President Pratibha Patil (Patil, 2012). In order to create a sustainable world, we must begin to empower women and girls. Empowering women empowers her family and in turn her community which translates to a powerful force that can change the world in significantly positive ways. Also, bringing more equality to mankind balances the strengths and weaknesses of men and women to complement each other.

Empowerment has come to denote women's increased control over their own lives, bodies, and environments. In discussions of women's empowerment, emphasis is often placed on women's decision-making roles, their economic self-reliance, and their legal rights to equal treatment, inheritance and protection against all forms of discrimination, in addition to the elimination of barriers to access to resources such as education and information. (Kishore 2008)

Women's empowerment can be seen as a process in which the following elementsare involved: awareness/consciousness, choice/alternatives, resources, voice, agency and participation. These dimensions of women's empowerment is linked to enhancing women's ability to make choices over the areas in their lives that matter to them, both the strategic life choices that Kabeer (1999) has discussed and to choices related to daily life Charmes and Wieringa (2003). The overall status of women in terms of gender gap index prepared by World Economic Forum in 2012 is presented as follows:.

Gender Gap sub-Indices	*India*		*Sri lanka*	
	Rank	*Score*	*Rank*	*Score*
1. Economic Participation and Opportunity	123	0.4588	105	0.5596
2. Educational Attainment	121	0.8525	108	0.9946
3. Health and Survival	134	0.9612	1	0.9796
4. Political Empowerment	17	0.3343	22	0.3151
5. Overall Index	105	0.6442	39	0.7122
Gender Gap Index -2012 (Out of 135 Countries)				

Source: World Economic Forum (2012) Global Gender gap Index-2012, pp. 10-11.

The table shows the status of low level of attainment of women in various fields of their participation. The Global Gender Gap Report by the World Economic Forum in 2009 ranked India 114th out of 134 countries for inequality between men and women in the dimensions of economy, politics, health, and education. On equal economic opportunities and women's participation in the labour force, India ranked 127th and 122nd respectively (Upadhyay, 2014). According to Census-2011, India has reached the population of 1210 million. The sex ratio was 0 930 in 1971 and it has increased to 0 940 according to 2011 Census. The female literacy also increased from 18.3 per cent in 1961 to 65.46 per cent in 2011 and male-female literacy gap decreased from 26.6 per cent in 1981 to 16.7 per cent (Census, 2011). But Women empowerment in India is heavily dependent on many different variables that include geographical location (rural/urban), educational status, social status (caste and class) and age. Policies on women empowerment exist at national, state and local levels in many sectors including health, education, economic opportunities, and gender based violence and political participation. The scope and coverage of the schemes launched has been expanding and include initiatives for economic and social empowerment of women and for securing gender equality (Nagaraja, 2013).

Importance of Women Education in India

Women education in India plays a very important role in the overall development of the country. It not only helps in the development of half of the human resources, but also in improving the quality of life at home and outside. Educated women not only tend to promote education of their girl children, but also can provide better guidance to all their children. Moreover educated women can also help in the reduction of infant mortality rate and growth of the population.

Women Empowerment through Education

Women play variety of roles in families and society and for all the roles that they perform education is the key support. While performing their roles one thing is certain, even with great challenges and seemingly impossible hindrances, they get the things done. When their sheer determination will get combined with the educational opportunities, there are no limits to what women can do for their family, society and nation. Empowering women and girls with education is fundamental to building a sustainable future for this planet. At the World Economic Forum (2012), U.N. Secretary General – Ban Ki Moon focused on the importance of female education. According to him education makes them productive and dynamic in life, they can contribute to the growth of society, and make their own decisions on different aspects of their life. A number of research shows that education improves women's life by opening their mind to the possibilities of what they may achieve, creating more income-producing work opportunities, improving their health and future generation's health, and giving them opportunities for economic independence. Education is vital to supporting the sustainable development initiatives. Only half of Indian women fall into the category of empowered, in terms of having higher education, exposure to mass media, decent job and freedom of movement. A large number of women don't have sufficient independence to make choices concerning their own life and most of their decisions and actions do not reflect their authentic interests or desires.

In India, women perform a central role in family, community and society. Still they remain unseen and unheard. Women more than men have to balance the complexities of surviving in extreme poverty, yet these women are excluded from discussion because they are often illiterate, they lack confidence and they lack mobility. Women Empowerment is a global issue and discussion on women rights are at the forefront of many formal and informal campaigns worldwide.

The concept of women empowerment was given impetus in the international women conference at NAIROBI in 1985. Education is milestone of women empowerment. Education makes them aware of their roles, empowers them to respond to challenges and express themselves. We can't disregard the significance of education with regard to women empowerment. India's dream of becoming a superpower, a developed economy can be achieved in reality only when the women of this nation become empowered.

India presently accounts for the largest number of illiterates in the world although Literacy rates in India have risen sharply from 18.3 per cent in 1951 to 74.04 per cent in 2011 in which enrolment of women in education have also risen sharply from 7 per cent to 65.46 per cent, this is due to its ever burgeoning population. Within the framework of a democratic polity, our laws, development policies, plans and programmes have aimed at women's advancement in difference spheres. From the fifth five year plan (1974–78) onwards there has been a marked shift in the approach to women's issues from welfare to development. In recent years, the empowerment of women has been recognised as the central issue in determining the status of women. The National Commission of Women was set up by an Act of Parliament in 1990 to safeguard the right and legal entitlements of women. The 73rd and 74th Amendments (1993) to the constitution of India have provided for reservation of seats in the local bodies of Panchayat and Municipalities for women, laying a strong foundation for their participation in decision making at the local level.

Conclusion

Empowering women means to enable them to stand on their own and transition from a weak position to that of the ability to suitably address and do away with the weakness. Education of women is the most powerful tool to effect their positive change of position in society. Educated women will be aware of the ill treatment of society and can come forth for reduction in disparities and improve their status within the family, society and the nation. The society will make satisfactory progress only when women will be given equal opportunities. once Pt. Jawaharlal Nehru said, "To awaken the people, it is women who must be awakened; once she is on the move, the family moves, the village moves and the nation moves." Therefore women must be brought in the mainstream for the development of India. Education of women must be encouraged at district, state and central level by establishing school, colleges and universities exclusively for women and they must be made aware of their rights so that they can raise voice in case of disparities. Education can offer opportunities for direct, interactive communication even with those who lack skills, are illiterate, lack mobility and have little self-confidence. Proper education can only empower women in the true sense.

References

- Census of India, 2011
- Charmus, Jacques & Wieringa, Saskia (2003): Measuring Empowerment: An Assessment of the Gender Related Development Index and the Gender 'Empowerment Measure', Journal of Human Development and Capabilities, Vol. 4, No. 3, pp. 419-435.
- Kabeer, Nailà. (2005): Gender Equality and Women's Empowerment: A Critical Analysis of the 'Third Millennium Development Goal', Gender and Development, Vol. 13, No. 13, No. 1, Millennium Development Goals (March, 2005), pp. 13-24.
- Kishore, Sunita, Subaiya, Lekha. (2008): Understanding Women's Empowerment: A Comparative Analysis of Demographic Health Surveys (DHS) Data DHS Comparative Report No. 20, Calverton, Maryland, USA: Macro International INC.
- Malhotra. Anju, Schuler R. Sidney and Boender, Carol (2002): Measuring Women's Empowerment as a Variable in International Development 'Background Paper Prepared for the World Bank Workshop on Poverty and Gender: New Perspectives.
- Nagaraja. (2013). Empowerment of Women in India: A Critical Analysis. Journal of Humanities and Social Science (IOSR-JHSS), 9(2), 4, www.Iosrjournals.Org
- Narayan, (2002): Empowerment and Poverty Reduction, Washington, DC, World Bank.
- Patil, P. P. (2012). Spewww.ibtimes.co.in/articles/287807/20120126/india-president-republic- day-speech-pratibha-patil.htm
- Sen, Amartya. (1999): 'Development as Freedom', Oxford: Oxford University Press.
- Upadhyay, R. (2010). Women's Economic Opportunities in India. www.asiafoundation.org
- World Economic Forum (2012), The Global Gender Gap Report 2012, www.weforum.org/reports/global-gend......

Chapter-11

The Role of Education in Empowering Muslim Women in South Asia

—*Amit Kumar Dutta*

Abstract

The objective of education is the holistic development of human personality and empowerment to all sections of society. Education is a great leveller because it helps to remove all barriers of caste, community, race and gender. Moreover, education being a social process, its true role in human empowerment varies according to the society and the State in which it is practiced. This chapter analyses the role of education in the empowerment of Muslim women in South Asia with special reference to the interface between Muslim religion and women education and the continuous struggle of Muslim women in South Asia for education, gender equality and empowerment. In this chapter author has analysed the state of affairs of Muslim women education in South Asia in the context of their position in Islam. The objective of this chapter is to highlight and assert the role which education can play in the socio–economic betterment of large sections of Muslim women in South Asia.

Key Words: *Education, Empowerment, Social Process, Muslim Women, Muslim Religion, South Asia.*

Introduction

South Asia is no ordinary land mass. It is a cradle of human civilisation. Since the dawn of history, groups and communities from various cultures and religions have settled and flourished in this part of the Asian continent. South Asia is an ocean where rivers of different faiths, ideologies, beliefs and religion have converged and created an ocean of humanity. Islam, which is one of the most popular religions of the world, was brought to South Asia by the invading Arabs. It enjoyed state patronage under the Delhi Sultanate and the Mughals. Even though South Asia is the birth place of Hinduism, Buddhism, Jainism and the Sikh religion, the difference between these religions and Islam is that the preachers and propagators of Islam were singularly determined and focused in converting large sections of the South Asian non Muslim population into Islam. Despite the greatness of Islam as a religion preaching oneness of God, respect and equal treatment to women and universal brotherhood, sadly, with the passage of time, certain aspects of the religion have been misinterpreted and manipulated by the mullahs and zealots to suit their vested interests resulting in unfair and unequal treatment to women.

Literature Study

(1) Dr Jamal Badawi in his essay, The *Status of Women in Islam,* has discussed the status of women in the pre Islamic era as well as the position of women in Islam from different perspectives such as spiritual, social, economic and political.

(2) In a short booklet written by Muhammad Zafrulla Khan entitled *woman in Islam,* which is largely based on the original Quranic teachings, the author has discussed the rights enjoyed by Muslim women and concepts like marriage, divorce and polygamy and the preservation of social and moral values in Islam.

(3) The book *Women in Islam and Refutation of Some Common Misconceptions* written by Dr Abdul – Rahman Al – Sheha deals with certain questions and issues such as the condition of women through the ages, matters in which men and women are equal in Islam, status and rights of women in various stages in Muslim society and certain misconceptions and their refutation about certain rights and obligations about women's rights in Islam.

(4) In a report on Muslim women in India, the author Seema Kazi has discussed the condition of Muslim women in India within a historical framework and discusses issues concerning gender discrimination and backwardness of Indian Muslim women. The author recommends certain measures to improve the condition of Indian Muslim women.

(5) In the final report *Pakistan : Country Gender Profile prepared by Sustainable Development Policy Institute*, Pakistani reporter discusses the socio-economic profile of women in Pakistan.

(6) The authors M. Shahidul Islam and Suvi Dogra in their paper *Women Empowerment in Bangladesh: the Rise of the Other Half* have studied women empowerment in Bangladesh in comparison with other countries in South Asia, China and Vietnam and have attempted to find out how the gender related development factors can help Bangladesh in achieving a higher growth path.

(7) The country report *Status of Women: Afghanistan* prepared by Wali M. Rahimi discusses the situation of women in Afghanistan and related issues.

(8) The authors Dr Syed Mussawar Hussain Bukhari and Muhammad Asim in their article *Women Empowerment in a Muslim Society: A Practical Observation* highlight women empowerment in Muslim society by specially focusing on international standards mentioned by United Nations Wing (UNIFEM). The authors conclude that the standards mentioned by UNIFEM are practically observed by Iran in all socio-economic and political fields.

(9) The authors Dr Syed Waseem A. Ashraf and Ayaz Ahmad in their study *Muslim Women Education and Empowerment in Rural Aligarh (A Case Study)* attempt to analyse the Muslim women education and empowerment in rural areas of Aligarh district. The authors conclude that socio-economic conditions are the major determinants of women empowerment than religion.

(10) Author Azra Abidi in her paper *Muslim Women and their Representation in South Asian Politics* discusses the

participation and representation of Muslim women in politics in India, Pakistan and Bangladesh.

(11) The authors Dr. David Tyrer and Fauzia Ahmad in their summary report *Muslim Women and Higher Education: Identities, Experiences and Prospects* have dealt with the findings of a qualitative study of Muslim women's experiences of studying in Higher Education Institutions (HEI) across the UK.

(12) Dr Shakeel Ahmed and Dr Malika Mistry in their study *Modern Education and Socio-Economic change (a case study of Muslim women in Pune city, India)* have concluded on the basis of a sample survey of Muslim women in Pune that attitudinal changes are noticeable among Muslim women due to the influence of better educational background of their parents and rapid changes in the outside world.

Research Methodology

This Chapter has been prepared by referring to various secondary data such as journals, books, websites, etc.

Position of Women in Islam

Islam does not differentiate between man and woman on the ground of gender. However, the religion accepts the inequality due to the biological differences of the two genders created by nature. The religion has a broad outlook towards women and accepts her importance to the human race. As a matter of fact, the religion of Islam has a progressive approach in allowing liberty to women in different spheres of life.

Islam considers man and woman equal in the eyes of God. A woman is allowed to participate in religious obligations, such as the Daily Prayers, Fasting, Pilgrimage, etc. During the days of the Prophet, women went to the mosque and offered prayers on Friday, which is compulsory for men. Islam teaches respect to women and therefore considers female infanticide as crime. It believes that women should be treated with kindness and fairness. According to the Prophet Muhammad–

"Whosoever has a daughter and he does not bury her alive, does not insult her, and does not favour his son over her, God will enter him into paradise."

(Ibn Hanbal, No. 1957)

Islam recognises marriage as a sacred institution whose objective is to perpetrate the human race through love, affection and care. Love and respect for each other's emotional requirements are the foundation of marriage. According to Islamic law, a woman cannot be compelled to marry any one without her consent. She has every right to be protected at the time of marriage, has complete right to her Maher, which is a marriage gift presented to her by her husband and is included in the nuptial contract and that the ownership of Maher does not pass on to her husband or father. Moreover, a woman has a right to dissolve an unsuccessful marriage if it she does not want to carry it on any more. Islam teaches respect to mothers. A famous saying of the Prophet is–

"Paradise is at the feet of mothers." (In Al'Nisa'I, Ibn Majah Ahmad)

In the economic sphere of life, Islamic Law allows a woman a right to her money, real estate or other properties. She is free to pursue any employment of her choice befitting her qualifications and ability. Since, Islam believes in equality between men and women, a woman enjoys equal rights in matters of nomination to political offices and posts. Therefore, it can be concluded that the religion of Islam has a liberal, tolerant and progressive view towards women. Islam believes that man and woman should complement each other and that the duty of a man is to provide leadership and guidance to women without exerting his masculinity.

Socio-Economic Profile of Muslim Women in Some South Asian Countries

1. *India*

The Democratic Republic of India is home to the second largest Muslim population of the world. Unfortunately, despite several years of independence from British rule, Muslims who enjoy minority status in this country remain backward. The Constitution of India provides certain safeguards to the minorities such as Article 16 which provides all minorities equal rights in public employment, Article 30 that allows the minorities the right to administer their own educational institutions, etc. Despite Constitutional safeguards, Indian leaders and politicians have had the tendency of considering Muslims as vote banks. The issues which have kept the Muslim community in general and Muslim women in particular, backward, are yet to be addressed.

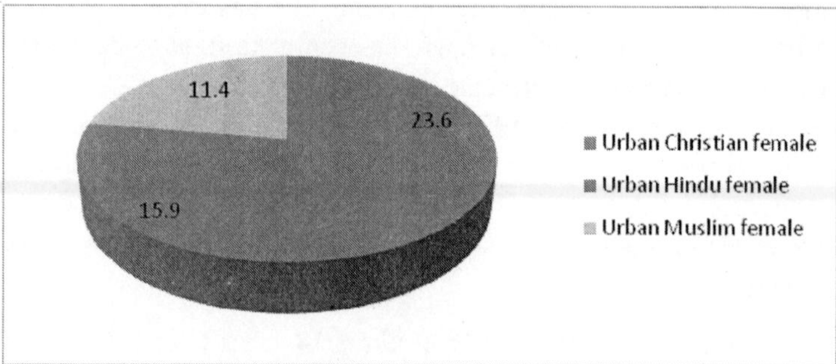

Source: The National Sample Survey, 43 Round, 1987 – 88, Schedule 10

Figure 1– Work Participation Rate (WPR) of Urban females from different communities.

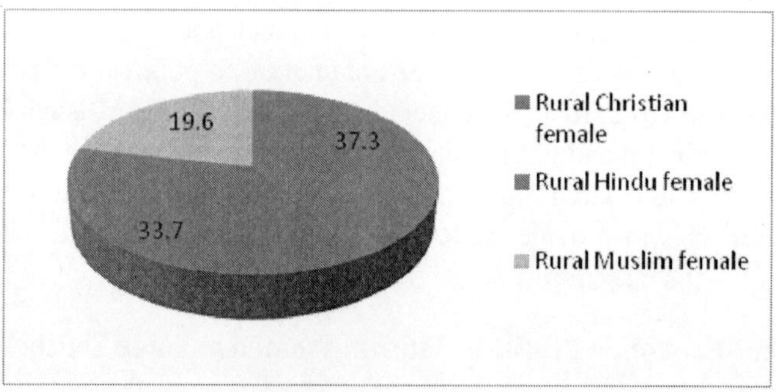

(*Source*: The National Sample Survey, 43 Round, 1987 – 88, Schedule 10)

Figure 2– Work Participation Rate (WPR) of Rural females from different communities.

Due to lack of data and few studies on the Muslim community, it is very difficult to get a clear picture of their socio–economic profile. Moreover, numerous data based on census reports, which are in the possession of the Indian government are yet to be made public. However, based on whatever data is available about the Muslim community, it is beyond all reasonable doubt that this community lags behind on all social parameters.

Muslim women have the lowest work participation rate (WPR) among all three categories of communities with large differences between the WPRs for Muslim women and Hindu or Christian women. Large sections of Muslim women do not participate in India's formal economy as either they are engaged as self – occupied employees or found to work in other informal sectors of the economy. Moreover, the literacy level of Indian Muslim women in comparison with women of other communities is significantly low.

A landmark event in the history of Independent India concerning the rights of Muslim women is the Shah Bano Case. [1985 AIR 945, 1985 SCC (2) 556]. Shah Bano, a 62 year old woman from Indore, was divorced by her husband in 1978. Unable to support herself and her five children, she moved the courts for grant of maintenance from her ex–husband. The Supreme Court ruled in favour of granting alimony to Shah Bano. Despite the case drawing widespread criticism from the Muslim community who saw it as a threat to the Sharia law, it led to the passing of the Muslim Women (Protection of Rights on Divorce), Act, 1986, by the government. The outburst and hue and cry of Muslim men on the rulings of the Shah Bano case and the subsequent move by the Government of India to accommodate their sentiments vindicates the fact that even today genuine concern for welfare of Indian Muslim women is held hostage by male chauvinism of the Muslim community.

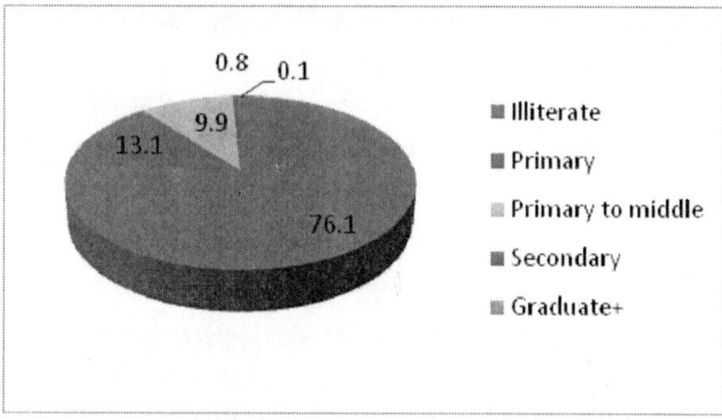

Source: The National Sample Survey, 43 Round, 1987 – 88, Table 31.4

Figure 3–Education in Rural India for Muslim women, 1987 – 88 (by per cent).

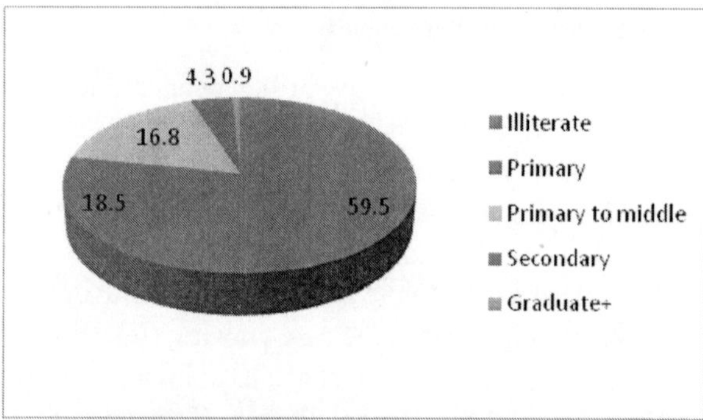

(Source: The National Sample Survey, 43 Round, 1987 – 88, Table 31.4)

Figure 4–Education in Urban India for Muslim women, 1987 – 88 (by per cent).

2. *Pakistan*

The condition of women in Muslim majority Pakistan is no better than what they are on the other side of the Wagah border. The Constitution of Islamic Republic of Pakistan gives equal rights to both women and men, but in practice women are lagging behind. The socio economic profile for Pakistani women is extremely poor. The female literacy rate for population of 10 years and older (2006 – 07) was 42 per cent and the female literacy rate for population of 15 years and older (2006 – 07) was 38 per cent. The Maternal Mortality Ratio (per 1,00,000 live births) in 2002 was 350. According to the Human Development Report 2007/2008 the Gender Empowerment Measure (GEM) rank of Pakistan among 93 countries registered with UN is 82. This in itself reflects the sorry state of women in Pakistan.

3. Bangladesh

Our eastern neighbour Bangladesh, which emerged after a bloody civil war against Pakistan, has yet to create an environment conducive for the progress and development of women. Women in Bangladesh are at the receiving end of several forms of blatant gender discrimination, exploitation and social taboos which have prevented them from making any meaningful contributions to the Bangladeshi society. The maternal mortality ratio (deaths per 100,000 births) is 320. (Source: National Institute of Population and Research Training, Bangladesh Maternal Health and Maternal Mortality Survey (BMMS) 2001, (Dhaka 2003). The per cent of unemployed women aged 15-49 is 65 per cent (Source: National Institute of Population and Research Training, Bangladesh Demographic Health Survey (BDHS) 2007, (Dhaka 2009). Moreover, the proportion of women aged 15 – 49 who were married before age 15 is 33 per cent and proportion of women aged 20 – 49 who were married before age 18 is 74 per cent Source : UNICEF and BBS Multiple Indicator Cluster [Survey (MICS) 2006, Bangladesh 2007].

Almost all social indicators point to the deplorable condition of women in Bangladesh. They are considered to be a liability for their parents and therefore, are married at an early age. Bangladesh has the highest rate of child marriage and adolescent motherhood in the world. Moreover, women lack security as they are victims of sexual abuse, intimidation, trafficking and other forms of crime against women.

The Role of Education

Islam does not forbid education of women. During the days of the Prophet Muhammad, the history of Islam suggests that there were educated women who excelled in different spheres such as literature, artistic skills, state craft, etc. However, if one ponders over the following statistics – the literacy rate of Muslim women in India is 51.1 per cent (South Asia Report, 2001), in Pakistan 36 per cent (according to the UN Report Press International Reports, 2005, Pakistan) and in Bangladesh 35.6 per cent (Education Watch, 2002, Education in Bangladesh: Need for a new Vision, June, 2003), one may easily conclude that the religion of Islam is responsible for the sorry state of women education in South Asia. The question is, is the conclusion correct? In order to get an answer, we need to understand the interface of Islam as religion and the customs and traditions of Islamic society where the role of women needs to be understood.

It is difficult to distinguish between Islam as religion from the customs and practices of the Islamic religion because Islam is more than a religion; it is a way of life. It is not the religion Islam, but various socio-economic factors, unique to Islamic community, which are responsible for the backwardness of Muslim women in South Asia. Islamic society in South Asia is a male dominated, patriarchal society, where women do not enjoy any freedom. Due to the poor-economic situation of majority of the Muslim women, they are dependent on their husbands and fathers for decision making. Being a patriarchal society, where men still have a feudal mindset, Muslim families have a preference for boys over girls. Moreover, the female members of a family are denied the basic necessities for growth and development such as nutritious food, proper education, socialisation, etc. The women are made to stay indoors which restricts their mobility for employment and better opportunities in life. The poor educational profile of Muslim women in South Asia makes them unsuitable for employment in the formal sector of the economy and this is why they are forced to work in low quality jobs in the informal sector. In short, the feudal, patriarchal mindset of Muslim men and the despotic mindset of the *Maulvis* and *Imams* are solely responsible for backwardness and exploitation of Muslim women in South Asia.

Education can play an important and crucial role in empowering South Asian Muslim women. It is an irony that despite Islam granting various rights to women, due to illiteracy and ignorance, the women are unaware of their rights. This puts them at the mercy of men, who exploit them for their narrow vested interests. Education can have two kinds of impact – short-term and long-term. In the short-term, through education women can get awareness about various things which are around them. In the long-term, education can facilitate in the creation of a large pool of educated manpower equipped with the necessary skills to be self reliant.

There are many examples of successful South Asian Muslim women, who have achieved the zenith of success in their respective fields. Some of them are Razia Sultana, Fatima Beevi, Mohsina Kidwai, Dr Najma Heptullah, Mehbooba Mufti, Shabana Azmi, Zeenat Aman, Katrina Kaif, Sania Mirza from India, Benazir Bhutto, Fatima Bhutto, Asma Jehangir, Mallala Yousufzai from Pakistan, Sheikh Hasina, Khaleeda Zia, Tasleema Nasrin from Bangladesh. Besides these personalities, there may be other names which we may not know. The reason why these South Asian Muslim women achieved success is that they could get themselves empowered. One should not discount the role of the family behind these successful and empowered Muslim women. Some enlightened Muslim families shed their orthodox views in getting their daughters the best of education and facilities so that they can be on their feet.

The goal of achieving empowerment through education may not be an easy task for millions of South Asian Muslim women. They have to continuously and consistently wage a battle against their orthodox community who will put barriers on their ways. South Asian Muslim women can draw inspiration from the struggle for women education by Mallala Yousufzai, the teenage Pakistani Nobel laureate, who has defied every obstacle for propagating women education. The purpose of education is enlightenment and through enlightenment one achieves empowerment. The objective of empowerment is to create equality and education could just be the catalyst for South Asian Muslim women to achieve gender equality and dignity.

Conclusion

It is an accepted fact that education leads to empowerment and various researches on the impact of education on Muslim women corroborates it. Despite attempts made by the governments of South Asian nations to solve the socio-economic problems of the Muslim women, their misery continues. This is because the socio economic and family structure of Muslim community is to be held responsible for their sorry condition of their women folk. Therefore, the government should directly intervene by granting financial assistance, encouraging the family members of Muslim community to shed their narrow outlook towards women, providing scholarships and grants to women from poor families, supporting female education, revamping the education system in the Madras as through introduction of information technology, Science, Mathematics, English, etc. and focusing on skill based and technical education so that women can be self reliant.

The benefits of education may be slow and time consuming but it can definitely pave the way for empowerment, gender equality and freedom. An illiterate mother nurtures illiterate children and illiterate mothers nurtures an illiterate race. Therefore, the Muslim community in South Asia must realise the significance of imparting education to their daughters and mothers because only through female education the Muslims in South Asia can put themselves on the road to empowerment and progress.

References

- Badawi, Jamal. *The Status of Women in Islam.*
- Khan, Muhammad Zafrulla. (1991). *Woman in Islam.* Islam International Publications Limited.
- Al – Sheha, Dr Abdul – Rahman. *Women in Islam and Refutation of some Common Misconceptions.*
- Kazi, Seema. (1999). *Muslim Women in India.*Minority Rights Group.
- Sustainable Development Policy Institute. (2007 – 2008). *Pakistan: Country Gender Profile.*
- Islam, M. Shahidul, and Dogra, Suvi. Women Empowerment in Bangladesh: The Rise of the Other Half. *ISAS Working Paper, No. 119,* 6 January 2011.
- Rahimi, Wali M. (1991). *Status of Women: Afghanistan,*UNESCO.
- Bukhari, Dr Syed Mussawar Hussain, and Asim, Muhammad. Women Empowerment in a Muslim Society: A Practical Observation. *Inter-disciplinary Journal of Contemporary Research in Business, Vol 5, No. 1,* May 2013.
- Ashraf, Dr Syed Waseem A., and Ahmad, Ayaz. Muslim Women Education and Empowerment in Rural Aligarh (A Case Study). *International Journal of Scientific and Research Publications, Volume 2, Issue 4,* April 2012.

- Abidi, Azra. Muslim Women and their Representation in South Asian Politics. *Islam and Muslim Societies: A Social Science Journal, Vol. 6, No. 2,* 2013.
- Tyrer, Dr David, and Ahmad, Fauzia. *Muslim Women and Higher Education: Identities, Experiences and Prospects.* Liverpool JMU.
- Ahmed, Dr Shakeel, and Mistry, Dr Malika. Modern Education and Socio–Economic Change (A case study of Muslim women in Pune city, India). *Researchers World – Journal of Arts Science and Commerce, Vol. 1, Issue 1,* October 2010.

Chapter-12

Women Empowerment through Distance Education: An Accelerating Action

—Meenakshi Dwivedi

Abstract

The concept of empowerment of women means psychological sense of personal control in the person's domestic, social and political realms. It is a process by which one is authorised to think, act and control resources in an autonomous way. The most important tool for women's empowerment is found to be education. It leads to improved economic growth, low fertility rate, better health and sanitation and an awareness of factors that empower woman. Work participation rate and political participation also grows with women empowerment. In this regard, distance education plays a vital role. This chapter explains how distance education helps in empowering women and contributes in women's intellectual development which eventually manifests women's autonomy in decision-making, freedom of expression and control over resources.

Key Words: *Empowerment, Control, Autonomy, Expression.*

Status of Women in India

The origin of the Indian idea of appropriate female behaviour can be traced to Manu in 200 BC: ***"By a young girl, by a young woman, or even by an aged one, nothing must be done independent, even in her own house"***

India is a multifaceted society where no generalisation could apply to the nation's various regional, religious, social and economic groups. Nevertheless certain broad circumstances in which Indian women live affect the way they participate in the society. A common denominator in their lives is that they are generally confined to homes, with restricted mobility, and live in seclusion. Other, unwritten, hierarchical practices place further constraints on women. Throughout history, women have generally been restricted to the role of a home-maker; that of a mother and wife.

Despite major changes that have occurred in the status of women in some parts of the world in recent decades, norms that restrict women to the home are still powerful in India, defining activities that are deemed appropriate for women. They are, by and large, excluded from independent life. In spite of India's reputation for respecting women, including treating her as a Goddess, history tells us that women were also ill-treated. There was no equality between men and women. This is true of ancient, medieval and early modern times barring some revolutionary movements such as that of Basaweshwara, the Twelfth century philosopher in Karnataka, who advocated equality, casteless society, status for women, and betterment of the down trodden. Reform movements in the nineteenth and twentieth centuries led by great social reformers provided boost to women's legal status in India.

Independence of India heralded the introduction of laws relating to women. The Constitution provided equality to men and women and also gave special protection to women to realise their interests effectively. Special laws were enacted to prevent indecent representation of women in the media and sexual harassment in workplaces. The law also gives women equal rights in the matter of adoption, maternity benefits, equal pay, good working conditions etc.

Although since independence some progress has been made in the field of women's education, but we cannot be satisfied with this progress, as much has yet to be achieved. The Indian women at present are far behind when compared to their counterparts in U.S.A., Russia and Germany. Much of the responsibility for this state of backwardness rests on the society. Various scientific and psychological experiments have proved that men and women can do equally good work in many spheres. The cause of backwardness of Indian women lies in the inherent flaws of the Indian society and its conservative outlook. So the society has to be purged of these evils and thus reformed early. A large section of the Indian society considers the home to be the only field of women's activities. Some people hold the view that unemployment will increase if women's education spreads. All these views are misleading. For the national development along with the women's development, the old values of society will have to be changed. It is also necessary to change the present social system and make it more fruitful for women.

Need for Women Empowerment

Women Empowerment is a global issue and discussion on women political rights are at the fore front of many formal and informal campaigns worldwide. The concept of women empowerment was given impetus at the international women conference at NAIROBI in 1985. The term Women Empowerment refers to the enhancement of the spiritual, social, political or economic strength of all women. It is frequently seen that the empowered in their capacities develop confidence. Empowerment of women is:

- Having the power of making decisions for self.
- Having access to resources and information for proper decision making.
- Having numerous options to choose from (instead of yes/no, either/or).
- Ability of showing assertiveness while making decisions collectively.
- Ability to think positively to bring about a change.
- Ability of developing new skills for group power and self improvement.
- Ability of using democratic means to change perceptions of others.
- Adopting changes and a growth process that are self initiated and continous.
- Overcoming stigma and staying focused on increasing positive self-image.

Today, women share equal status as men. More stress should be laid on empowering rural women and their development. A special focus should be there on empowering girls and women, since it will lead to a change in the society which would be sustainable and will be in effect for ages to come. A united approach must be followed while empowering women; it is a social cause that requires stewardship and continuous attention from every individual. Society needs to enhance its efforts for women empowerment and to boost the progress being made by women. It is society's constitutional, moral and social responsibility to confirm women's progress giving women equal opportunities and rights. India is poised to becoming superpower, a developed country by 2020. The year 2020 is fast approaching; it is just five years away. The vision can be realised only when the women of this nation become empowered.

Role of Education in Women Empowerment

The only way to remove this social evil of illiteracy is to encourage women's education so that they may realise their responsibility and make efforts to regain their proper place in society. Despite shortcomings and difficult conditions the present educational systems has produced some Indian women who are far ahead when compared to women in many other highly advanced countries.

It shows that what is needed for the progress of Indian women is education, and through its help, they can achieve their lost position in the society. The Education Commission has stressed the need of women's education at all stages. The Radhakrishnan Commission (1948-49) in its reports laid particular emphasis on women's education and observed that Indian women can work like men in all spheres.

It is true that women have many special tasks in life and their spheres of duties are different from those of man. But we should remember that these tasks also need training and education. Unless women get proper education their prospective faculties get crippled. It is only by imparting proper education to them that we can expect them to discharge their duties nicely and decently. Childhood is an impressionable stage and anything good or bad makes a great in influence on a child's mind. We cannot have educated ideal citizens when the mothers themselves are foolish and ignorant. Every woman is a potential mother. The future of a child depends on how it is brought up and educated in child hood. An educated mother is naturally expected to bring up and educate her children better than an uneducated mother. Napoleon Bonaparte once said that—

"Give me an educated mother, I will give you an educated nation."

There was a time when people thought that it was not necessary to educate girls. Now we have begun to realise that girls' education is essential. The modern age is the age of awakening of girls. They are trying to compete with men in all spheres of life. There are many people who oppose girls' education. They say that the proper sphere of girls is the home. So, they argue that the money spent on girl's education is wasted. This view is wrong, because girl's education can bring about a silent revolution in the society.

Distance Education for Women Empowerment

Distance education is a field of education that focuses on the pedagogy and andragogy technology, and distance based instructional systems design modules taking into consideration the aim to deliver education to students who are not physically present in formal learning situations. In a distance education based learning environment teachers and students are separated by place and time. They communicate at their own times of convenience and by exchanging printed or electronic media, or through technology that allows them to communicate in real time and through other online ways.

Distance education is less a philosophy and more a method of education. Students can study in their own time, at the place of their choice (home, work or learning centres), and without face-to-face contact with a teacher. Technology is a critical element of distance education.

Distance education has several stages of development. Taylor (1999) has proposed five generations of distance education:

- Correspondence education.

- Integrated use of multiple, one-way media such as print, broadcasting or recorded media such as video-cassettes.
- Two-way, synchronous tele-learning using audio or video-conferencing.
- Flexible learning based on a synchronous online learning combined with online interactive multimedia.
- Intelligent flexible learning, which adds a high degree of automation and student control to a synchronous online learning and interactive multimedia.

Open and Distance Education has emerged as a powerful instrument for augmenting opportunities of many learners, especially women. Women comprise the largest section of the underprivileged group in India and continue to shoulder all domestic responsibilities. Women in India face restrictions in the form of traditional patriarchal attitudes. Therefore, the educational programmes through distance mode are recommended primarily for women learners who discontinued their studies for financial or other reasons and also who stay in rural areas. It also paves a way for those who want to continue learning after marriage to improve their social and economic status. At present the number of women students has considerably increased, thanks to the Open and Distance Learning initiative which women find convenient, economical and beneficial.

The changes in women's educational and career attainment may have multifaceted characteristics. Women might have increased their enrolment in colleges compared to men, but women may still differ in terms of the types of subjects in which they are enrolled. Distance learning is becoming increasingly attractive for women, as shown by some research studies. Namely, more than 60 per cent of those over 25 years of age and females opt for this type of developmental and educational initiatives. The reason for this lies in the fact that this method of learning offers numerous advantages. Among the most prominent benefits, the following may be pointed out:

- The flexibility of the learning process (students study at the time most convenient to them).

- Achieving a better balance between personal and other commitments (they may spend more time at home with their families).
- Minimising costs. (both time and money savings are made);
- A deeper sense of self-fulfilment (acquiring relevant and useful knowledge and achieving professional goals).

Importance of Distance Education for Women Learners

Distance learning aims to empower women through education, especially women who for some reason are unable of studying through the regular mode. It seeks to break the boundaries which block women from pursuing education by taking education to the homes of women who cannot go to regular colleges. It reaches to every woman who desires it. It aims to extend not only equal but equitable opportunities of education to women who desire the privilege of education, to be pursued at their own place and time, simultaneously with the demand of a job or domestic commitments. It is a boon for career women who aspire to enhance their personal and professional competence, home bound women who wish to profitably use their time and resources to satisfy their deferred academic aspirations and the rural girls who have no access to the mainline educational system.

Hence, distance education is important for the following major reasons:

Confidence in dealing with family members and outsiders: Stay-at-home women who pursue their education through distance mode are much more likely to be in touch with their children and other family members and are thus better placed to supervise them or even just know when something is wrong. A stay-at-home woman is much more likely to participate in the daily learning and exploring activities of her child such as field trips and special events both during and after school. Education lets stay-at-home women start to believe more in themselves and act with the inner feeling of confidence, coolness and self-esteem.

Increased career opportunities: A major concern that women have when they contemplate pursuing a distance education degree is the value of the degree with respect to employment opportunities. Most of the universities offering distance education have now established dedicated "placement cells" that actively seek to get their students placed in reputed multinationals, government jobs, non-governmental organisations (NGOs) and the private sector. These placement cells make sure that all registered students get help with job placements, counselling for employment and even self employment.

Enhancement in social esteem through attainment of higher qualifications: The main social objective of education is to complete the socialisation process. The distance education also serves this purpose. The positive appraisal, compliments, praises and acceptance of an educated woman by a social group or society enhance her social esteem. Enhancement in women's social esteem and social leadership not only help them to live the life that they truly want, but also help deepen their relationships with others. It also helps in enhancing their career or work life, and ultimately it helps a woman become a happier person because social interactions and relationships are key to happiness.

Second chance for the earlier drop-outs: Many girl students do not complete the study of their curriculum and consequently the time, money and energy expended on such students prove to be sheer wastage. This happens due to economic causes like poverty, social causes like early marriage, orthodox parental attitude and various educational causes like high university fee, defective examination system etc. but distance learning is likely to improve the drop out rate for these non-conventional students. Distance learning allows drop-out women learners who have employment, family and other responsibilities to update knowledge and skills related to their job by saving travel costs and allowing a flexible schedule.

Acquisition of knowledge: Knowledge is power, and education is the fundamental precondition for political development, democracy and social justice. Education is a process of gaining knowledge for some useful application whereas knowledge is facts acquired from good education, peers, consultations and extensive reading. Distance learning provides this opportunity to women learners where one comes to know various facts, ideas, theories and its applications. Distance education is a formal process of gaining knowledge whereas knowledge is informally acquired through experiences.

Changed socialisation process: Socialisation has been referred to in some quarters as the process by which a biological human being becomes socially human. One of the primary aims of socialisation is to make the individual acceptable to the society. Therefore distance learning aims at the reformation of attitudes wrongly developed by women already in the modern society. It is the function of distance education to see that unfounded beliefs, illogical prejudices and unreasoned loyalties are removed from the learner's mind. Distance education prepares the women learners for future occupational positions so that learners should be enabled to play a productive role in society.

Fosters Participant Democracy: Distance education fosters participant democracy. Participant democracy is very important as far as the women education is concerned. Distance education gives them the platform where Flexible delivery allows women learners to fit study around work, social or family commitments.

Occupational Placement: Education is an instrument of livelihood and also it helps the individual for earning his livelihood. It enables the students earn their own livelihood. Distance education also prepares the students for future occupational positions and enables learners to play a productive role in society. Accordingly, great emphasis is placed on vocational training too. The companies are hiring women force in more numbers since they have shown excellence in dedication towards their work as well as striking a perfect balance between their social, personal and professional life.

Developed ability to think critically: Critical thinking is the ability to think clearly and rationally. It includes the ability to engage in reflective and independent thinking. Critical thinking is not an isolated goal unrelated to other important goals in education. Critical thinking enables women to live rationally, reasonably, empathically and also helps in making decisions and in carrying out high level responsibilities.

Beside above mentioned advantages, some other benefits of distance education to women are:

- Better decision making ability.
- Respect in family and community.
- Better communication skills.
- Empowerment to change the politico-socio-economic perception of society.
- Enablement of promotion of literacy in neighbourhood.
- Enablement of participation in local bodies.
- Facilitation of the acquisition of variety of knowledge through the print and the non-print media.
- Enhancement of the means and methods of empowerment of women.
- Better dissemination of legal literacy and information relating to women's rights and entitlements in society so as enable women to participate on an equal footing in all areas.

Conclusion

Women are keen to embark on self-development initiatives without being hampered significantly by the social or cultural inhibitions imposed on them. Better and easily accessible educational opportunities and the impact of communication technologies on the social and cultural environment are making substantial difference to their attitudes, values and concerns. In the changing scenario, women are likely to benefit much more from improved access to education. Keeping in mind the changing needs of our society, the distance education offers courses to equip women to enter new areas in the world of Management, Business Administration, and Information Technology in addition to offering add-on programmes in traditional disciplines. It has also extended its frontiers by offering Diploma and Certificate courses to those who work among the women at the grass root level in NGO management, Self Help Groups, Community Health Workers, Women Leaders in Political and Civic Administration. Thus, the distance education is committed to provide access to affordable, supportive and flexible but quality education to all women seekers of knowledge from all walks of life.

References

- Joseph, Kochurani (2005), Women Empowerment A conceptual Analysis, Vimala Books and Publications, Kanjirapally.
- Beteta, C. Hanny (2006): What is Missing in Measure of Women's Empowerment?, Journal of Human Development and Capabilities, Vol. 7, No. 2, 221-241.
- Hall, Margaret (1992), Women and Empowerment. Strategies for Increasing Autonomy. Washington, D.C.: Publishing Corporation.
- Soni, Jaspreet Kaur (2008), Women Empowerment the substantial challenges, Authors press Delhi.
- Nussbaum, Martha. (2000): Women and Human Development: The Capabilities Approach. New York: Cambridge Press.
- Sahay, Sushama (1998), Women and Empowerment- Approach and Strategies, Discovery Publishing House, Delhi.
- www.unesco.org
- www.careindia.org
- www.caesjournals.org
- www.amrita.edu
- www.ifuw.org

Chapter-13

Empowered Women, Empowered Nation Still a Dream in India

—Yogendra Pal Bharadwaj

Abstract

India today is at the cusp of a paradigm change with respect to its growth and position in the world. We must act decisively to capture this opportunity. We need to think big and scale up rapidly in each and every area, be it education, infrastructure, industry, financial services or equality of both genders. For around two centuries, social reformers and missionaries in India have endeavoured to bring women out of the confines in which centuries of traditions had kept them. Empowerment is a process, by which women gain greater control over material and intellectual resources which assist them to increase their self-reliance and empower them to assert their independent rights. Women account for more than fifty per cent of population and are the main drivers behind the economy. Women as the motherhood of the nation should be strong, aware and alert. Therefore, the constitution not only grants equality to women, but also empowers the state to adopt measures of positive discrimination in favour of women. The concept of empowerment is very complex in itself indeed very fuzzy also; different scholars hold different definitions of empowerment according to the need of their work. Women's agency, autonomy and empowerment are widely used ideas in development literature and capability approach. But there exists substantial ambiguity in conception of these ideas. While women's well being and women's agency is sufficiently distinguished from each other, there seems to be a large overlap between agency and empowerment and between agency and autonomy. The present chapter examines various conceptions of empowerment of women on a large scale which needs to be redressed clearly by taking into consideration overlapping zones and distinguishing features of the respective concepts.

Keywords: *Empowerment, Distinguished Factors, Sound Development.*

Introduction

India today is at the cusp of a paradigm change with respect to its growth and position in the world. We (both men and women) must act decisively to capture this opportunity. We need to think big and scale up rapidly in each and every area, be it education, infrastructure, industry, financial services or equality of both genders. For around two centuries, social reformers and missionaries in India have endeavoured to bring women out of confines in which centuries of traditions had kept them. Empowerment means to inspire women with the courage to break free from the chains of limiting beliefs, patterns and social or religious conditions that have traditionally kept women suppressed and unable to realise their true beauty and power. Women account for more than fifty per cent of population and are the main drivers behind the economy. Women as the motherhood of the nation should be strong, aware and alert. Therefore, the constitution not only grants equality to women, but also empowers the State to adopt measures of positive discrimination in favour of women.

India might be the world's largest democracy, but it's also one of the most gender-skewed. Women remain under represented at every level, starting from the electorate to elected representation in the legislature representation of women here is among the lowest in the world. For instance, the average Indian woman has the odds stacked against her from birth, if she is allowed to be born in a son-centric society. She is denied food, education, health-care and above all, the right to choose her own life partner. After marriage, she is denied the right to protest against sex preference of her children, decide the number of children she will have, the right to gainful employment, the right to her fair share of property and in old age the right to a life of dignity.

The democratic process in India has created the awareness among the women about their plightful condition. The principle of gender equality is enshrined in the Indian Constitution in its preamble, fundamental rights, fundamental duties and directive principles. The constitution not only grants equality to women, but also empowers the State to adopt measures of positive discrimination in favour of women. The 73rd and 74th Amendments (1993) to the Constitution of India has provided for reservation of seats (at least one-third) in the local bodies of Panchayats and Municipalities for women. Another Constitutional Amendment (84th Constitutional Amendment Act, 1988) reserving 33 per cent seats for women in Parliament and State Legislatures is in the pipeline.

Empowerment enabling atmosphere, a level playing field, greater representation across all spheres, are some of the terms we hear. Every year we celebrate International Women's Day (8th March). This day is an opportunity for women across the world to fight for equality and justice. I don't think we need any day as a special day to celebrate women's day. Every day should be an occasion to respect the women in our lives and accord them respect and dignity. Our attitude as women should be a no-nonsense one. Will all the meetings, debates, speeches, mock-artistry and of course articles on women across India who routinely face hardships and oppression solve their problems? Not at all, in fact, it his time we recognise the importance of their economic upliftment.

Gender equality plays a crucial role in uplifting women. Rather, gender inequality certainly needs to be abolished. Gender-based discrimination and disparity are evident from various dowry cases and sexual harassment incidents. The idea of equal employment opportunities is still lingering unimplemented in several remote areas. Women in some inaccessible areas are yet confined to their household routines while their spouses go for work. India has the lowest percentage of women employees (23 per cent), followed by Japan (24 per cent), Turkey (26 per cent) and Austria (29 per cent), according to the Corporate Gender Gap report brought out by the World Economic Forum. Women must be given freedom to choose their interest of work and discharge their duties unbiased. Survey confirms various percentages of employed women in distinct sectors–the financial services and insurance (60 per cent), professional services (56 per cent) and media and entertainment (42 per cent). The sectors that flaunt the lowest percentage of women in the twenty economies are automotive (18 per cent), mining (18 per cent) and agriculture (21 per cent). Besides employment, gender inequality is clearly observed at temples wherein only entry of male devotees is sternly followed. One of such temples is *Sabarimala* temple where women are not at all allowed. Such biasness creates imbalance between men and women.

Scope of the Study

The purpose of the study is to examine the impact of various factors which led to the propagation of women empowerment either as a boon or bane in the society and why this is still to be considered as a dream for Indian society.

Objectives of the Study

Following are the objectives of the present study:–

1. To exemplify the factors which have led to the prominence of women empowerment.
2. To highlight the general plight of women towards emancipation.
3. To overcome all the barriers which do not allow women to develop in the society.
4. To develop an action-based agenda for the thematic priorities of women in the Indian society.

Literature Review

For accelerating the development process of a welfare state, women empowerment is the matter of concern for both developing and developed world. But it is necessary to develop proper way by which empowerment could be measured quantitatively as well as qualitatively to formulate effective action plan for the betterment of the societal condition. Plenty of research work has been carried out at national as well as international level covering multidimensional nature of women empowerment.

- Das (2011) has identified various constraints of women empowerment among Karbi tribes of Assam, viz. social, political, economic, technological and psychological constraints. He further argues that 'lack of knowledge about new technology and information' was the main reason behind poor empowerment of such tribal women.
- The constitution of India grants equity to women in various strata of society by means of reservation and ensuring better involvement in various development projects. But a large number of women are either ill equipped or not in a position to propel themselves out of their traditionally unsatisfactory socio-economic conditions (Deshpande *et. al.* 2010).
- Kabeer (2005) defines it as a process by which those who have been denied the ability to make choices acquire such ability. The elements required in enabling one to gain power, authority and influence over others, institutions or society. Although the present world has taken much more attention in achieving the equity of power between men and women, the women in developing world are still in darker position. To ensure the empowerment among the women it is necessary to change long back traditional socio-cultural norms along with redefining the concept of patriarchal societal pattern.
- Kishor *et. al.* (2004) have proposed various strategies to combat these problems, such as increasing women's access to land and other assets.
- Malhotra *et. al.* (2003) made a pioneer study of measuring and analysing women empowerment by putting six commonly used dimensions, viz. economic, socio-cultural, familial-interpersonal, legal, political and psychological including their potential operationalisation in the household, community and broader arenas has been put forth. These dimensions cover a broad range of factors, and thus women may be empowered within one of these sub domains. For instance, the socio cultural dimension covers a range of empowerment sub domains, such as marriage systems, norms regarding women's physical mobility, non-familial social support

systems and networks available to women. After reviewing all the studies, I found no such work which exemplifies the emancipation of women in modern era that define why this is still a dream for us.

Statement of the Problem

India has been working towards empowering her women ever since independence, and especially since the 1990s. The government and non-government sectors have both been pushing ahead with programmes aimed at imparting education to women, giving them better health care, providing them with means of livelihood and opportunities to participate in the decision making process at home and in the society. Special attention is being paid to improve the lot of the girl child giving her better chances of survival and opportunities for living a life of fulfilment.

Empowerment being an ongoing process, there is no final goal. One does not arrive at a stage of being empowered in some absolute sense. It is always relative and situation specific in context. Because of its complex and dynamic nature, defining and measuring empowerment either as a boon or bane is a challenge in any development study. Some studies suggest a linear cause-effect model while others resort to a more process based approach. The dynamic process might be broken into key components for a comprehensive understanding of empowerment. Here the process is separated into components (such as enabling factors/ parameters, agency and outcomes) in identifying policy interventions to support empowerment, and for evaluating the impact of such interventions. Therefore, utmost attention has been taken in identifying the key empowerment parameters for women and measures that will propagate its significant emancipation level.

Statistical Figure of Women All Around the World:

- Of the world's 1.3 billion poor, nearly 70 per cent are women.
- Between 76-80 per cent of the world's 27 million refugees are women and children.

- Women hold only 10.5 per cent of the seats in the world's parliament.
- Of the World's One billion illiterate, two thirds are women.
- Two-thirds of 130 million children worldwide, who are not in school, are girls.
- In most countries, Women work approximately twice the unpaid time men do.
- Rural Women produce more than 55 per cent of all food grown in developing countries.
- The value of Women's unpaid house work and community work is estimated at 35 per cent of GDP worldwide.
- HIV is increasingly affecting Women. Today about 42 per cent of the estimated cases are those of women.
- 20 million unsafe abortions are performed every year resulting in the deaths of 70,000 women.

Females in India

Killing of girl foetus is still rampant in prosperous states with India's Sex ratio for girls being 933 for 1,000 boys. About 50 per cent girls of the total number of enrolment drop out before reaching class VI. Only 36.22 per cent girls complete secondary education. Of the total infant mortality cases, 59 per cent are girls. In low-income groups, 49.78 per cent girls are married before attaining the legal marriage age of 18. There are more girls than boys as child labourers. A number of girl children are trafficked for prostitution as well as for domestic help. Highest child labour is among scheduled tribes and Muslims followed by scheduled castes. It is really a matter of shame for the nation which has ambitions of becoming a superpower in the near future to tolerate such social injustices.

Why Empowered Women and Empowered Nation is Still a Dream in India?

India has come a long way economically since the 70s. But this gallop has failed to keep pace with another crucial social indicator that determines a country's overall well being; the status of its women speaks of the approach of illusion of this empowerment issue through these case studies.

Case Study (1) –

Amita is luckier, her mother is determined to take her to school so that one day she would become a doctor. However, in her class, there are 70 pupils and the teacher (one teacher) never shows up for most parts of the lessons. The facilities at the school are poor; the drinking water is so filthy that pupils have to bring along their own water to school. And what's more, Amita confesses that the toilets are very dirty that she has never used them since she got enrolled in that school. Though she does not understand, her mother saves at least 900 rupees so that she can get coached in 3 subjects where she is not doing well.

Case Study (2) –

Amla did not tell her parents when the older boys started to harass her on the one- hour long walk to school from their apartment in Madanpur Khadar, South of Delhi. They occasionally grabbed her hands and demanded that the little girl kiss them. She knew that the blame would be placed on her, as if she was somewhat encouraging them to do so. But she was pretty right as when her family found out about her plight, they literally "banned" her from ever going back to school again, worried about the effects on their "honour" in the event that she was sexually assaulted. Guess what, now the plan is to marry her off once she reaches 16 years of age.

Case Study (3) –

Sumen, a woman who is 35 years old is battling with her daughter's future. The little girl who is only 9 years has learning disabilities and her mother has tried every year to enrol her in schools but with very little success. Luckily, the authorities have agreed that the little girl should get some education, but it's only once in 7 days. Sumen, who is a housewife, wonders if she should try to teach her daughter herself. The question is this; how she will teach her when she never went to school herself? It's sad how she was quoted- "But if I have not studied myself, how much value will I add to her life?"

On the basis of these case studies, do we not live in a so called civilised society, where empowerment is still a dream?

Committee to Study Status of Women

Government has set up a 15 member High Level Committee, HLC, on the status of women to undertake comprehensive study to understand the status of women since 1989 as well as to evolve appropriate policy interventions based on a contemporary assessment of women's needs. The Committee will be chaired by Justice Ruma Pal.

The HLC will conduct an intensive literature survey to take stock of published data, reports, articles and research from about 1989 onwards, on the status of women in India. The Report will also bring out the interconnectedness of these aspects in terms of their impact on women and recommended measures for holistic empowerment of women. The committee will examine the overall status of women including the socio-economic, health and nutritional, legal and political status, disaggregated by rural/urban, economic and social position (e.g. APL/ BPL, SC/ST, single women, disabled women, migrant women) and wherever possible by minority status (e.g. Muslims/others). The analysis would take account of cross-regional differences and focus on inequalities both within and outside the household. It would also assess the impact made by existing policies and legislative changes on equality, security and holistic empowerment of women, and will identify inequalities in policy and legislation as well as gaps in implementation.

The committee will examine women's access to and participation in formal and informal paid employment; emerging areas of participation, geographical pattern of their economic activity, unpaid work/care economy, etc. and access to micro-finance, bank credit, training and skill up gradation, marketing etc. and constraints on increase in productivity.

Significant Areas Need To Be Focused Upon

1. **Judicial Legal Systems:** It should be made more responsive and gender sensitive to women's needs, especially in cases of domestic violence and personal assault. New laws need to be enacted and existing

laws reviewed to ensure that justice is quick and the punishment meted out to the culprits is commensurate with the severity of the offence.

2. **Decision Making:** Women' equality in power sharing and active participation in decision making, including in political process at all levels should be ensured for the achievement of the goals of empowerment.

3. **Mainstreaming a Gender Perspective in the Development Process:** Policies, programmes and systems should be established to ensure mainstreaming of women's perspectives in all developmental process, as catalysts, participants and recipients.

4. **Economic Upliftment:** Steps should be taken for mobilisation of poor women and convergence of services by offering them a range of economic and social options, along with necessary support measures to enhance their capabilities.

5. **Micro Credit and Social Development:** Strengthening of existing and new micro credit mechanism should be undertaken so that adequate flow of credit will ensure easy accessibility. Equal access to education, steps to eliminate discrimination, increased enrolment ratio and development of occupational/ vocational/technical skills by women are needed.

6. **Health:** A holistic approach to women's health which includes both nutrition and health services is required and special attention should be given to the needs of women. Women should have access to comprehensive, affordable and quality health care.

7. **Rights** : The rights of boys and girls as per the Convention on the Rights of the child should be ensured and protected.

Conclusive Remark

Women's concerns have to be kept at the centre of public policy, developmental planning and governance, with recognition of their role as critical growth agents and as ambassadors of social change. The approach of addressing issues related to empowerment of women from a holistic and macro point of view acknowledging the cross cutting linkages between economic, social and political identity of woman presents a new hope. There is increasing recognition that these factors are deeply intertwined and if efforts in any one dimension remains absent or weak, the outcome and momentum generated by the other components cannot be sustained, and that it is only when all these factors are addressed simultaneously and made compatible with each other can women be truly empowered. Therefore, for the holistic empowerment of women, all ministries and departments would need to energise synergistic measures through more effective use of tools such as gender budgeting and platforms such as the National Mission for Empowerment of Women. The gender convergence mantra also holds a key to inclusive governance and our cherished dream of growth with justice and equity.

The discussion brings a major interpretation to light that the status of women can be improved by women themselves and nobody else. It is the modern era of satellites, achievements and technology-based gadgets. Why should women be left behind? Women will have to empower themselves 'from below' in order to compel the government to empower them 'from above'. Further, there is a need for a change of values and behaviour in the society, a need for positive socio cultural and economic empowerment and above all the will power and strong determination of women to join each and every sphere of life.

Last but not least, our efforts should be directed towards the all round development of each and every section of Indian women, not confining the benefit to a particular section of women in society, by giving them their due share. It is a must to protect their chastity, modesty and dignity and ensure their dignified position in society. Without removing social stigma, enduring progress and development cannot be achieved. For this, the governmental and non-governmental organisations including media should come forward and play an active role in creating awareness in society.

Thus, it is no real surprise that women empowerment in India is a hotly discussed topic with obviously known solution looming in the horizon and that is to doubly redouble efforts and continue to target the sources of all the ill-will towards women. Swami Vivekananda once said, "Arise away and stop not until the goal is reached."

Thus, our country should thus be catapulted into the horizon of empowerment of women and revel in its glory. The task is not too difficult to achieve. The honesty and sincerity on the part of those involved is a must. If the lots of women change, definitely it will have a positive impact on society.

References

- Alkire, Sabina (2007): Measuring Agency: 'Issues and Possibilities', Indian Journal of Human Development, Vol. 1, and No. 1.
- Acharya, M and Ghimire, P (2005) "Gender Indicators of Equality, Inclusion and Poverty Reduction", Economic and Political Weekly, October 29.
- Beteta, C. Hanny (2006): What is Missing in Measure of Women's Empowerment? 'Journal of Human Development and Capabilities, Vol. 7, No. 2, 221-241.
- Bhuyan, Dasarathi (2006), "Empowerment of Indian Women: A Challenge of Twenty first Centuary," Orissa Review, January -2006, Accessed 18 March 2013, URL: http://orissa.gov.in/emagazine/Orissareview/jan2006/engpdf/Empowerment_of_India.pdf
- Burkey, S. (1993), People First: A Guide to Self-Reliant, Participatory and Rural Development. London, Zed Press.
- Burgess, Robin, & Stern, Nicholas (1999). Social security in developing countries: What, who and how? In Ehtisam Ahmad, J. Dreze, J. Hills & A.K. Sen (Eds), Social security in developing countries (pp. 41–80). New Delhi: Oxford University Press.
- Collier, Women in Development: Defining the Issues, Policy, Planning and Research Working Paper 129, Population and Human Resources Department, World Bank, Washington, DC, 1998.
- Deshpande S. and Sethi S. (2010). Role and Position of Women Empowerment in Indian Society, International Referred Research Journal, Vol. 1(17), pp. 24-27.
- Desai, NGOs Gender mainstreaming and urban poor communities in Mumbai. Gender and Development, 2005, pp. 90- 98.
- Gabriel, T. (1991), The Human Factor in Rural Development. Belhaven Press, London and New York: 41-57.
- Handya and Kassamb. (2004) Women's empowerment in rural India. Paper presented as the ISTR conference, Toronto Canada.
- Kabeer, N. (2005): "Gender Equality and Women's Empowerment": a Critical Analysis of the Third Millennium Development Goal. *Gender and Development*, 13 (1): 13-24.
- Mahajan, N (1992) "Women's contribution in economic growth," Kurukshetra, March.

- Mayoux, Tackling the down side: Social Capital, Women's Empowerment and Micro- Finance in Cameron, Development and Change, pp. 435-436.
- Sen, A (1983) 'Development: Which Way Now?" Economic Journal, December.
- Sharma, Sheetal (2006), "Educated Women, powered, women" Yojana Vol. 50, No. 12.
- Sadik, Women, the Centre of Development, Development, 1998, Vol.1, pp. 30-31.
- Peerzade, Sayed Afzal and Prema Parnade, 2005, 'Economic Empowerment of Women,' Theory and Practice' Southern Economist, March- 1, pp. 9-10.
- Vishawanathan, NGOs and Women's Development in Rural South India: A Comparative Analysis, 1991, p. 24.
- Tripathi T. (2011). Women's Empowerment: Concept and Empirical Evidence from India, paper presented at annual conference ('Winter School') of the Centre for Development Economics, Delhi School of Economics, December 10-13, 2011.

Chapter-14

Women, Education and Empowerment: Anandibai Joshi, the Brave Woman

—Swati Basak

Abstract

This chapter is dedicated to Anandibai Joshi, the first woman doctor who was honoured with MD degree from USA. Born in a Maratha Brahmin family, Anandi was married to a person who was twenty years older than her when she was just nine. She did not receive formal education before marriage. Her husband Gopalrao Joshi, an enlightened Indian and a strong supporter of women's education aimed at educating her. Both of them realised that in our country women did not get proper health treatment because of scarcity of women doctors. When their only child died Anandi decided firmly to become a doctor and from then her journey started. She was just fourteen years old when their child died. In this chapter author wants to bring out the fact that how Gopalrao helped in fulfilling her dreams and the positive role of patriarchy. Without the effort of Gopalrao, Anandi could not achieve more because during that time women were kept almost under seclusion. I am not denying the talent and potential of Anandi what her feminist biographers like Kashibai or Caroline Dall wanted to declare but like them I cannot blame Gopalrao for her distress. I am not ready to make him the villain of the whole story. In this way this chapter establishes a relation between women's education and empowerment and there is no doubt that without proper education women cannot be empowered. Anandibai's story is a good example of women's education and empowerment. Though I have supported patriarchy in the case of Anandibai but we cannot deny the fact that an egalitarian society can only make our world peaceful and we have to try for it.

Key Words: *Nine years, Fourteen years, Husband, Education, Empowerment*

Anandibai Joshi, the first woman doctor in India who got a MD degree from USA is an inspiration to all of us and more prominently to all women of India who have to face a lot of hurdles in their daily life to acquire their rights and assert their independence and dignity. It was the middle of nineteenth century when the British started dominating India politically, economically and socially. Some social reformers influenced by the ideas of western thought and knowledge were in favour of promoting women's education. They even started establishing female schools to educate our women. In this situation Anandibai Joshi was born on 31st March, 1865. Her early name was Yamuna Joshi. Her father was the landlord in Kalyan, a small town near Mumbai. But they lost their land. Anandi was married to a person who was twenty years senior to her. She got married when she was just nine years old to Gopalrao Joshi who was a postman by profession. Her name was changed to Anandi after marriage.

Anandi did not receive formal education in her childhood days before marriage. She was able to read Marathi before her marriage but her husband Gopalrao aimed at teaching and educating her. He was enlightened with the ideas of western knowledge and thoughts and so he realised the necessity of educating womenfolk. He married her on one condition that he would educate her. Soon after their marriage he started educating her but it was not so easy during those days. A husband could not speak with her wife in front of the presence of other persons. So, it was a difficult as well as a challenging task to educate women. But Gopalrao was adamant. He was very strict at his motive. Family support is very much necessary for a person's success. Though patriarchal family in those days were not in favour of women's education but some enlightened persons like Gopalrao supported educating women for which he had to struggle throughout his life. Once Gopalrao said Anandibai "Try and go to America somehow. I want you to be a doctor. No Indian lady has yet gone to America, not for education surely." J. S. Joshi wrote what Gopalrao told his twelve years old wife, "You will have to be wiser than I am. You are going to learn what I don't know and what none of these men [orthodox Hindus] will ever know." Anandibai was lucky enough to get a husband like him who wanted to become a "social reformer" and "progressive thinker" and patriarchy worked positively in her situation. Gouri Srivastava in her book *Women Who Created History* wrote "The structure of the patriarchal family did not change and men continued to have the decisive say in family matters but in reformed families women were respected and their opinions and views were valued. Similarly, as far as marriage was concerned it was companionship that was gradually emphasised. Men in reformed families taught their wives and even encouraged them to take to higher education i.e. Gopalrao Joshi taught Anandibai and even encouraged her to do her doctorate in medicine from America. This kind of relationship that was emerging between husband and wife was gradually breaking the walls of segregation within a patriarchal household. However, this was extremely limited in nature." This pattern of companionship within the patriarchal family model helped in empowering women in those days. In those days most of the people thought that women should keep in seclusion and work inside the house but some enlightened reformers like Gopalrao thought that it was the proper education that would empower and would abolish all the grievances of women.

Before discussing patriarchy and its role in educating and empowering women I just want to finish the life story of Anandibai. Gopalrao admitted Anandi to a missionary school but that did not work out. So they shifted from Kalyan to Alibag, then Kohalpur and at last reached Calcutta. After sometime she became able to read Sanskrit and also to read and speak English. Gopalrao wished to give her higher education. Anandi lost her son when she was just 14. Soon she and her husband realised that in our country common women did not have access to female doctors and they were reluctant to visit male doctors which were also the reasons of increasing child mortality rates. So she decided to become a doctor and she got full support from her husband. She submitted her thesis on the topic "Obstetrics among Aryan Hindoos."

Gopalrao tried hard to admit her in some Universities in America but failed. Finally she got help from Mrs Carpenter. They became very close to each other and Anandi started calling her 'mavashi' (aunt). Finally after a long struggle and controversies Anandi reached America in June 1883 and met Mrs Carpenter. She got admitted at the Women's college at Philadelphia. She was offered a scholarship of $600 for the total three years. But life in America was not smooth at all. She also met with some problems there. The most serious problem was the weather. She was not comfortable with the winter clothes of America but the Maharashtrian attire was not enough to cope up with the cold of America. Her health started deteriorating. She managed to take her final exams but her health was not good. At the convocation she was declared and honoured as the first woman doctor in India. She had tuberculosis and finally died from this disease after returning back to India.

Now I come to my point. In our country patriarchy decides everything in our family and outside our family. Patriarchy decides the role of male and females in our society and this is a story of more than two hundred years ago when the society was more conservative and more orthodox. Women were under the tutelage of male members in the family and they were denied their access and right to education. Here Anandibai took a bold step towards women's education and became a doctor. What is more interesting here that patriarchy worked positively in her case. She could not become a doctor if she would not have married Gopalrao Joshi. Her inclination towards education was created by her husband who had the desire to educate his wife properly. His fight against society in favour of women's education was not so easy. Gopalrao even left his father because Vinayakrao threatened him that he would not see his face as Gopalrao had started educating his wife. After Gopalrao and Anandi left home, Vinayakrao died but Gopalrao was still adamant. He realised the necessity of women's education and the submissive situation of the women in our society. Only proper education can empower them and restore their position in society.

While discussing on women and empowerment I must quote from the article on 'Women and Empowerment' written by P.R. Panda.

The author said, "From time immemorial women have been confined to the home and hearth. Individuality is the inner voice that commands you to be different. It is the strength that can move any mountain-respect its power, recognise its potential. United force of women will change the shape of India." "In India through centuries women have been playing second fiddle to the whims and fancies of man. In short I am agreeing that gender discrimination exists even today i.e. in the twenty first century. But at the same time I will say that men are not entirely selfish because one political leader alone who was a man has brought about significant changes and amendments for empowering women." She also quoted the words of Napoleon "Give me a good mother; I will give you a good nation." So women education and empowerment can build up a nation. She also declared that women played a significant role in the development of nation. So it's our responsibility to show respect to them. The author also commented that "The strategy for strengthening woman's economic status is to add the twin objectives of increasing income and solidarity of women. Moreover to increase the status of women they must be empowered socially, economically and politically. Women are one wheel of a cart or one side of a coin. If we look at Ancient India starting from Vedic period up to present women have played vital roles in all spheres of life."

In our society we need to empower women for not only their own well being but also for the welfare and development of our society. We have to increase the decision making powers of the women in our families and which women like Anandibai showed us. Education and empowerment are interlinked and they can increase the status of our women in the society. Patriarchy played a positive role in the case of Anandibai where she was lucky enough to have a husband like him and without his help, effort, inspiration and motivation she could not have become a doctor. So, it is time to review the role of patriarchy in our society though we cannot deny the negative side of it.

It is true that we have patriarchal family where it is the norm of the society that the male members of our family are the bread winners where as the female members are the care givers of the family. So it can be said that "gender inequality rather than egalitarianism is the characterisation of the relationship between husbands and wives in the division of household labour. Moreover, in the face of dramatic social changes, men's power in making family decisions has remained at a substantial, if not constant level. Once again contrary to Goode's claim, the macro-level shifts do not seem to be able to overcome men's resistance and a convergence towards egalitarianism has yet to come into being.

Several scholars supported Anandi's effort, dedication and courage and made her husband villain with whom a person like Anandibai could not stay anymore. The first biography of Anandibai was written by a male novelist in 1962 named J.S. Joshi who has been criticised by several feminist scholars because of his inclination towards Gopalrao. Joshi glorified the role of Gopalrao and tried to suppress the efforts of Anandi. The first Marathi biography on Anandibai was written by a woman writer named Kashibai Kanitkar. Kashibai was the first woman biographer of Anandi who wrote her book in 1889 just after the death of Anandi. Another female biographer who wrote on Anandi in 1888 and also knew her is Caroline Dall. The other biographer who portrayed Anandi was another Marathi woman named Anjali Kirtane. She wrote her book in 1997. Anjali was a trained researcher while the first Marathi woman–Kashibai did not receive formal education. Her biographer Caroline Dall glorified her role as the first woman doctor of India and questioned the role of her husband Gopalrao. When Dall first met Anandi in 1886, she saw Gopalrao and his negative attitude towards missionaries and colonialists. I must quote this attitude from 'Through A Changing Feminist Lens: Three Biographies of Anandibai Joshi' written by Prachi Gurjarpadhye. She wrote, "His public lecture delivered in the US and letters published in the American press were harsh indictments of Western racism and while Dall takes no offence at Anandi's mild reservations about the Christian assumptions about non-believers expressed in her private letters and dialogues with her friends, it is not so easy to take that point from the aggressive public articulations by Gopalrao. At a time when it would have been becoming to bask in the glory that the American public was all eager to lavish on Anandibai and her husband and to be properly grateful to even function as the mascots of Western civilisation, Gopalrao seems to have cringed from that expectation and was being difficult by debunking the myth of Western progressivism." Dall fully blamed Gopalrao for his behaviour and attitude and questioned that how would Anandibai restart her married life with the person of such irritating behaviour especially after passing a quality time in the liberal atmosphere of the West. Dall also made him responsible for her death. The three biographers of Anandibai like Kashibai Kanitkar, Anjali Kirtane and Carole Dall glorified her role, made her the heroine of the age and presented her 'as an ideal of Arya Hindu womanhood' and portrayed her husband Gopalrao as the villain of the story.

I want to establish in this chapter the valorous role of Anandibai who has created a history and built up her own agency and also the positive role of patriarchy and Gopalrao Joshi in fulfilling her dreams. Despite the criticisms of her biographers, I want to say that without the effort and support of Gopalrao, Anandi could not have proceeded far. So we cannot deny the role of Gopalrao while building her own agency and empowering her. Prachi Gurjarpadhye pointed out "When it became clear that it may not be feasible for financial reasons for both of them to go to America for Anandi's education, it was Gopalrao's suggestion that in that case she should go alone and set an outstanding example for their wretched society. Anandi was all ready for it. She had acquired enough poise by then to deliver, at the age of 18, her first public lecture ever in English at Serampore justifying her decision to go abroad to study medicine when no other Hindu women had done such a thing before. Attended by important dignitaries and widely covered by the press, it reads today as a remarkably sensible speech not only for its content and maturity but also for its tenor that shows an amazing awareness in Anandi of exactly where she stood. This speech sealed Anandi's success. It was not very difficult for the reformists after this speech to raise funds for her education." Though Prachi Gurjarpadhye is not ready to give any credit to Gopalrao, she declared that it was Anandi's efforts and potential that made her great. She said: "There is no doubt that this is Anandi speaking and not Gopalrao. Here was an able young individual spreading her wings and ready to take off towards a future of her own making." But it was Gopalrao's effort which gave Anandibai her due fame.

In another place Prachi declared that for the betterment of his wife's education Gopalrao sought transfer to different places like Bombay, Kohalpur, and Calcutta. He met different British officers also for his wife's education and explained them his objective of making his wife a doctor. This type of sacrifice and dedication cannot be denied though it was not new in the nineteenth century India. Once Anandi left a missionary school because the teacher forced her to study Bible but Gopalrao said to her that it was nothing bad to know about other religions and it would enrich her properly. After that Anandi was sent back to the same school. So, it is clear from the quotation that Gopalrao tried hard to give proper education to his wife. He wanted to make her independent which means that he helped in empowering her. Prachi wrote in another place that Gopalrao sent her to different places alone so that she could walk alone or more clearly he wanted to make her independent. She travelled long distances by train or walked alone on the streets and had to face several problems, people looked at her and made many comments but Gopalrao did it to make her independent. He realised that education is the only avenue to empower women and he wanted to prove the fact. These types of experiences of Anandi helped her when she was alone in America and she was able to live independently there. Prachi stated "Anandi surprisingly, proved equal to the challenge Gopalrao had placed before her. She studied single mindedly, learnt, not just to obey, but increasingly to argue, question and debate. She picked up as many as seven languages and gradually began to feel certain that her calling was medicine."

This chapter is about the story of a woman who was born in a simple Marathi Chitpavan Brahmin family and married to a person who was twenty years senior to him and also a widower. She stared her journey to become a modern educated woman under the tutelage of her husband and after long efforts she reached America and became a doctor. This story is very much inspiring to all woman of India. Her efforts, vivacity, talent and challenge helped her to reach at a height. In the nineteenth century India where women were not in a better position in our society because of patriarchal norms and colonialism, she has created an example, she was an exception because there were very few women in India who received such opportunity like her and her husband had played a significant role in empowering and building up her own agency. Actually we want an egalitarian society where both men and women work together. Patriarchy or matriarchy cannot be the good option for our society. We need education for both men and women and we cannot deny the role of father for a child's education. Without a mother a child cannot be grown up properly and father also plays a significant role for rearing him/her. So we cannot be biased towards anybody. We can dream of a society and country where women can survive independently and according to their will, where there would be no gender discrimination and no atrocities towards women. Education is the only thing which would empower a person and especially the womenfolk and Anandibai's story is the best example of women's education and empowerment.

References

- Bagchi, Ashoke, K. (1994), *Great Women of Science*, New Delhi, Konark Publishers Pvt. Ltd.
- Dall, Caroline. (1888), *The Life of Dr Anandibai Joshee, a Kinswoman of the Pundita Ramabai,* Boston, Roberts Brothers Publication.
- Gurjarpadhye, Prachi. (August, 2014), "Through a Changing Feminist Lens: Three Biographies of Anandibai Joshi" in *EPW*, vol.XLIX, No. 33.
- Geetha, V. (2007), *Patriarchy*, Calcutta, STREE.
- Haj-Yahia, Muhammad, M. (November, 2005), "On the Characteristics of Patriarchal Societies, Gender Inequality, and Wife Abuse: The Case of Palestine Society" in *Adalah's Newsletter,* Vol. 20, pp. 1-6.
- Kosambi, Meera. (1994), "The Meeting of the Twain: The Cultural Confrontation of Three Women in Nineteenth Century Maharashtra" in *Indian Journal of Gender Studies*, New Delhi, Sage Publications.
- Mukherjee, Sujata. (August, 2012), "Medical Education and Emergence of Women Medics in Colonial Bengal" in *Occasional Paper*, Kolkata, IDSK, pp. 1-40.
- Panda, P, R. (2009), "Women and Empowerment" in *Orissa Review,* pp. 46-47.
- Srivastava, Gouri. (2000), *Women's Higher Education in the nineteenth Century*, New Delhi, Concept Publishing Company.
- Thakar, Pooja. (January, 2009), "Lilavati's Daughters: 2. Dr Anandibai Joshi" in *Nan-politan.*
- Joshi, Janardan, Srikrishna. (1962), *Anandi Gopal*, translated by Asha Damle in 1992, US, the University of Michigan.
- Joshi, Raghunath. (1988), *Anandibai Joshi, Triumph and Tragedy,* Span.

(Section – F)

Linking Girl Education with National Development

Chapter-15

National Mission for Empowerment of Women-2010: Providing Educational Base for Socio-Economic Development of Women

—*Deepa Awasthi*

Abstract

India has experienced rapid growth and development in the past years. Across the globe educating women and giving them the ability to stand on their own feet has been a priority. Education is the most vital element for socio-economic development of individual as well as country. It is an instrument of social change which eliminates gender disparities and creates equal opportunities. In this context, National Mission for Empowerment of Women (NMEW) through its social empowerment and education domain ensures gender mainstreaming in the education sector in order to empower women holistically and the nation building through her. NMEW is also named as Mission Poorna Shakti. In present chapter author has described various features of NMEW, its focus areas, key strategies etc. In present chapter various educational schemes and efforts of government are also discussed which are available under the umbrella of NMEW. Different facilities available for women at different levels of education i.e. elementary, secondary, higher etc. have also been highlighted in detail, which provide basis of socio-economic development of women.

Key Words: *Empowerment, Development, Opportunity, Schemes.*

Introduction

The National Mission for Empowerment of Women (NMEW) was launched by the government of India on International women's day 2010, with the aim to strengthen the overall processes that promotes all round development of women. It has the mandate to strengthen the inter-sector convergence; facilitate the process of coordinating all the women's welfare and socio-economic development programmes across various ministries and departments. The mission aims to provide a single window service for all programmes run by the government for women under aegis of various central ministries.

In the light of its mandate, the mission has been named ***Mission Poorna Shakti***, implying a vision for holistic empowerment of women. National Resource Centre for women has been set up which functions as a National Convergence Centre for all schemes and programmes for women. It acts as a central repository of knowledge, information, research and data on all gender related issues and is the main body servicing the National and State Mission Authority.

Mission Statement

NMEW will achieve gender equality, gender justice and holistic development of women through inter sectoral convergence of programs relating to women, forging synergy between various stakeholders and creating an enabling environment conducive to social change.

Focus Areas of the Mission

- Access to health, drinking water, sanitation and hygiene facilities for women.
- Coverage of all girls especially those belonging to vulnerable groups in schools from primary to class 12.
- Higher and professional education for girls/women.

- Skill development, micro credit, vocational training, entrepreneurship, SHG development.
- Gender sensitisation and dissemination of information.
- Taking steps to prevent crime against women and taking steps for a safe environment for women.

Key Strategies

- Inter-sectoral convergence of schemes for women; monitoring and review of progress.
- Strengthening institutional framework for greater efficiency in support to women.
- Focused research, review of schemes, programmes and legislations, and gender audits for evidence based policy making.
- Investment in skill and entrepreneurship development, micro-credit, vocational training and SHG development for economic empowerment of women.
- Support to Panchayati Raj institutions; women's movements and community representatives for strengthening of local bodies, 360 degree approach on media and communication for behaviour change and social mobilisation for gender equality.

Poorna Shakti Kendra

The Poorna Shakti Kendra (PSK) is the focal point of action on ground through which the services to women at grassroots level would be facilitated; village coordinators at the Kendras would reach out to the women with the motto ***'Hum Sunenge Naari Ki Baat'***. It–

- Provides information on all the government programmes/schemes/services for women.
- Maintains a database of target population.
- Does awareness generation on legal rights and entitlements.
- Facilitates the availability and access to government programmes/schemes/services across health, education and livelihood sectors.

- Imparts training and capacity building on various issues like leadership, legal rights etc.
- Organises women into collectives to access various resources.
- Coordinates the outreach of services of various departments.

Some Schemes of Government under NMEW

- Mahatma Gandhi National Rural Employment Guarantee Scheme (MGNREGS)
- Public Distribution System for Food (PDS)
- Integrated Child Development Services Scheme (ICDSS)
- National Rural Health Mission (NRHM)
- National Rural Livelihood Mission (NRLM)
- Sarva Shiksha Abhiyan (SSA)
- National Literacy Mission (NLM)
- Rajiv Gandhi Scheme for Empowerment of Adolescent girls (SABLA)
- Rashtriya Swasthya Bima Yojna (RSBY)
- Indira Gandhi Matritva Sahyog Yojna
- Total Sanitation Campaign
- Indira Gandhi National Widow Pension Scheme
- Indira Gandhi National Old Age Pension Scheme
- Support for Training and Empowerment Programme for Women (STEP)
- SWADHAR
- Janani Suraksha Yojana
- Panchayat Mahila evam Yuva Shakti Abhiyan
- Scheme for Leadership Development for Minority Women
- Science and Technology for Women
- Adivasi Mahila Sashaktikaran Yojna of NSTFDC

NMEW: Socio-Economic Development of Women and Education

Education is the most vital element of socio-economic development. A well educated population, adequately equipped with knowledge and skill is not only essential to support economic growth, but is also a precondition for growth to be inclusive, because it is only the educated and skilled person who can stand to benefit most from the employment opportunities generated due to growth. Improvements in education are not only expected to enhance the efficiency but also augment the overall quality of life. Education is an instrument of social change and eliminates gender disparities and ensures equal opportunities.

In this context, National Mission for the Empowerment of Women (NMEW) through its Social Empowerment and Education domain ensures gender mainstreaming in the education sector in-order to empower women holistically and through her the nation building. Social Empowerment and Education domain aims at converging and linking various schemes of Government of India focusing on women with special reference to the flagship programs of Ministry of Human Resource Development (MHRD). The domain will review existing studies, policies, programmes, schemes and also commission research studies of various programmes/ schemes on education for better implementation.

The National Policy on Education-1986, revised in 1992(NPE): emphasises the need to use education as an agent of basic change in the status of women. The NPE proposes national education system to play a positive interventionist role in the empowerment of women, fostering the development of new values through redesigning of curriculum, text book, training and orientation of teachers, decision making and administration and active involvement of educational institutions. These will be an act of faith and social engineering. Women studies will be promoted as the part of various courses and education institutions will be encouraged towards taking up active programs for women's development.

Removal of women's illiteracy and obstacles inhibiting their access to, and retention in elementary education will receive overriding priority, through provision of special support services, setting up of time targets and effective monitoring. Major emphasis will be laid on women's participation in vocational, technical and professional education at different levels. The policy of non-discrimination will be pursued vigorously to eliminate gender stereotyping in vocational and professional courses so as to promote women's participation in non-traditional occupations as well and in existing and emergent technologies.

The National Policy of Empowerment of Women of 2001 has endorsed the provisions of NPE 1986. The policy prescribes:

- Equal access to education for women and girls.
- Special measures for eliminating discrimination.
- Universalisation of education.
- Eradication of illiteracy.
- Creation of a gender-sensitive educational system.
- Increasing enrolment and retention rates of girls.
- Improving the quality of education.
- Development of occupation/vocation/technical skills by women.
- Reducing the gender gap in secondary and higher education.

Schemes

Education provides a strong base for building of self sufficiency and development. Government has launched various schemes covering every aspect of education i.e. elementary, secondary, higher and technical education. These schemes are not only for providing means of education but through these schemes social and economic development can also be ensured. After getting a particular type of education a girl is able to get certain type of vocational self sufficiency which provides economic independence and social recognition. These schemes can be discussed as below–

Elementary education: Elementary education has been accorded priority and Sarva Shiksha Abhiyaan (SSA) was launched during 11th Plan as a part of Universalisation of the elementary education. The goals of SSA were:

- All children to be in a regular school, Education Guarantee Scheme, Alternative Innovative Education, or "Back to School' camp by 2005.

- Bridging all gender and social category gaps at primary level by 2010.
- Universal retention by 2010
- Free textbooks to all girls up to class VIII (Rs 300 per girl at primary level and Rs 450 per girl at upper level).
- Recruitment of 50 per cent women teachers.
- Gender–sensitive teaching-learning materials, including textbooks.
- Districts with Gender Gaps in enrolment receive attention under SSA focus on elementary education of requisite quality with emphasis on education for life.
- Separate toilets for girls
- Bridge courses for older girls.
- Early Childhood Care and Education Centres in/near schools/ convergence with ICDS programme etc.
- Teachers' programmes to promote equitable learning opportunities.
- Intensive community mobilisation efforts.
- 'Innovation fund' per district for need based interventions for ensuring girls' attendance and retention.

SSA has brought primary education to the door steps of millions of children and have enrolled them including first generation learners. During these period major schemes like district primary education program and the national program of nutrition support to primary education (Mid-day meal scheme) was also launched. Schemes related exclusively for girls under Elementary education are as follows:

1. Mahila Samakhya Scheme.
2. National Program for Education of Girls at Elementary Level (NPEGEL).
3. Kasturba Gandhi Balika Vidyalaya (KGBV).

The schemes for girls like Mahila Samakhya Scheme, National Program for Education of Girls at Elementary Level (NPEGEL) and Kasturba Gandhi Balika Vidyalaya (KGBV) Scheme have been launched by MHRD. Mahila Samakhya Scheme established Mahila Sangas or "Women Collectives" to empower women in rural areas especially from socially and economically marginalised groups. The program focussed on creation of awareness which has resulted in increasing the enrolment and retention rates of girls in school. NPEGEL focuses on "Hardest to Reach" girls, especially those not in school. The scheme is being implemented in educationally backward rural blocks (EBBs). For the promotion of the girl education KGBV scheme provides support for establishment of residential schools in each district. Both the schemes are operationalised where the female literacy rate is less than the national average and gender gap is higher than the national average.

The National Programme for Education of Girls at Elementary Level (NPEGEL) needs to be focused on blocks with Rural Female, Literacy Rate (RFLR) below 30 per cent as per 2001 Census as well as the existing criteria of the scheme [i.e. educationally backward blocks (EBBs) where the level of rural female literacy is less than the national average and the gender gap is above the national average; in blocks of districts which are not covered under EBBs but are having at least 5 per cent SC/ST population and where SC/ST female literacy is below 10 per cent; and also in select urban slums].

Under MSS, The Mahila Samakhya Scheme is currently being implemented in nine States viz. Andhra Pradesh, Assam, Bihar, Jharkhand, Karnataka, Kerala, Gujarat, Uttar Pradesh and Uttaranchal spreading over 83 districts and covering more than 20,380 villages. The scheme is covering a total of 339 blocks and out of these 233 are Educationally Backward Blocks. MS Societies have also been registered in Madhya Pradesh and Chhattisgarh and the programme is to be initiated in these States also.

Under KGBV scheme out of 3572 sanctioned, 2567 schools are operational (as on 30.09.2010) in 27 states with enrolment of 2.15 lakh girls of whom 27.07 per cent girls belong to SC, 28.08 per cent to ST, 26.23 per cent to OBC, 8.62 per cent to Muslims and 10 per cent to BPL category.

Under NPEGEL, in 3,297 Educationally Backward Blocks (EBB) covering 41,103 clusters around 40,623 Model cluster schools have been opened (2011); 4,367 ECCE centres are being supported, 24,593 additional classrooms have been constructed, and 2,14,731 teachers have been given training on gender sensitisation, remedial teaching to 24,18,036 girls, bridge course covering 6,57,622 girls, Meena activity covered 32,35,753 girls, exposure visits covered 9,10,499 girls and including additional incentives like uniforms etc. were provided to about 10,80,110 girls.

Secondary Education

There are various schemes to provide incentive to girls to complete secondary education. Secondary education provides extension to basic knowledge of girls. It provides basis for vocational and higher education. It empowers girls to be self dependent. Specific efforts for girls in the field of secondary education are as below–

Incentives to girls for Secondary Education: According to the scheme, a sum of Rs 3000 is deposited in the name of the unmarried eligible girls as fixed deposit, who are entitled to withdraw it along with interest thereon on attaining 18 years of age and passing Xth class examination. During the period from 1st January, 2013 to 31st March, 2014] an amount of Rs 99.02 crores have been sanctioned covering 3,30,076 girl students.

Girls' Hostel Scheme: Girls Hostel Scheme was launched in 2008-09 and is being implemented from 2009-10:The scheme envisages construction of a hostel with the capacity of 100 girls in each of about 3,500 Educationally Backward Blocks (EBBs) in the country. Students passing out of KGBVs will be given preference in admission in hostels. At least 50 per cent of girl students should be from SC, ST, OBC and Minority Communities. 1647 girls hostels were sanctioned and Rs 1006.78 crores grant was released till 31.3.2014.

Setting up of Model School at block level as benchmark of excellence: The objective of the scheme is to have at least one good quality senior secondary school in all the 6,000 blocks of the country. As on 31.3.2014, about 1.47 lakh students were enrolled in these

1184 functional schools. It is expected that after the operationalisation of 2266 model schools, which have been approved so far under state sector component, a total number of 12.68 lakh students would be benefited from 560 students per school.

Considering the demand generated out of universalisation of primary education, the need to set up a mission for universalisation of secondary education was envisaged and Rashtriya Madhyamik Shiksha Abhiyaan (RMSA) has been launched by the MHRD to widen access to women, SC/STs, and other deprived categories of children. Schemes like Model schools, ICT Schools, Inclusive education for disabled at secondary state, National merit cum means scholarship have also been implemented.

For the promotion of the girl education at secondary level, the scheme for incentives to girls for secondary education and scheme for establishment of girls' hostels have been implemented. The schemes of incentives promote the enrolment of girl child belonging to SC/ST communities in secondary schools and ensure their retention up to the 18 years of age. Girls' hostel scheme envisages construction and running of hostels in educationally backward areas for the promotion of the access and retention of girls at Secondary and Senior Secondary level.

Adult Education

Adult education is very important aspect of education covering millions of illiterate women and providing them confidence of literacy and education. There are various schemes which give opportunity to become literate without consideration of age.

Saakshar Bharat: It is continuity of the earlier National Literacy Mission but with revised design and structure with principal focus on women and excluded groups like SCs, STs and Minorities etc. The mission has four broad objectives, namely, to:

(a) Impact functional literacy and numeracy to non literate adults.

(b) Enable the neo literate adults to continue their learning beyond basic literacy and acquire equivalency to formal education system.

(c) Impart non and neo literates relevant Skill development programmes to improve their earning and living conditions.

(d) Promote learning society by providing opportunities to neo literate adults for continuing education.

Under Saakshar Bharat, accordingly, 410 districts qualify for coverage including 35 LWEA districts. 167 districts were covered during 2009-10. NIOS has conducted three Learner's Assessment Examinations in which 97 lakh learners appeared for exam out of which 32 lakh students have been cleared and certified. Targeted women population is 60 million. 115 districts were sanctioned during 2010-11 and another 90 districts were sanctioned during 2011-12. By March, 2012, the programme was sanctioned in 25 States and 1 UT covering about 1.61 lakh Gram Panchayats of 372 districts. During 2012-13, the programme was continued in these 372 districts. While, 11 bifurcated districts got sanctioned during 2013-14 expanding the reach of programme in 383 districts.

Jan Shiksha Sansthan: It has been established to promote vocational training to disadvantaged groups of adults such as neo-literates, less-educated slum dwellers, SC and ST and women etc. to raise their efficiency and increase their productive ability. Majority of the beneficiaries are women.

Shiksha ka Haq Abhiyan: In October 2011, the National Advisory Council (NAC) for RTE took a decision to launch a country wide campaign for RTE. The Prime Minister of India addressed a letter to the children of the country, which was read out on the occasion of National Education Day, 11th November 2011, at a special function organised at Nuh, Mewat Haryana.

Higher and Technical Education

Higher and technical education is the upper most step of educational ladder. It not only establishes a woman in the academic and professional world but it also provides her with an opportunity to become a role model for other women. There are various schemes of government which help women to avail higher education. Some of them are:

Women's Hostel in higher education institutions: Under this scheme women's hostels are established in the areas where there are significant population of weaker section and minorities. The grant for this purpose is provided by University Grants Commission (UGC). Under Hostel Scheme, during 2012-13, a total grant of 184.98 crores to 1010 state colleges had been released.

Women's Study Centres in Universities and Colleges: The Women's Studies Programme which was initiated in VIIth plan period, was promoted, strengthened and given direction to over various plan periods by establishing Women's Study Centres in the University System. As on 31.03.2012, as many as 159 Women's Study Centres (82 in universities and 77 in colleges) including 28 centres set up in 2010-11, have been functioning in the University system. Approximately 80 proposals for opening the Women's Study Centres are lying pending with the Commission in 12th plan.

Women Polytechnics: As per AICTE, 168 Polytechnics for women are operational in various states.

Women Hostels in Polytechnics: Under this scheme, 481 polytechnics have been provided partial financial assistance of Rs 202.00 crores till 31.01.12.

Establishment of New Model Degree Colleges: There is a scheme for establishing model degree colleges in Educationally Backward Districts with Low (GER) (UGC).

Capacity Building of Women Managers in Higher Education: The scheme of Capacity Building of Women Managers in Higher Education was initiated by UGC in the Xth Plan period. The overall goal is to facilitate the constituencies of women faculty, administrators and staff within the higher education system so as to increase the participation of women in higher education management for better gender balance, to sensitise the higher education system through policies and procedures which recognise women equity and diversity and to involve the women capable of becoming administers for the qualitative development of higher education. 35 Sensitisation/Awareness/Motivation (SAM), 3 Training of Trainers (TOT) and

9 Management Skills Enhancement Module (MSEM) workshops have been organised during 2012-13 under this scheme.

Establishment of Special SC/ST Cells in Universities: The Commission has been providing financial assistance to universities for the establishment of SC/ST Cells to ensure effective implementation of the reservation policy for SC/ST in admissions, recruitment of both teaching and non-teaching positions. Up to 31st March, 2013, as many as 127 SC/ST Cells had been functioning in various universities.

Residential Coaching Academy for Minorities and SC/ST/OBC (non-creamy layer/Minorities viz.)/women: Under this scheme Universities and Colleges establish Residential Coaching Academy for UG/PG level students to prepare them for NET and coaching them for entry into services covered under Central and State Governments.

Girls' Hostels in Minority Concentration Areas: UGC has sanctioned 284 women's hostels during 11th plan in 90 Minority Concentration Districts/Areas. Out of total allocation of Rs 366.49 crore, Rs 201.55 crores have been released till July 15 2011.

Merit Scholarship Scheme: Under this scheme students are provided a scholarship amount of Rs 2000 per month for a period of two years (i.e. 10 months in a year) and scholarship amounts are directly credited to the bank account of the student beneficiaries.

Indira Gandhi Scholarship for Single Girl Child for pursuing higher and technical knowledge: This scheme supports higher education through scholarships of only single girl child families for promoting small family norm. Girl students up to the age of 30 years at the time of admission of Postgraduate courses are only eligible. The number of slots for scholarships available under the scheme is 1200 p.a. The scholarship amount is @' 2,000 p.m. for 20 months. As many as 1803 students who have taken admission in 2012-13 academic sessions have been selected for providing the scholarship. An expenditure of Rs 2,66,80,763/- was incurred during the reporting year 2012-13.

Tuition Fee Waiver for Girl Students: The AICTE has launched a scheme to encourage tuition fee waiver for girl students by providing incentives to Technical Institutions in the form of sanctioning additional intake capacity up to 10 per cent, if the institutions provide tuition fees waiver to at least 10 per cent students, belonging to economically-weaker sections, physically challenged categories and women. With this, the AICTE has also relaxed its norms for establishment of Technical Institutions exclusively for women.

Post-doctoral fellowship for women: The scheme provides for a scholarship of Rs 25,000 pm for fresh Ph.D and Rs 30,000 to Ph.D with 5 years of experience and associate ship for 5 years and a grant of Rs 50,000 p.a is given. Rs 2000 p.m. (fixed) is also provided to physically disabled & blind candidates for Escorts/Reader assistance. Under the Post-doctoral fellowship for women, 100 slots per year are available. During 2012-13, Rs 5.39 crores have been distributed.

Conclusion

Education has changed the vulnerable condition of women in to the empowered one. National mission for empowerment of women has provided women an opportunity to avail various schemes promulgated for them. Through various educational schemes women have developed socially as well as economically. Educated women not only help their family economically but they provide proper guidance to their children. Social and Economic scenario of India has undergone a huge change, and so has the status of women. The contribution of women has always been omnipresent. In every field they have made notable contributions towards the growth of the Indian economy. Indian women play an important role in initiating socio-economic progress of the country. NMEW is providing strong support for socio-economic development of women and also for the country.

References

- Burchi, F. (2006). Identifying the role of education in socio-economic development presented in International Conference on Human and Economic Resources, Izmir. www.die-gdi.de
- National Mission for Empowerment of Women, www.nmew.gov.in
- Role of women in socio-economic growth of country, www.carrierride.com
- www.india.gov.in
- www.thehindu.com

Chapter-16

Role of Girl Education in Socio-Economic and Political Development of India

—Mehnaz Najmi

Abstract

Education is learning, knowing and exploring. It is a tool of changing mindset of society. It pushes one out from darkness to light. Therefore, it is very important for the development of any nation or society. First Prime Minister of India, Pandit Jawaharlal Nehru said "If you educate a man you educate an individual, however, if you educate a woman you educate a whole family. Women empowered means mother India empowered." *Education is a universal human right. Article 21(a) says that the State shall provide free and compulsory education to all children in the age group of 6 to 14. Education empowers girls by helping them achieve other basic human rights and paves way for a spiral of power in their lives, grounded in education. But beyond the attainment of individual rights, girls' education has also proven to be a remarkably effective catalyst for social development and economic growth in developing countries. Education helps us understand ourselves better; it helps us realise our potential and qualities as a human being. It helps us to tap into latent talent, so that we may be able to sharpen our skills.*

Keywords: *Education, Empowerment, Girl-education, Social development, Economic development, Political development.*

Introduction

Definition of Education in its general sense is a form of learning in which the knowledge, skills, values, beliefs and habits of a group of people are transferred from one generation to the next through storytelling, discussion, teaching, training, and research. Education may also include informal transmission of such information from one human being to another. Education frequently takes place under the guidance of others, but learners may also educate themselves (autodidactic learning). Any experience that has a formative effect on the way one thinks, feels, or acts may be considered educational.

Education is learning, knowing and exploring. It is a tool of changing mindsets and society. It pushes one out from darkness to light. Therefore, it is very important for the development of any nation or society. First Prime Minister of India, Pandit Jawaharlal Nehru said "*If you educate a man you educate an individual, however, if you educate a woman you educate a whole family. Women empowered means mother India empowered.*" His statement was visionary. If a mother is educated, she is able to look after and bring up her children in a better manner. She is more capable of taking better decisions for herself and others. Education not only gives her a degree and economic power but also empowers her by enriching thought process.

Education is a universal human right. It empowers girls by helping them achieve other basic human rights and initiates a spiral of power in their lives, grounded in education. But beyond their attainment of individual rights, girls' education has also proven to be a remarkably effective catalyst for social development and economic growth in developing countries. So it is in some sense not only the individual girl who is empowered – it is the broader society. Our first PM stressed on women education, the constituent assembly since its inception gave a lot of importance on education. A lot of provisions and amendments have been made by the Government to make Right to Education especially for women more effective.

Constitutional Provisions for Women's Education in India

The Constitution of India not only grants equality to women but also empowers the State to adopt measures of positive discrimination in favour of women for neutralising the cumulative socio-economic, educational and political disadvantages faced by them.

Article 21(a) says that state shall provide free and compulsory education to all children in the age group of 6 to 14 years in such manner as the state may, by law, determine. Fundamental Rights, among others, ensure equality before the law and equal protection of law; prohibits discrimination against any citizen on grounds of religion, race, caste, sex or place of birth, and guarantees equality of opportunity to all citizens in matters relating to employment. The Right of Children to Free and Compulsory Education Act, 2009, commonly known as the Right To Education (RTE) Act, is being seen with much hope for bringing about the long awaited changes in education of children aged 6-14 years and addressing disparities of access and quality. The Act came in force from 1st April, 2010. While stating the duties of appropriate Government authorities at various levels, the Act has also included duties of parents and guardians to get their children /wards admitted for elementary education in neighbourhood schools.

Educational Provisions in Centrally Sponsored Schemes in School Education

Major schemes for Elementary Education include:

1. Operation Black Board
2. Teacher Education
3. Education Guarantee Scheme and Alternative and Innovative Education (EGS & AIE)
4. Mid-day Meal Scheme
5. Sarva Shiksha Abhiyan (SSA)
6. Kasturba Gandhi Balika Vidyalaya (KGBV)
7. Shiksha Karmi
8. Mahila Samakhya
9. District Primary Education Programme (DPEP)
10. National Programme for Education of Girls at Elementary Level (NPEGEL)
11. Lok Jumbish

12. Janshala Programme
13. Padhe Bitiya Badhe Bitiya
14. Ladali Scheme

Major schemes for Secondary Education include:

1. Access and Equity
2. Quality Improvement in Schools (QIS)
3. ICT in Schools
4. Integrated Education for Disabled Children (IEDC)
5. Vocationalisation of Education

Present Day Situation

The biased parental attitude towards girl child is a reason of lesser enrolment of girls despite so many governmental efforts. The Indian society since long has practiced biased approach towards girls. Secondary status has been given to her, which starts right from providing educational avenues to other rights in the society. This discrimination can only be erased through education. Generally parents send their daughters to government schools and sons to private schools (another case of discrimination). Since government schools are free and private expensive, therefore, male child is send to private and expensive schools (also considered better qualitatively). It is a general misconception of parents that girls are burdens and they are only to be married off, hence no need to spend on their education whereas male child will live with them and will look after them in their old age, therefore, the benefits of better education needs to be given to them. Besides, there are other problems that are faced by girls in school due to which parents are not much inclined to send them for higher education. Most of the government schools are over-crowded as it is mandatory to give admission to all the students. There is hardly any proper sitting space for all the students whether girls or boys. Infrastructure has become a major problem in these schools. Teacher-student ratio is also poor. In any government school of Delhi it is 55-60 students per teacher. It is just not possible to provide equal time and attention to all the students in a class of thirty minutes. Teachers are not appointed on regular basis and school appoints guest teachers in bulk where quality compromise takes place. Therefore, the quality of teaching gets affected and is generally substandard as compared to private facilities.

Another big problem in government schools is sanitary condition of schools. Young girls need hygienic sanitary conditions which are missing here. Despite the govt. scheme of distributing free sanitary napkins to girls every month, the hygiene standards are not at all maintained. Toilets are dirty, in pathetic conditions and most often than not they don't have proper water supply. Generally girls avoid attending school during this period. Frequent absenteeism affects their overall performance and parents feel that they are not good in studies. Consequently, they are told again and again to concentrate on house hold chores so that their future lives are hassle free.

The growth of women's education in rural areas is very slow. Gender inequality is reinforced in education which is proved by the fact that the literacy rate for the women is only 65.46 per cent against 82.14 per cent of that of men, as per 2011 Census.

Literacy Rate in India

Year	*Persons*	*Males*	*Females*
1901	5.3	9.8	0.7
1911	5.9	10.6	1.1
1921	7.2	12.2	1.8
1931	9.5	15.6	2.9
1941	16.1	24.9	7.3
1951	16.7	24.9	7.3
1961	24.0	34.4	13.0
1971	29.5	39.5	18.7
1981	36.2	46.9	24.8
1991	52.1	63.9	39.2
2001	65.38	76.0	54.0
2011	74.04	82.14	65.46

Source: Census of India (2011).

According to the Table above, the pre-Independence time literacy rate for women had a very poor spurt in comparison to literacy rate of men. This is witnessed from the fact that literacy rate of women rose from 0.7 per cent to 7.3 per cent where as the literacy rate of men rose from 9.8 per cent to 24.9 per cent during the four decades spanning 1901 to 1951. During the post- independence period literacy rates have shown a substantial increase in general. However the literacy rate of males has almost tripled over the period e.g. 25 per cent in 1951 and 76 per cent in 2001. Not so surprisingly the female literacy rate has increased at a faster pace than the male literacy during the decade 1981 -2001. The growth is almost 6 times e.g. 7.9 per cent in 1951 and 54 per cent in 2001. This can be attributed to very low literacy levels of females in the beginning and concentrated efforts of the Government to raise the same.

From this analysis one can infer that still the female literacy rate (only half of the female population is literate) is lagging behind male literacy rate (three fourths of the male population are literates). The rate of school drop outs is also found to be comparatively higher in case of women. This higher rate of illiteracy of women is undoubtedly attributing for women dependence on men and their subjugation. The lack of education is the root cause for women's exploitation and negligence. Only literacy can help women to understand the India's constitutional and legislative provisions that have been made to strengthen and uplift them. Thus promoting education among women is of great importance in empowering them to accomplish their goals at par with men in different spheres of life.

Social-Economic and Political Development through Girl Education in India

Social Development: The psychological and social control over women to keep her in "*her place*" resulted in subordination and subjugation of the half of the human population. The physical strength and alleged dominance of men has been an important instrument of controlling women's freedom of action. The traditional image of male as protector of women had to be maintained by telling her again and again that she couldn't defend herself. Consequently men became in-charge of their lives. Men have been deciding what job a woman can do and what she cannot. All the household chores, rearing and bearing of children, looking after young and old, taking care of the needs of family members have been thrust upon women as their primary responsibility and consequently women became economically dependent on men. Their movements got restricted. With the evolution of Indian society their lives became more difficult. With the advent of Muslim rulers new traditions came in our *Manuvadi* society. Life of women folks became much more difficult. They were forced to follow *Pardah* system also in addition to their age old customs. Another reason for subjugation was internal pressure from the women-group themselves. From generation to generation mothers teach their daughters to please men. Over the centuries women have played the role of most ardent and loyal follower of tradition. It is them who mastermind all the rituals and are mainly responsible for showing preference to male children. All these prejudice and injustice can be eradicated through education. These immaturities and illiteracy is self-incurred, which needs to be removed.

Education as a tool of Self Empowerment: According to philosopher Kant, *"Emergence of an individual from self-incurred immaturity is enlightenment."* Not receiving or providing education to children is one such immaturity which keeps us backward. Good education helps in empowerment, thus making one strong enough to look after children in any given situation. It keeps one aware of given surrounding as well as the rules and regulations of the society we are living in. It's only through knowledge that one can be able to question authority for its negligence or discrepancies. It is only then that one can avail rights as a citizen and seek improvement in the structural functioning of governance and economy. It's only when a citizen is aware about the policies of its government can he be able to support or protest the change. As a whole, people can bring about development only when they know where improvement is necessary for the greater good of mankind. Education helps us understand ourselves better; it helps us realise our potential and qualities as a human being. It helps us to tap into latent talent, so that we may be able to sharpen our skills.

Dignified Life: Education helps us in gaining sufficient academic qualification so that one is able to get suitable employment at a later stage. A decent employment would be combined with hard-earned remuneration or salary through which one can look after their personal expenses. While one earns, she gradually begins to realise the true worth of money and how hard it is to earn. One realises the significance of saving for a rainy day and for unforeseeable contingencies. One feels empowered because there is a new sense of worth that develops within, and one feels the need to be independent and free from any further financial support. One takes pride in the fact that she is earning for self, and is not obligated to anyone. Well-documented evidence shows that educating girls and women also yields significant social and health benefits. Educated women are more likely to send their daughters to school. Countries with higher levels of female secondary-school enrolment have lower infant mortality rates, lower fertility, lower rates of HIV and AIDS, and better child nutrition. More education reduces the rate of violence against women, enables them to leave abusive relationships, and empowers them to reject adverse cultural practices, such as female genital mutilation.

Economic Development: Todaro, (2007) asserts that gender discrimination, in education, hinders economic and social development, and that it needs to be eliminated by maximising educational opportunities due to following four reasons:

- The rate of return in women's education is higher than that of men's.
- Increasing women's education not only increases productivity in the fields but also results in greater labour force, lower fertility and improved child health and nutrition.
- Improved child health and nutrition and more educated mother lead to multiplier effects on the quality of a nation's human resources for many generations to come.
- Women carry a disproportionate burden of poverty and landlessness that permeates developing societies, so that any significant improvement in their role via education can have an important impact on breaking vicious cycle of poverty and inadequate schooling.

Women's educational empowerment is essential for economic development, growth, and poverty reduction not only because of the income it generates, but also because it helps to break the vicious cycle of poverty. Educating girls and women is critical to economic development. Female education creates powerful poverty-reducing synergies and yields enormous intergenerational gains. It is positively correlated with increased economic productivity, more robust labour markets, higher earnings, and improved societal health and well-being. For developing countries in particular, women represent a previously untapped source of human capital, and countries that have adopted aggressive policies to promote gender equality in education can be expected to reap higher social and economic benefits. Greater investment in girls' education is vital for increasing female participation and productivity in the labour market, especially in non agricultural wage employment. Greater productivity means higher economic growth and more effective reduction of poverty. Whether self-employed or earning wages, working women help their households escape poverty. When women have more schooling, the returns flow not only to themselves, but to the next generation as well.

Human capital theory suggests that just as physical capital (machines) augments people's economic productivity, so human capital acquired through education improves the productivity of individuals. Studies of the sources of economic growth demonstrate persuasively that education plays a major role as a factor in the rise of output per worker. The new growth theories in economics place education and human resource development at the centre of their explanation for long-term economic growth. Confidence has grown in the belief that education affects economic growth because many studies have shown the positive correlation between a country's educational effort and its economic status, and causality has been attributed to education. Prominent examples of this are the so-called "miracle" economies of East Asia. If female schooling raises human capital, productivity, and economic growth as much as male schooling does, then women's disadvantage in education is economically inefficient. Research world-wide shows that, in general, the economic benefits from women's education - calculated as the economic rate of return to education - are comparable to those from men's education. Thus, from the point of view of economic efficiency, the gender gap in education is undesirable and should be filled.

Political Development: It seems evident that formal education should be strongly associated with political participation for women and for men. Women have the right to participate in decisions that affect their families, their societies, and particularly their own well-being. Yet despite recent progress, women in India are still largely absent from national and local decision-making bodies. Globally, fewer than 20 per cent of representatives to national legislative bodies are females, and women continue to face countless challenges to participation in the civic and political life of their countries. Beyond the numbers, the quality of women's participation is often hindered by discrimination within organisations or limits on women's access to mentoring, training, technology, and other resources. Strengthening women's rights and addressing barriers to political participation are critical steps toward empowering women, reducing poverty, and achieving our development goals. Participation is on two levels: one- as a representative and two- as a voter.

Education fosters participant democracy. Participant democracy in any large and complex society depends on literacy. Literacy allows full participation of the people in democratic processes and effective voting. Quotas and reservations for women in national-level politics are generally enjoyed by women who have long been active in politics, have good contacts, elite family backgrounds, and differ little from elite male politicians in being highly educated and financially secure. It is in efforts to increase the numbers of women participating in local politics that we see an influx of women to politics with significantly lower endowments than men in human and social capital and in material assets. For example in India we have reservation for women at Panchayat level. Few years back I made a research study on women Panchayat heads of Faridabad, Haryana and their powers. The findings were shocking as 4 out of 5 women *sarpanch* worked as proxies of their husband or father in law who attended meetings with villagers and Block Development Officer instead or with the ladies. Women *Sarpanch* stayed at home as any other house-wife. They were called to sign papers or put thumb impression as and when required by the "*Real Heads*." One *sarpanch* who did not behave as proxy was seen as untouchable and woman of bad character by the patriarchs of village.

She was an educated woman. Education brought the difference in her approach. She knew her powers, responsibilities and role very well. Despite opposition she was able to lead the village because of education.

Similarly, In Delhi state assembly elections of 2015, women voters voted for change and supported a new party whereas men preferred a ruling party. They were able to vote for change without any force or coercion. They openly spoke about the issues that affected them like electricity rates, gas or water supply. They were ready and open to deal with all the political leaders who came knocking their doors demanding votes. Such power and confidence comes from education but this was a case only of the capital city.

But it is also a reality that political institutions such as political parties and the formal institutions of state work in a distinctive way in this respect, showing more resistance to women's participation than do institutions in the labour market. The marked hostility of parties the world over to women has been observed by many feminists, but has yet to be fully explained. The resistance of voters to accept women as political leaders has also been noted, and has mainly been explained with reference to the rather general variable of 'culture'. The cultural acceptability of women in politics is held to be a function of the timing of women's suffrage, where early suffrage has given the electorate more time to adjust to the idea of women's political participation, and has given women an extended apprenticeship in political competition. Religious practices are also held to shape the cultural acceptability of women in politics. But such lines of discrimination can be erased through educational empowerment. Recent changes that came in politics are evident enough to predict that more the exposure of women to education and technology, more the empowerment.

Conclusion

Girl education is an instrument of bringing change in the society from a developing one to developed, from backward to uplifted and empowered. For this purpose a multidimensional and comprehensive approach is required to address gender equality and quality in education. The curriculum of the school, its extracurricular activities and the informal relationships amongst students and teacher communicate social skills and values, which needs to be strengthened. Quality educational content for girls must also include the information and skills that girls need to make informed decisions about their sexual and reproductive health. Training in life skills should be comprehensive and well designed, ensuring that school grounds, classrooms, and corridors are places where girls feel physically safe and psychologically at ease. Lack of access to water and sanitation facilities in schools particularly affects girls' education. Adolescence and puberty can be difficult times for all young people. For girls, however, in emergencies, chronic crises, and early reconstruction contexts, puberty—and especially the onset of menstruation—pose particular challenges, due to this lack of adequate restrooms and water at school girls find it difficult to comfortably change sanitary pads or other materials and wash themselves in private. Quality, retention, and achievement are essential elements of an education strategy designed to ensure that girls maximise their full potential. The present Gender Equality status in the Educational Framework indicates towards the need of addressing issues of insufficient access so as to ensure that boys and girls receive the maximum benefit from their education. Getting children into school is crucial; ensuring that they stay in school, learn, and achieve requires more efforts. The four dimensions of the framework provide planners with a systematic way of addressing the components necessary for ensuring a relevant, high quality education for all learners. Seizing these opportunities will help move closer to making education not just a lofty ideal, but a reality for millions of girls in India. Once, these ideals of making education girl-friendly are achieved and gender disparity is decreased, the girls of India will take the nation forward to new heights.

References

- Government of India, Census of India 2001.
- Government of India, Census of India 2011.
- Gupta, N.L. (2003). Women's Education Through Ages, Concept Publications Co, New Delhi.
- Karat, B. (2005). Survival and Emancipation: Notes from Indian Women's Struggles, Gurgaon, Three Essays Collective.
- Mahajan, V.D. (2010). Modern Indian History, Delhi, S. Chand.

- Michael P. Todaro (2007) Economic Development Edition.
- Nair, J. (1996). Women and Law in Colonial India: A Social History, Delhi, Kali for Women (published in collaboration with the National Law School of India) University, Bangalore.
- Rao, R.K. (2001). Women and Education, Kalpaz Publications, Delhi.
- Selected Educational Statistics (2003-04). Planning, Monitoring & Statistics Division, Department of Secondary and Higher Education, Ministry of Human Resource Development, Government of India.
- S. P. Agarwal (2001), Women's Education in India (1995-98) Present Status, Perspective, Plan, Statistical Indicators with Global View, Vol. III Concept Publications Co., New Delhi.
- Women in Indian Religions (Ed.) (2002). Arvind Sharma, Oxford University Press.
- www.demographic-research.org/Volumes/Vol3/3.
- www.portal.unesco.org/education
- www.unesdoc.unesco.org/images/0014/001467/146770e.pdf

Chapter-17

Girl Education and Development of India

—Meera Thakur and Anupama Katoch

Abstract

The destiny of a nation is shaped through its education and in this the girls' education has a strategic importance. Definitely education is a silver bullet for empowering women and girls worldwide. Offering girl education is a sure way of giving them much greater power of enabling them to make genuine choices over the kinds of lives they wish to lead. However, there are also important benefits for society as a whole. Education of women is the most effective channel for reducing the inequalities between men and women and ensuring the maximum participation of women in the development process. In other words, we can say that the education of girls and women is an integral part of national development. It plays an important role in the overall development of the country and not only helps in the development of half of the human resources, but in improving the quality of life. An educated woman has the self-confidence, information and skills that she needs to be a better parent, worker and citizen. Educating girls helps to make communities and societies healthier, wealthier and safer. Education has a profound effect on girls' and women's ability to claim other rights and achieve status in society. All of these occurrences are imperative to national development, and they can be accomplished by giving education to girls.

Keywords: *Education, Girls Education, Empowerment, National Development and Global Development.*

Introduction

Education is an essential human virtue and helps people to earn respect and recognition. The importance of education is undeniable for every person. Education has a positive effect on human life. It empowers people and strengthens nations. In other words, education is central to development and improvement of the nation's welfare. As a matter of fact, everything we create today is based on the knowledge that we obtain throughout our life by way of education. Education is considered as an important instrument through which processes of modernisation and social change come to existence. Education gives birth to intelligent people, guides for innovations, and creates a peaceful and harmless society. These ways are prerequisites for development of a nation.

Though education is important for every individual living on this earth, but it is more significant for girls and women. Educating girls is not only important because it gives them an opportunity to earn but the most important reason of educating girls is because they are the one who develop the whole family. The education of a girl is necessary for the girl herself, for society and for the nation. The emphasis with regard to girls' education should be to equip their multiple roles as citizens, housewives, mothers, and contributors to family income, builders of new society and nation. Hence to think about harmonious development is impossible without educating girls. Before coming on the role of girl education in development of India, we must think about the place of girls and women in society. Women constitute almost half the human race. As per their social status is concerned, they are not treated as equal to men in all the places. Since the older times, women have been treated as second class citizens all across the globe. The situation is almost the same everywhere and which in many ways is comparable with that of racial minorities irrespective of the development status of a country (developed/undeveloped), caste, community, colour or creed.

Revolutionary changes have taken place in the position of women in India after independence. The Constitution of India is provided with special steps to be taken by the government to improve the condition of women. The Constitution of India guarantees certain fundamental rights and freedoms such as protection of life and personal liberty.

Indian women are the beneficiaries of these rights in the same manner as the Indian men. In the post-independent India we had series of laws passed for the upliftment of women. These legislations have been brought in order to give women equal rights and privileges as men, to eliminate discriminations against women, remove inequality between sexes, and remove external barriers on the way of their self-realisation and development. The important Acts passed for the upliftment of women are:

- The Hindu Marriage Act of 1955
- The Hindu Adoption and Maintenance Act of 1956
- The Hindu Minority and Guardianship Act of 1956
- The Hindu Succession Act of 1956
- The Dowry Prohibition Act of 1961
- The Hindu Women Right to Property Act of 1973
- The Equal Remuneration Act of 1976

Besides legislations, 'education' was regarded as an important factor in raising the status of women in society. Therefore, active steps were taken to promote women's education. Various committees and commissions emphasised the need for equalisation of educational opportunities. The status of Indian women through the ages has been changing and the status, which was lost during the middle ages and earlier parts of nineteenth century, has been regained somewhat. Subsequently Indian women have gradually moved towards self-reliance and independence.

Status of Female Education

Although in the Vedic period women had access to education in India, they had gradually lost this right. However, in the British period there was revival of interest in women's education in India. Various socio religious movements led by eminent persons like Raja Ram Mohan Roy, Iswar Chandra Vidyasagar, Mahatma Jyotiba Phule, Periyar and Baba Saheb Ambedkar emphasised on women's education in India. They took various initiatives to make education available to the women of India. However, women's education got a fillip after the country got independence in 1947 and the government has taken various measures to provide education to all Indian women. As a result women's literacy rate has grown over the three decades and the growth of female literacy has in fact been higher than that of male literacy rate. While in 1991 only 32.17 per cent of Indian women were literate, and in 2011, 65.46 per cent female were literate, the growth of female literacy rate is 33.29 per cent as compared to 29.40 per cent of that of male literacy rate. The Indian government has expressed a strong commitment towards education for all. Though there has been seen a substantial increase in the number of literate women and this gap is narrowing, it still persists. Among such figures, there exists a ray of hope as well.

According to the 2011 census, since year 2011, 110 million additional women had become literate as compared to 107 men that mean the number of literate women is increasing. Females constitute about 50 per cent of country's human resource but lack of education snatches their chance to be a part of the progress and development of India. This means our pace of progress is less than the required pace. The Indian government's commitment to education is stated in its constitution with an article promising "free and compulsory education for all children until they complete the age of 14." The National Policy on Education, which was updated in 1992, and the 1992 Program of Action both reaffirmed the government's commitment to improving literacy levels, by providing special attention to girls.

Literacy Levels Improving Over Time

Although literacy levels are low, there has been progress in improving educational attainment for both sexes in India over the last several decades as shown in Table No. 1:

Table-1: Literacy Rate of India as per census data 2011

S. No	*Year*	*Total (per cent)*	*Male (per cent)*	*Female (per cent)*	*Male-Female Gap in Literacy rate*
1.	1901	5.35	9.83	0.60	9.23
2.	1911	5.92	10.56	1.05	9.51
3.	1921	7.16	12.21	1.81	10.4
4.	1931	9.50	15.59	2.93	12.66
5.	1941	16.10	24.90	7.30	17.60
6.	1951	16.67	24.95	9.45	15.50

(Contd...)

7.	1961	24.02	34.44	12.95	21.49
8.	1971	29.45	39.45	18.69	20.76
9.	1981	36.23	46.89	24.82	22.07
10.	1991	42.84	52.74	32.17	20.57
11.	2001	64.83	75.26	53.67	21.59
12.	2011	74.04	82.14	65.46	16.68

India's literacy levels have increased by 9.21 per cent in the past 10 years to reach 74.04 per cent, according to the 2011 census. Interestingly, female literacy level saw a significant jump as compared to males. Female literacy in 2001 stood at 53.67 per cent, it has gone up to 65.46 per cent in 2011. The male literacy in comparison rose from 75.26 to 82.14 per cent. There is a dramatic difference in the female literacy rate based on various regions in India (Table-2). Kerala has the highest female literacy rate with over 92 per cent of literate women in 2011. The state with the second highest female literacy is Mizoram, where nearly 89.40 per cent of women are literate. Rajasthan (52.7 per cent as per 2011 census) has the lowest female literacy rate in India. States such as Uttar Pradesh (59.3 per cent as per 2011 census) and Bihar (53.3 per cent as per 2011 census) that are the most populated states in India show low levels of female literacy. These literacy levels are highly correlated with the health status of the population. Kerala has the lowest infant mortality rates and the highest life expectancies of all the states. Bihar and Uttar Pradesh have a high mortality rate and the lowest life expectancies.

Table-2: Male-Female Literacy Rates of Indian States and Union Territories as per Census Data 2011.

S. No.	*State*	*Literacy Rate (2011 Census)*	*Male Literacy Rate (2011 Census)*	*Female Literacy Rate (2011 Census)*
1.	Andaman & Nicobar Islands	86.3 per cent	90.1 per cent	81.8 per cent
2.	Andhra Pradesh	67.7 per cent	75.6 per cent	59.7 per cent
3.	Arunachal Pradesh	67.0 per cent	73.7 per cent	59.6 per cent
4.	Assam	73.2 per cent	78.8 per cent	67.3 per cent
5.	Bihar	63.8 per cent	73.5 per cent	53.3 per cent
6.	Chandigarh	86.4 per cent	90.5 per cent	81.4 per cent
7.	Chhattisgarh	71.0 per cent	81.5 per cent	60.6 per cent
8.	Dadar and Nagar Haweli	77.7 per cent	86.5 per cent	65.9 per cent
9.	Daman and Diu	87.1 per cent	91.5 per cent	79.6 per cent
10.	Delhi	86.3 per cent	91.0 per cent	80.9 per cent
11.	Goa	87.4 per cent	92.8 per cent	81.8 per cent

(Contd...)

12.	Gujarat	79.3 per cent	87.2 per cent	70.7 per cent
13.	Haryana	76.6 per cent	85.4 per cent	66.8 per cent
14.	Himachal Pradesh	83.8 per cent	90.8 per cent	76.6 per cent
15.	Jammu and Kashmir	68.7 per cent	78.3 per cent	58.0 per cent
16.	Jharkhand	67.6 per cent	78.5 per cent	56.2 per cent
17.	Karnataka	75.6 per cent	82.8 per cent	68.1 per cent
18.	Kerala	93.9 per cent	96.0 per cent	92.0 per cent
19.	Lakshadweep	92.3 per cent	96.1 per cent	88.2 per cent
20.	Madhya Pradesh	70.6 per cent	80.5 per cent	60.0 per cent
21.	Maharashtra	82.9 per cent	89.8 per cent	75.5 per cent
22.	Manipur	79.8 per cent	86.5 per cent	73.2 per cent
23.	Meghalaya	75.5 per cent	77.2 per cent	73.8 per cent
24.	Mizoram	91.6 per cent	93.7 per cent	89.4 per cent
25.	Nagaland	80.1 per cent	83.3 per cent	76.7 per cent
26.	Orissa	73.5 per cent	82.4 per cent	64.4 per cent
27.	Puducherry	86.5 per cent	92.1 per cent	81.2 per cent
28.	Punjab	76.7 per cent	81.5 per cent	71.3 per cent
29.	Rajasthan	67.1 per cent	80.5 per cent	52.7 per cent
30.	Sikkim	82.2 per cent	87.3 per cent	76.4 per cent
31.	Tamil Nadu	80.3 per cent	86.8 per cent	73.9 per cent
32.	Tripura	87.8 per cent	92.2 per cent	83.1 per cent
33.	Uttar Pradesh	69.7 per cent	79.2 per cent	59.3 per cent
34.	Uttarakhand	79.6 per cent	88.3 per cent	70.7 per cent
35.	West Bengal	77.1 per cent	82.7 per cent	71.2 per cent
	INDIA	74.04 per cent	82.14 per cent	65.46 per cent

Low female literacy rate means an overall sluggish growth of India, as it impacts every arena of the development. India is struggling hard to stabilise its growing population through family planning programs. Growing population is one of the root causes of instability in the country. But if females are illiterate, then this has a direct and negative impact on these initiatives. When a girl or a woman is not educated, it is not only she who suffers but the entire family, society and also country has to bear the consequences of her illiteracy.

Issues and Challenges Related to Girl Education

The problem of Girls'/women's education in India is one which attracts our attention immediately. In our country, due to conservative traditionalism, women's status has, through ages, been considered to be lower than that of men. Illiteracy and ignorance is prevalent more in women folk than in men-folk and this evil is rampant especially in rural areas and backward communities. Under the fast changing conditions in the country in the recent times increased attention is being paid to their education. Though different commissions and committees appointed at times suggested for the solution of the problems of women's education and for its expansion, even though, certain problems still persist in that field. The negative attitude of parents towards the girl child and her education is one of the major reasons of low female literacy rate in India. In most of the families, boys at home are given priority in terms of education but girls are not treated in the same way. Their education is just considered as wastage of money as well as time. Poverty is the root cause of many problems in India and also of low female literacy rate. More than one-third of population in India is living below the poverty line. Though government is putting efforts to make the primary education free but still parents are not ready to send their girls to school. In most of the rural areas lack of easy accessibility to school is another reason for low female literacy rates. Even if schools are there then lack of adequate school facilities becomes a hurdle. Some of the schools are really in pathetic conditions and do not have even basic facilities. The other problems facing girls' education are:

- Scarcity of lady teachers
- Need of suitable curriculum for the education of girls
- Lack of consciousness among women
- Lack of physical facilities
- Unwillingness of lady teachers to serve in rural areas
- Financial difficulties
- Problem of transport
- Problem of wastage and stagnation
- Problem of co-education
- Lack of enthusiasm and interest of the officials in charge of education

In spite of all reasons, women must understand and realise that education can actually end the vivacious cycle of poverty and their misfortune so that they can live a life with pride. In case of any misfortune in life, it is education that would help them, not anything else. We should encourage the girl child in getting education to create a balanced and an educated society.

Provisions for Girls' Education in India

The Constitution of India in Article 15(1) on right to equality provides the basic policy framework that enshrines the vision of girls' education and the spirit in which their education is to be provided. Until 1976, education was a State subject. Since its transfer to the Concurrent List by the 42nd Constitutional Amendment in 1976, the Central Government has played a more proactive role in the sector through several centrally sponsored schemes that had a distinct bearing on promoting education for girls. A new thrust was provided to girls education in the National Policy on Education 1986, (as modified in 1992) which provided a holistic vision for the education of women and girls and recognised the cross cutting issues that inhibited the realisation of this goal. It aims at using education as an agent of basic change in the status of girls and women in society.

The 86th Constitutional Amendment Act, 2002 has made elementary education a Fundamental Right for children in the age group of 6-14 years by providing that "the State shall provide free and compulsory education to all children of the age of six to fourteen years in such manner as the State may, by law, determine." This has been a path breaking legislation in India, where such a major commitment to the cause of elementary education has bound governments, community based organisations and civil society into a common resolve to achieve universal elementary education. Drawing upon the Constitution and other policy statements articulated in the years that followed, the Government of India in partnership with State Governments has designed different strategies, interventions, schemes and programmes with specific objectives that impinge on girls' education.

Major Schemes for Elementary Education:

- Operation Black Board
- Teacher Education
- Education Guarantee Scheme & Alternative and Innovative Education (EGS & AIE)
- Mid-day Meal Scheme
- Sarva Shiksha Abhiyan (SSA)
- Kasturba Gandhi Balika Vidyalaya (KGBV)
- Shiksha Karmi
- Mahila Samakhya

- District Primary Education Programme (DPEP)
- National Programme for Education of Girls at Elementary Level (NPEGEL)
- Lok Jumbish
- Janshala Programme
- Padhe Bitiya Badhe Bitiya
- Ladali Scheme

Major Schemes for Secondary Education:

- Access and Equity
- Quality Improvement in Schools (QIS)
- ICT in Schools
- Integrated Education for Disabled Children (IEDC)
- Vocationalisation of Education

To encourage the education of girls at all levels and for dilution of gender bias in providing education, government established schools, colleges and universities even exclusively for women. To bring more girls, especially from marginalised families of BPL, into mainstream education, the government is providing a package of concessions in the form of providing free books, uniforms, boarding and lodging, clothing for the hostelites mid-day meals, scholarships, free circles and so on. Education for All (EFA) programme and other many educational programmes are providing various facilities to enhance the education for girls, these programmes are very helpful for improving the girls' education in India.

Girl Education and Development

Girls' education has a direct and proven impact on the goals related to child and reproductive health and environmental sustainability. Education also promotes economic growth, national productivity and innovation, and values of democracy and social cohesion. Investment in girl education benefits the individual, society, and the world as a whole. Broad-based education of good quality is among the most powerful instruments known to reduce poverty and inequality. With proven benefits for personal health, it also strengthens nations' economic health by laying the foundation for sustained economic growth. For individuals and nations, it is key to creating, applying, and spreading knowledge—and thus for the development of dynamic, globally competitive economies and it is fundamental for the construction of democratic societies. We can outline the importance of girls' education in nation's welfare as an enabler of:

- **Increased productivity and earnings:** Research has established that every year of schooling increases individual wages for both men and women by a worldwide average of about 10 per cent. In poor countries, the gains are even greater.
- **Economic competitiveness:** An educated and skilled workforce is one of the pillars of the knowledge-based economy. Increasingly, comparative advantages among nations come less from natural resources or cheap labour and technical innovations and the competitive use of knowledge. Studies also link education to economic growth. Education contributes to improved productivity which in theory should lead to higher income and improved economic performance.
- **Poverty reduction:** Education can vitally contribute to the attainment of the Millennium Development Goals. While two of the goals pertain directly to education, education also helps to reduce poverty.
- **Improved health and nutrition**: Education greatly benefits personal health, is particularly empowering for girls, profoundly affects reproductive health and also improves child mortality and welfare through better nutrition and higher immunisation rates.
- **Democratisation:** Educated women are more likely to participate in political discussions, meetings, and decision-making, which in turn promote a more representative, effective government.
- **Decreased population explosion**: Women with formal education are much more likely to use reliable family planning methods, delay marriage and childbearing, and have fewer and healthier babies than women with no formal education. A

study of UNESCO found that literate women had an average of 2 children while illiterate women had an average of six children.

- **Lower infant and child mortality rates**: Women with some formal education are more likely to seek medical care, ensure their children are immunised, be better informed about their children's nutritional requirements, and adopt improved sanitation practices. As a result, their infants and children have higher survival rates and tend to be healthier and better nourished.
- **Lower maternal mortality rates:** Educated women (with greater knowledge of health care and fewer pregnancies) are less likely to die during pregnancy, childbirth, or during the postpartum period. Increased education of girls also leads to more female health care providers to assist with prenatal medical care, labour and delivery, delivery complications and emergencies, and follow-up care.
- **Protection against HIV/AIDS infection:** Girls' education ranks among the most powerful tools for reducing girls' vulnerability. It slows and reduces the spread of HIV/AIDS by contributing to female economic independence, delayed marriage, family planning, and work outside the home as well as greater information about the disease and how to prevent it.
- **Improved socio-economic growth**: Educated women have a greater chance of escaping poverty, leading healthier and more productive lives, and raising the standard of living of their children, families, and communities.

Conclusion

Girls' education enables girls/women to participate and contribute to their societies and economies more broadly. Education helps change their lives for the better. Women education in India plays a key role in the social and economic development of the country. As we know the present day girl is the mother of tomorrow. She must be given all the necessary education. Ignoring her, keeping her illiterate means we are creating an illiterate and ignorant generation. It is a fact that any educated woman will definitely support the education of her children especially a girl child and provide a better guidance to her children. An educated woman will easily imbibe an independent and progressive outlook in her children. There is not a single field where women do not play a role in spite of several adversities. It is up to the men to understand and respect the role of a woman and reciprocate to them with the support they need. Great men are actually created by women who teach them moral values including equality and respect for one and all. Development cannot be accelerated unless girls are given right education in right direction.

References

- De, A. (2012). Education: Key to women empowerment. Education India Journal: A Quarterly Refereed Journal of Dialogues on Education. Vol. 1, Issue- 2.
- Desai, M., and Takkar, U. (2001). Women in Indian Society, New Delhi: National Book Trust.
- Government of India, Census of India 2011. Gupta, N.L. (2003). Women's Education Through Ages, Concept Publications Co, New Delhi.
- Johnson, Pamela S. & Johnson, Jennifer A. (2001). The oppression of women in India. Violence against Women, Vol. 7, No. 9, pp. 1051-1068.
- Parveen, S. (2008). Female education and national development: As viewed by women activists and advocates. Bulletin of Education & Research, Vol. 30, No. 1, pp. 33-41.
- Rao, R. K. (2001). Women and Education, Kalpaz Publications, Delhi.
- http://www.census.gov/population/international/files/wid-9801.pdf
- http://planningcommission.nic.in/plans/planrel/fiveyr/10th/volume2/v2_ch2_2.pd
- http://www.mapsofindia.com/my-india/society/low-female-literacy-rate-and-its-impact-on-our-society-2

Chapter-18

Girls Education and Development: A case study on the Juang Tribe in Odisha

—Madhusmita Sahoo

Abstract

Education is the key to the development of human resources along with provision of basic amenities like safe drinking water, adequate shelter and health care and an optional level of nourishment. The tribal children of the present society are the future present. Development of all the capacities in the individual to control his/her environment and fulfil possibilities becomes possible only through education. The all round development in respect of physical, mental and spiritual dimensions in the tribal child and adult can be effected only through education. As per the 1991 census the percentage of literacy among the Scheduled Tribe population was 22.31 per cent as against the national literacy rate of 52.21 per cent and the percentage of literacy of the Scheduled Tribes was 22.31 per cent as against the State literacy of 49.09 per cent. Education is a cultural process, which includes schooling as well as training agencies other than schools. It varies from culture to culture, time to time and space. In this chapter an attempt has been made to explain about the Juang tribal education system in Keonjhar district in Odisha state. The study is mainly focused on the girls' education of the tribe and how education can influence their society. The study has been conducted in the in the hilly Juang area in Keonjhar district.

Key Words: *Education, Women, Culture, Odisha.*

Introduction

India is a multi - racial and multi lingual state. This is also reflected in India's tribal population. The pre-history and ancient history of this country is replete with instances of interaction between the natives and the outsiders arriving in the country with their distinctive racial features, language, and culture. The tribal are beset with numerous problems and challenges. They have been neither empowered by economic development to tackle the challenge nor have they been converted into a different way of life by plentiful opportunities. Geographically, Odisha in Eastern India is divided into two parts: the coastal belt near Bay of Bengal, and the hilly regions. Odisha has a total population of 3, 68, 04, and 660 according to the census of 2001. The total number of persons in the scheduled tribe population is 81,45,081 (Male - 40, 66,783, Female - 40, 78,298).

The tribals are the indigenous auto-ethnos people of the land who occupy the relatively more inaccessible regions of forests and hills. As a result, we find tribes who, for centuries have lived far away from the mainstream in their relatively isolated, inaccessible, less fertile and less agriculturally productive regions of forests, hills and mountains. The isolated nature of the tribal and wide spread poverty is acting against their integration into the mainstream. The tribal people continue to remain economically and educationally backward and are languishing at the bottom of the economic ladder. Due to lack of education, the STs lag behind in acquiring new skills required in the use of appropriate technology and other opportunities and remain backward perpetually. The position of literacy among the ST is extremely poor and poorest among the ST females. If the literacy level does not improve in general and girls in particular, it would be a herculean task to effect any social and economic change among the tribals.

Education is a dynamic concept. It's meaning changes from time to time. The word education has been derived from the Latin word "educatio" which means imparting training for bringing up or rearing.

Education is the prime ingredient and irrefutably the heart of human resources development. Literacy rate is the measuring rod to determine the status of education in India, even though it does not explain the level of scholastic achievement required to equip people with knowledge and skills. Literacy in India means that a person must have bare minimum reading and writing skills. In most cases, it covers those who can write and sign their own name. The sole purpose of this is to encompass more people in terms of literate, even if they are not so in the usual sense of the term of 'literacy'. The literate and literacy rate is computed for 7+ age group populations.

The National Policy of Education (1986) has strongly advocated that the new policy will lay special emphasis on the removal of disparities and equalise the educational opportunities by attending to the specific needs of those who have been denied so far. Therefore, residential schools, including ashram schools were established on large scales.

It is almost obvious that education is not only a means of development but it is also an end in itself. Education leads a man from darkness to light. Education accords perfection to life. It is closely associated with socio-economic development of a country or society. The rate of literacy varies considerably across gender, across regions and across social groups. For the tribal communities, who at a critical stage of their history are facing a new situation to adjust themselves to the changes, education is of special significance. Even in the rural areas, particularly in the tribal regions, the lack of educational facilities has left the children of these people centuries behind. Low enrolment ratio and high drop-out rates lead children, especially girls, into illiteracy, rendering futile the efforts and investments made in improving literacy. The drop-out rate at the elementary level is high especially in the case of girl students. The main reasons for this situation in the tribal areas is that girls are engaged in household works, lack of parents interests, poverty, language and communication and lack of tribal teachers and also women teachers.

The total tribal population of the Odisha states is 7,032,214 as per the 1991 census, and out of these only 361,708 live in urban areas and the rest reside in rural areas. All the 62 scheduled tribal communities of the Odisha state are classifiable into three categories, namely, (i) Indo-Aryan; (ii) Austro-Asiatic (*Mundari*) and (iii) Dravidian. The dialects of tribal communities of the Indo-Aryan category are the variant dialects of the regional language; whereas each of the tribal communities of the other two categories has its own distinctive dialect.

The constitution came into operation in 1950. Article 45 of the constitution states that the state shall endeavour to provide for free and compulsory education for all children until they complete the age of 14 years. This has no doubt given the tribal community an impetus for attaining education. But there is a lot more to be done. Primary education continues to be prominent among the neglected sectors. Its impartation has continued over the years in a humdrum routine like manner. Along with the growth of literacy rate in the country the number of illiterates is also constantly rising. India is said to have entered the twenty first century with the maximum number of illiterates in the world.

There is a wide difference between the national literacy rate and the literacy rate of the Scheduled Tribes of the country. As per the 1991 census the percentage of literacy among the Scheduled Tribe population was 22.31 per cent as against the national literacy rate of 52.21 per cent. The percentage of tribal women was dismal. Another difference was also noticed in respect of the literacy rate of urban and rural tribal women. When one examines the State level percentage of literacy of Odisha with that of the Scheduled Tribes in the state, a similar difference emerges. According to 1991 census the percentage of literacy of the Scheduled Tribes was 22.31 per cent as against the State literacy of 49.09 per cent. The literacy rate of Schedule Tribes' men was 34.94 per cent as against 63.09 per cent for men in the state during the same census year. Likewise; the percentage of literacy of tribal women was 10.21 per cent as against 34.68 per cent for total women of the State. However, these are effective literacy rates and refer to the population which is in the age group of seven years and above.

Adivasis are found throughout India but are primarily based in the mountain and hill areas, away from the fertile plains. The Indian government has a special programme for the welfare of tribes which it has classified as "primitive" tribes. These are Adivasis engaged in pre-agricultural technology and shifting cultivation with either a static or declining population. In 1988 there were 73 such tribes totalling over one million people.

Education is a key factor of progress and achievement in the society or in any community. It propagates knowledge which is inevitable in understanding various forces of life-situation. Education so to speak kindles the light of consciousness. It animates perception and there by the persons concerned acquire the capacity for improving thought patterns and activity orientation. There is no denying of the fact that for the overall development of the tribal people they must be given the requisite light of education. It is due to their ignorance arising out of literacy that they have fallen under the clutches of exploitation and poverty. The tribal people throughout the state of Odisha as well as India are low in literacy levels due to various unfortunate situations.

Education has been in consideration as the cardinal aspect of socio-economic development, both at the micro and macro levels, since a long time. But more specifically modern education has proved itself to have greater implications on the shaping of the overall development goals at the level of individuals, families, communities, and finally nation as a whole. Socio-economically, a nation is more advanced if its people are more literate and educated than other nations.

Review of Literature

Behura has authored some scientific papers on the tribal education in Odisha. In one paper (1982) he has explained the problems of the tribal education in this state with respect to two different categories of constraints: (i) internal constraints, and (ii) external constraints, he speaks of how medium of instruction, communication gap and relation between teachers and pupils, inappropriate curriculum and text books, inadequate methods of teaching and supervision have been responsible for the poor schooling atmosphere in tribal areas. Under the second category of constraints, he says that local ecological conditions, poor economic condition of parents and lack of motivation and aspiration etc constitute major roles in disorienting the tribal people from school education.

Panda undertook a vast study in the year of 1998. It constituted samples from as many as 52 schools located in North and South Odisha.

The main objective of his study was to locate the factors that stand against the way of tribal education. He has vividly discussed some of the pivotal aspects in his study pertaining to the educational background of parents, school and home environments, local economy etc. and found that language, inadequate availability of educational facilities in predominant tribal areas, irrelevant course content, lack of motivational factors for the students, severe poverty, uncongenial home environment etc. are the major impediments that beset tribal education. He has suggested some action plans concerning all these problem areas.

Mahapatra (2007) has made a study among three primitive tribal communities, namely the *Bonda, Dongria Kondha* and *Juang*, who reside in compact hilly and forest dominated areas of Odisha. He has conducted this study in a total number of nine villages, three each for the above communities. His work is primarily based on empirical observations. He has gone into the depth of finding out the field reality on the aspects of the entire schooling system surrounding the tribal children and how the parents, friends, teachers, pedagogy etc. are in one way or other related to the success or failure of the whole system of tribal education among the primitive tribal communities of the state.

According to the census 1991, the tribal population in Odisha was estimated to be 70.32 lakhs, which constitutes only 22.21 per cent of tribal population of the State. The tribal population is estimated to have reached 84.45 lakhs in 2001, which is 22.10 per cent of the tribal State. The literacy rate of the Scheduled Tribes of Odisha is 22.31 per cent but the male literacy is 34.44 per cent, where as the female literacy rate is 10.21 per cent.

One of the important factors for our country's laggard status is that our youth wealth is not productive; they badly need useful training programmes to improve their skills. Keeping this in mind vocational skill training programmes towards productivity improvement has been made an integral part of the educational system for the tribals.

Elementary education comprising the primary (class I-V) and middle school is (class VI-VIII) to be provided free by the State but unfortunately Secondary and H. Secondary education (class IX-XII) does not fall under the free education provision scheme.

Methodology

The present study is descriptive in nature. The study was based on the primitive tribes of the Bansapal block in Keonjhar district of Odisha. Unit of study are the families and schools. Students and teachers in the schools and parents in the family were contacted for gathering primary data. The present study employed observation and interview schedule for the collection of data. For the insightful primary data, both the observation and interview schedule method have been adopted. The secondary data has been obtained from books, journals, news-papers, web sources, and both published and unpublished statistical documents.

Objectives

The objectives of the study are following:

- To know the education status of the Juang tribe.
- To analyse the role of women in promoting education among the Juang.
- To focus on the status of tribal literacy in the region.

According to the Census of India, literacy rate among tribal people in Odisha is 37.37 per cent of the literates; males constitute 51 per cent and females 23.47 per cent. The total literacy rate of the state is 63 per cent out of which male literacy rate is 73 per cent and female literacy is 51 per cent. The overall gap of literacy is 38 per cent, in which the gap in male literacy is 41.25 per cent and the gap in female literacy is 54 per cent.

Majority of Scheduled Tribes live in hilly and forest regions. Their economy is largely subsistence oriented, non-stratified and non-specialised. Their social system is simple and aspirations and needs are not many. Though the Scheduled Tribes in Odisha have suffered from social, educational and economic backwardness due to geo-historical reasons, they have their own distinctiveness and social-cultural milieu. At one end of the scale there are nomadic food gatherers and hunters and at the other end, skilled settled agriculturists and horticulturists. The tribal areas of Odisha, therefore, present an extremely diverse socio-economic panorama.

Education Plan and Policy Implemented by Govt. of India

Article 45 of the constitution stipulates that the state shall endeavour to provide within a period of 10 years from commencement of the constitution, free and compulsory education for all children (including the girls of both ST and other communities) until they complete the age of 14 years. Article 46 enjoins upon the State to promote with special care the educational and economic interests of the weaker sections of the people, and in particular of the Scheduled Tribes and protect them from social injustice and all forms of exploitation, and with a view to fulfil these constitutional commitments, several commissions and several committees have been appointed and several policies have also been formulated and implemented for the spread of primary education depending upon the recommendation of these committees. Some of the major past and ongoing educational programmes of the department of education include: Sarva Shikhasha Abhiyan (SSA), District Primary Education Programme (DPEP), National Programme for Education of Girls at Elementary Level (NPEGL), Prarambhik Shiksa Kosh (PKS), National Institute of Open Schooling (NIOS), Jan Shikshan Sansthan (JSS), Mahila Samakhya, Education for Women Equality, National Programme for Nutritional Support of Primary Education, and some other schemes which accord priority to the areas of concentration of SCs, STs, OBCs, and minorities. Apart from all these, the Ministry of Tribal Affairs, also run various schemes for the educational development of ST students.

Gender Specific Schemes (Programmes)

India has implemented a total number of three gender specific programmes with a view to tackle the issues related to the educational problems of the female sex. These are: (i) Mahila Samakhya, (ii) Kasturba Gandhi Balika Vidyalaya (KDBV), and (iii) National Programme for the Education of Girls at the Elementary Level (NPEGEL).

Mahila Samakhya: With the prime objective of 'Education for women equality', this programme was first introduced in 1989 in five states. However, the programme focused on the educational development of the socially and economically marginalised women residing in rural areas. The programme endeavours to create a learning environment where women can collectively affirm their potential, gain strength to demand information and knowledge and come forward to face challenges and changes in their lives independently. The Tenth Five Year Plan indicates that a pool of aware women has been created through the Mahila Shikshan Kendra and there is an ever increasing demand for literacy and education for the daughter and granddaughters and the programmes were being implemented in about 9,000 villages in 53 districts spread over five states, by the Tenth Five Year Plan.

Kasturba Gandhi Balika Vidyalaya (KGBV): With a view to provide school facility at elementary level for the out of school girls belonging to the ST, SC and OBC and Minority sections, this programme took its birth during the Tenth Five Year Plan Period. The Programme however was meant for specific Educationally Backward Blocks (EBB). As per the 2001 census report the rural female literacy rate is below the national average and the gender gap in literacy more than the national average. The programme emphasised on setting up of residential schools with boarding facilities for the targeted children. In Odisha, by 2006-07, a total number of 49 special schools have been constituted under the programme in the identified areas.

National Programme of Education for Girls at Elementary Level (NPEGEL): This National Programme of Education for Girls at Elementary Level also took its birth during the Tenth Five Year Plan period as a special component of Sarva Shiksha Abhiyan, for the mitigation of the gender gap. It acts to provide education to the most vulnerable and hard to reach girls in the age group of 6-14 belonging to the categories like: never enrolled girl children, drop-out girls, working girls, adolescent girls - and thereby meets the goals towards UEE. It works in the educationally backward blocks where the level of normal female literacy is less than the national average and also in blocks that have at least 5 per cent of Scheduled Tribe or Scheduled Caste population and their literacy rate fall below 10 per cent.

In Odisha, this programme was launched in 2003-2004 in all the district excluding Baraghar, Jhasuguda, and Nayaghar, and at present it is in operation in a total number of 143 educationally backward blocks, 23 ST blocks, 13 urban slums and small towns of the states. So far a total number of 1651 Modal Cluster Schools (MCS) have been constituted in the identified areas and a total number of 1344 MCS co-coordinators have been appointed for undertaking the activities of this programme. This is one of the educational complexes that was made by the Govt. of India for the purpose of education of the Juang primitive tribal girls in Gonasika area in Keonjhar district of Odisha state.

Table No 1: Educational Complex of Tribal Girls for Juang (PTG), Gonasika

Sl. No	*Name of the scheme*	*Amount Allocation (Rs. in Lakhs)*	*Infrastructure created*	*Remarks*
1.	Article,275(1)	32.00	• Two storied Educational Complex building with 6616 sq ft plinth area. • School building with 1200 sq ft plinth area. • 100 seated hostel with 5000 sq ft. Plinth area. • Installation of transformer with internal electrification. • Bore well & Sanitary well with water supply system. • Kitchen complex • Additional Lavatory complex • Internal CC road with CD • Compound wall over Ac.6.00 of land	Total boarders staying 250.
2.	Periphery Development	39.50		
3.	BRGF	4.00		
4.	CCD Plan	8.50		
5.	Non Plan	4.00		
6.	SCA to TSP (JDA)	3.00		
7.	State Plan	35.00		
	Total	**228.38**		

This residential girls' school was constructed under convergence of different schemes in the year 2008-09 as follows. This only for girls' educational complex with hostel in the Juang PTGs in Gonasika in the Keonjhar district of Odisha has been functioning with effect from 2008-09 with 250 Juang girl's (PTG) boarders. They are being provided three times full meals and blanket, mosquito nets, utensils, colour T.Vs. etc. A compound wall has been constructed for the safety and security of the girl boarders out of the grant provided under the Periphery Development Scheme. All the girl boarders are getting 3 pairs of dresses, sweaters, shoes, sleepers, belts etc. from the fund provided by Govt. of India through OMTES. Similarly, electrification, provision of bore well and sanitary well, kitchen shed, toilets have also been made for convenience of the girl boarders. Construction of 100 seated new ST girls hostel is going on out of state plan of Rs 35.00 lakhs and PDS of Rs 10.00 lakhs for the accommodation of more PTG Juang girls in future.

Table No. 2: Enrollment Ratio of the Juang PTG Girls in Educational Complex in Gonasika

Year/class	*I*	*II*	*III*	*IV*	*V*	*VI*	*VII*	*VIII*	*Total*
2008-09	211	4	12	4	11	3	2	3	250
2009-10	132	83	3	12	4	9	4	3	250
2010-11	45	91	83	3	12	4	9	3	250
Total	**388**	**178**	**98**	**19**	**27**	**16**	**15**	**9**	**750**

This table presents the enrolment ratio among the Juang girls (classes I-VIII) in the educational complex from 2008 to 2010. The total strength of the school is 250 girls every year. In the academic year 2008-09 the number of students were 211 in class-I, 4 in class-II, 12 in class-III, 4 in class-IV, 11 in class-V, 3 in class-VI, 2 in class-VII and 3 in class-VIII. In the next academic year 2009-10 the total strength was also 250 with 132 in class-I, 83 in class-II, 3 in class-III, 12 in class-IV, 4 in class-V, 3 in class-VI, 4 in class-VII and 3 in class-VIII. In the year 2010-11, the total strength was 250 with 45 in class-I, 91 in class-II, 83 in class-III, 3 in class-IV, 12 in class-V, 4 in class-VI, 94 in class-VII and 3 in class-VIII.

Table No. 3: Dropout Rate in Juang PTG in Educational Complex in Gonasika

Year/Class	*I*	*II*	*III*	*IV*	*V*	*VI*	*VII*	*VIII*	*Total*
2009-10	25	1	1	1	2	0	0	1	31
2010-11	21	2	0	0	0	0	2	1	26
Total	**46**	**3**	**1**	**1**	**2**	**0**	**2**	**2**	**57**

Table 3 presents the drop-out ratio among the Juang girls in the educational complex only for Juang PTG. This table shows the drop-out rate in the educational complex for the academic years 2009-10 and 2010-11. In 2009-10 the total drop-out rate was 31, it is interesting to note that the drop-out rate for class I was very high at 25 but for all the other classes it was 1 or 2 or even nil. In the successive academic year also similar trend can be observed with a total dropout rate of 26, Class-I accounts for the largest drop-out rate of 21, in other classes drop-out rate is as low as 1 or 2 or nil. This suggests that students who once got well inducted into the educational system strived hard not to leave.

Conclusion

Free education and government aid is justifiable in terms of meeting social needs. The educational system under government control is more vulnerable to pulls and pressures from forces outside than is the private education system. Where education is concerned human resources have to be handled but these are unpredictable and not easily manageable collectively both at the national and state levels. The present system of our education is very rigid. The schools are following old age rules and procedures which are not easy to get rid of. No significant changes have occurred in the educational system, in spite of considerable changes in socio-economic and political environment of the country and significant scientific and technological developments. The essential role and function of educational endevours is to mould productive and responsible citizens through community development works as community life is an essential feature of the Juang tribes' educational system.

References

- Census of India, (2001), Government of India.
- Challam, K. S., (2008). *Modernisation and Dalit Education*, Rawat Publications New Delhi.
- Daesn, Pierre., & Akkari Abdeljalil (2008) *Educational Theories and Practices From The Majority World,* Sage Publication, New Delhi.
- Dutta, K. B., (2005) *Dynamics of Dalits*, Akansha Publishing House, New Delhi.
- Government of Odisha (2011) Economic Survey, Planning and Coordination Department.
- Khan, Mohd. M., (2007). *Reflections on Dalit and Minorities Issues*, Kanishka Publishers, New Delhi.
- Mallaiah, L. C., & Kumari, K. B. Ratna, (2008). *Dalits and Human Development*, Abhijeet Publications, Delhi.

- Ota A. B., (2009). *Critical Issues in Tribal Development,* Scheduled Castes & Scheduled Tribes Research Training Centre. Bhubaneswar.
- Puri, K. Harish., (2004). *Dalits in Regional Context*, Rawat Publication, New Delhi.
- Selvam, Paneer. S.K. (2009). *Primary Education*, A.P.H. Publishing Corporation, New Delhi.
- Setty, E. D., (2007). *Dynamics of Dalits Development*, Akansha Publishing House New Delhi.
- Shabbir, Mohamed, (2005) *Ambedkar on Law, Constitution and Social Justice,* Rawat Publication, New Delhi.
- Thorat, Sukhadeo, and Newman, Katherine (2010), *Caste: Economic Discrimination and Social Exclusion in Modern India,* Oxford University Press.

Chapter-19

Contribution of Girl Education in Nation Building: Challenges and Solutions

—Rashmi Gahlowt

Abstract

Women form an important and integral part of any country's development. Illiteracy of women can be a major obstacle when it comes to achieving the dream of a progressive and developing nation. Education is the cornerstone of women's empowerment because it gives them the essential tools to confront stifling social norms and to challenge pervading biases. Aspects of women's education are very varied in a country like India with its vast geography and different cultures. In India, it is the need of the hour to focus on strengthening and empowering women and girls. They are the worst affected by misery, poverty and discriminations. They are the objects of abuse and violations both inside and outside their homes. They are not aware of their rights had hence are unable to attain those. They have minimal access to resources. Educating girls will be the way to realise the objective of their empowerment and as a consequence the empowerment of nation and humankind as a whole. Literate and enlightened women raise better families in terms of health and education. They not only help their families but whole communities overcome poverty, marginalisation and social injustice. This chapter will investigate the issue from three angles which include assessment of how the promotion of girl's education will reduce the levels of poverty, what are the socio-cultural and economic hurdles encountered in way of girl's education and what initiatives and schemes have been undertaken by the government and private organisations like corporates and NGOs.

Key Words: *Female Literacy Rate, Women empowerment, Socio-cultural and economic factors, Literacy schemes, Women's rights advocacy.*

Introduction

Education is a major force in building a peaceful community in any part of the world. Educational systems and frameworks take up the responsibility of promoting pluralism and multiculturalism in any society. India has indeed made remarkable progress in the field of education. But there are gaping holes in the area of women's education. Despite of a significant rise in literacy and a substantial improvement made at primary, secondary and higher levels of education, there are three main hurdles which make the objective of achieving education for all difficult to meet. The first of these obstacles is educational progress made by different social groups and geographical regions differ vastly. Secondly, there is a difference in education levels in rural and urban India. The third hurdle is the gender gap in education which is still considerable. The percentage wise gender gap in urban areas is 13.5 per cent and 25 per cent in rural areas.

In the words of D.S. Kothari, "Knowledge is vitally important; but if it is to transform society from a state of relative stagnation to one of dynamism and progress, there must be a general willingness and determination to make use of it in the service of community. In Indian society girls and women are a disadvantaged group. To empower girls, there are various short-term and long-term solutions such as reforming the law enforcement systems, supporting women's upliftment movements, developing new structures of accountability and ushering in the social changes to challenge patriarchal set ups. Education can play an eminent and substantial role in resetting gender norms in India. For example, in marginalised and repressed societies, enlightened and educated girls fight and protest against early marriage.

India still has a long way to go when it comes to reaching the UN's Millennium Development Goal of quality education for all by 2015. If we want a better understanding of plight of girls in India, particularly of those residing in rural communities, then we must probe into the deep rooted cultural and societal norms. Girls are not considered for educating and they are not allowed to leave homes and towns to study in outstation schools and colleges. This chapter will have three pronged approach in discussing how:

- Promoting girl education will go a long way in bringing down poverty levels.
- The challenges faced in girl's education
- Steps taken by government and NGOs to address this problem.

Education gives necessary tools to girls to make better and informed decisions. It improves their physical and mental well-being. This positive change is then carried through to their families first, then societies and eventually to the nations at large. A society or a nation can never progress if girls' education and advancement is ignored. The social and economic goals can only be met if girls are brought out of their plight. Girl education has multi- pronged benefits, through education girls strive to not marry before reaching adulthood, have children at a later and healthier age, have fewer and healthier children, earn an income to support family, educate her children and to understand and exercise her rights.

The wellbeing of future generations of a country depends upon the well-being of girls and women. It has direct effects on infant mortality rates. Girls and young women understand the benefits of having smaller families and looking after their children in a better way. Educated mothers are also more likely than their uneducated counterparts to get their children immunized against deadly diseases and they don't fall prey to blind beliefs and superstitions prevalent in particularly rural societies. Educated girls and women also raise a voice against violence. They are not as much at risk of facing violence at home and society as uneducated and illiterate women. When women are educated, they increase earning potential of a family and ultimately push the economic growth rate of the country. Educated girls constitute productive labour strength. They possess entrepreneurial and job skills needed in an increasingly competitive market. They are able to fruitfully participate in the growth of both formal and informal economy.

When women have fewer children, the number of dependents on them decreases, the decline in the dependency rates causes a rise in per capita income and spurs up the rate of savings. Educated girls and women command higher wages, they are aware and informed about their rights and duties, they also take part actively in civic and political issues of the country and strive to become equipped for participating in community improvement programs.

India contains the largest number of illiterate people in any country of the world. The disparity in India occurs region-wise. Southern states are better off when it comes to women's literacy. The northern states have more numbers of women who are illiterate. Bihar, Rajasthan, Uttar Pradesh, Andhra Pradesh and West Bengal account for 70 per cent of India's illiterate population. Educating marginalised and tribal girls presents a huge challenge. Even in areas where primary schools are there, girl's attendance and dropout rates remains a worrisome factor. This is in addition to the lacunae present in the primary education system. Majority of girls enrolled in primary schools lack the reading, writing and numeric skills.

A study conducted by World Bank in 2006 showed that 50 per cent of 10 year old girl students could not do basic numeric calculations of addition and subtraction. The failing of the school system is due to poor teacher student ratio and teacher absenteeism along with the lack of content in textbooks that is not localised and hence incomprehensible to many students.

It is common knowledge that the condition and levels of education in the rural and tribal regions of India is extremely poor. Basic infrastructural facilities like school buildings, paucity of teachers and lack of qualified staff are pretty widespread. All these factors culminate in students dropping out of schools in high numbers, girls' drop-out rate is even more so. Right and access to education is a basic and fundamental right but poor backward students are deprived of it.

Literacy and education for all is an integral component of any democratic government. The central and state governments have started to take steps in the direction of providing education for all. Nevertheless, the gaps are still present when it comes to the implementation and follow up aspects of these initiatives and programs. The issues faced in implementations are several and range from inadequate infrastructure to socio-cultural challenges that girls face in their homes and societies.

When a nation fails to educate its girls, it is riddled with several problems such as gender discrimination and exploitation. The National Policy on Education clearly states that education remains an inseparable and essential tool for long-term women's equality. It stresses upon the necessity of education being used for fundamental social change and for decreasing the gender gap and removing gender bias.

The United Nations Children's Fund (UNICEF) in collaboration with the Ministry for Human Resources Development has framed a 'National Vision for Girls' Education in India - Roadmap to 2015. The objective of this draft is to construct an all-inclusive and far reaching program for girls' education. The Vision Document consists of a detailed framework for concrete steps to be taken for girls' education in India. The policy of action for the next one year will be the Shiksha Ka Haq Abhiyan (Mission for Right to Education) which will act as the key element for implementing the ambitious RTE program. The local governments will get the community, media and other stakeholders involved in order to forge a supportive climate and systems for girls' education.

Some of the most essential steps in this regard are to provide for capable and substantial legislation that make child labour a punishable offence and to stop gender based violence. It is pertinent to provide residential facilities, transport and such enticements and impetus for attracting qualified female teachers especially for schools in rural, backward and remote areas. The first and the foremost concerns should be to address safety issues of girls. Obstacles exist at every level beginning from homes. Communities and elders are not usually too keen on the idea of girls attending schools at the cost of household duties and chores.

It is the moral and social responsibility of the parents and community leaders to ensure that the children attend schools and make use of the quotas reserved under the RTE for them.

'Education for empowerment' will remain just a government catchphrase to promote the education of the girl child unless the thousands of tribal and backward girls are: relieved of their household and farming duties to an extent that they are able to attend school, not subjected to sexual violence or harassment by school staff and provided basic separate toilet facilities.

There has indeed been a significant rise in the admission of girls to school throughout India over the past decades, the school system has not been able to retain the girls or have them attend regularly and stop the dropouts from doing so. A recent study 'Gender Discrimination: Impact on Lives of Girls in School in Four States (Bihar, UP, Rajasthan and Delhi)' undertaken to find out the reasons for drop outs, states that more than 50 per cent girl students drop-out of schools after the primary level itself. As per the study the high dropout rate among girls is because girls have to take care of siblings, do household and farming chores and they also have to work to support the family financially. The lack of female teachers and staff also is a primary factor of lesser number of girls attending schools. Female staff is more empathetic and sensitive towards specific problems of girls. Elders in the family too are hesitant to send the girls to schools where the majority of teaching and support staff is male.

Mostly all commissions which have been formed to investigate into the specifics of girl education have been unanimous in their recommendations for recruiting female teachers. Apart from enlisting female staff, the issue of transportation also needs to be looked into. Primary schools are usually located near student's homes but secondary schools are usually fewer in number and located in other towns. Transportation and commuting thus becomes a major issue. It should be an integral part of infrastructural facility provided free of cost to students. For secondary and tertiary education, girls need to usually shift outstation. This poses a serious issue when it comes to their accommodation. There need to be hostel facilities for outstation girl students. Security and other concerns must be taken care of at hostels. Parents need assurance that their ward will be safe from all harm at hostels. The fear of sexual harassment also plagues many girls and their families are constantly worried about their safety. Incidents of rape, harassment and molestation of girls cause fear and intimidation in parents. They prefer girls to stay and home rather than go out to study especially after they attain puberty.

School hours for tribal and rural students should be flexible. Most children accompany the elders in the family to work at farms or do household work. The school system should be such that it accommodates the students when they are done with their home and farm duties. There has been a successful instance where the concept of flexible school timings has been applied. The Shiksha Karmi Project and Lok Jumbish, have implemented this and found the results to be good when it comes to girl's attendance.

These causes culminate in environments which make it very difficult for the girls to attend and remain enrolled in schools.

The government is very much aware of these challenges. Both at the central and state levels they have come up with effective sounding schemes and programs for encouraging the enrolment and retention of girls in schools. Now, more than ever before there are schools which are closer to homes, scholarships are offered to outstanding students and mid-day meals are provided in many schools. The government has also taken steps to orient and sensitise communities towards girls' education.

Factors causing such a miserable condition in girl education are both socio-cultural and economic in nature.

Socio-cultural: Parents and community do not attach much value to the education of girls. Their mind-sets are patriarchal and they feel little need to educate girls who would eventually only need to get married and look after home and hearth. Girls have several restrictions when it comes to mobility and travel. They are married off at a younger age. Elders in the family do not have knowledge about women's rights; the concern for their health is glaringly absent.

Economic: Primary enrolment is free but the secondary and tertiary education requires fees. This poses a hindrance. Infrastructural issues like absence of separate toilet facilities for girls is a contributing cause of girls shying away from school. Girls are also at a risk of facing sexual violence. Female teachers are noticeably absent. Quality of education is poor, overall. Content in textbooks is overwhelmingly sexist and reeks of gender bias. Stereotypical gender roles are much highlighted.

Central and State Government Initiatives

- **Sarva Shiskha Abhiyaan (SSA):** As part of this program, steps to establish schools which are closer to children's homes, scholarships to deserving students and midday meals provided a boost for enrolment in schools and a fall in drop-out rates. There is, however, a lack of complete implementation of the program.
- **Formation of Balika shivirs (residential girl camps):** This scheme provides for establishment of residential camps for the disadvantaged and underprivileged girls.
- **National program for education of girls at elementary level:** This initiative aims to appoint especially trained teachers to understand specific problems of girls.
- **Mahila Samakhyas (education for women's equality):** It aims to establish alternative learning centres for girls.
- **Total sanitation campaign:** This program specifically aims to construct toilet blocks for students.

Apart from the above initiatives by the government at state and central levels the Corporate as part of their Corporate Social Responsibility undertake several programs which aim towards social upliftment in general, girl education being an integral part of it. The Adolescent Girls' Initiative by Nike, Educating Women and Girls Initiative by ExxonMobil are two of the many international corporations that are investing in the cause. Non-governmental organisations like Akanksha, Nanhi kali, Child Relief and You, Teach for India and Prathma are actively engaged in educating disadvantaged children across India.

Strategies and Solutions to Combat Educational Challenges

The government, the NGOs and the corporate sector have initiated several activities and schemes specifically aimed at improving girl's education. These include offering incentives like scholarships, subsidised higher education, setting up literacy camps, formation of women centric policies, special training to sensitise teachers, providing teaching learning resources and infrastructure.

There is a consensus among the private and public sectors when it comes to educating girls. The aim of achieving economic progress and development would only be possible when the girls of a nation are educated. Some of the world's leading businesses are increasingly investing in girl's education. Access to education and opportunities will construct the world's human capital and its overall economy.

More and more companies now are starting to take note of the social and economic sense in investing in girls' education. Now it is not just through charities and philanthropic activities but also through main business activities by which companies are supporting the cause of girls' education. They are also proactively involved in advocacy steps and measures as well as being involved in framing public policy to push for a conducive environment to support girls' education and betterment.

Apart from these aspects, there is also a need to provide training in essential life skills and vocational skills which would equip them to compete in the job market, to develop critical reasoning, build self-esteem and become capable of taking independent decisions and act on them. Following are some of the ways in which all girls' education can be a reality in the country:

- Providing financial assistance to girl students in terms of scholarships and fees. Offering free/subsidised educational materials like textbooks, uniforms and stationary.
- Endorsement and advocacy of educating girls with a view to empower them for claiming their rights.
- Sustained initiatives towards improvement of quality of education like remedial classes, creation of gender sensitive teaching learning materials.

Community drives: Includes drives such as setting up of informal literacy centres and vocational training camps. These endeavours boost the much required connection between community and schools.

Conclusion

In addition to a strong intervention by the government and the private sector through various schemes and programmes constant aid and support of international organisations like the United Nations has also been present for the cause of girls' education. We need to identify the most disadvantaged and deprived sections of society and to frame and apply time-bound programmes specifically designed for girls. The special programmes should be intertwined with the formal school system. This will also give the major thrust to the girl children from the families belonging to below poverty line. On similar lines, time bound specific initiatives for education of adolescents should be undertaken, for those who have completed grade five and/or have dropped out of school. There needs to be a sustained focus on localised education, skill development, building of self-esteem and health education.

References

- www.unicef.org
- www.ssa.nic.in
- www.theguardian.com/education/2013/mar/11/indian-children-education-opportunities.
- Government of India, Census of India 2001.
- Government of India, Census of India 2011.
- Karat, B. (2005). Survival and Emancipation: Notes from Indian Women's Struggles, Gurgaon, Three Essays Collective.
- N. L. Gupta (2003) Women's Education Through Ages, Concept Publications Co., New Delhi.
- R. K. Rao (2001) Women and Education, Kalpaz Publications, Delhi.

Index